Read ALL the CAT WHO mysteries!

THE CAT WHO COULD READ BACKWARDS: The world of modern art is a mystery to many—but for Jim Qwilleran and Koko it's a mystery of another sort . . .

THE CAT WHO ATE DANISH MODERN: Qwill isn't thrilled about covering interior design for *The Daily Fluxion*. Little does he know that a murderer has designs on a woman featured in one of his stories . . .

THE CAT WHO TURNED ON AND OFF: Qwill and Koko are joined by Yum Yum as they try to solve a murder in an antique shop . . .

THE CAT WHO SAW RED: Qwill starts his diet—*and* a new gourmet column for the *Fluxion*. It isn't easy—but it's not as hard as solving a murder case!

THE CAT WHO PLAYED BRAHMS: Fishing at a secluded cabin, Qwill hooks on to a mystery—and Koko develops a strange fondness for classical music . . .

THE CAT WHO PLAYED POST OFFICE: Koko and Yum Yum turn into fat cats when Qwill inherits millions. But amid the caviar and champagne, Koko starts sniffing clues to a murder!

THE CAT WHO HAD 14 TALES: A delightful collection of feline mystery fiction from the creator of Koko and Yum Yum!

TURN THE PAGE FOR MORE CAT WHO

THE CAT WHO KNEW SHAKESPEARE: The local newspaper publisher has perished in an accident—or is it murder? That is the question . . .

THE CAT WHO SNIFFED GLUE: After a banker and his wife are killed, Koko develops on odd appetite for glue. To solve the case, Qwill has to figure out why . . .

THE CAT WHO WENT UNDERGROUND: Qwill and the cats head for their Moose County cabin for a relaxing summer—but when a handyman disappears, Koko must dig up the motive for a sinister crime . . .

THE CAT WHO TALKED TO GHOSTS: Qwill and Koko try to solve a haunting mystery in a historic farmhouse.

THE CAT WHO LIVED HIGH: An art dealer was killed in Qwill's high-rise apartment—and he and the cats reach new heights in detection as they find out whodunit . . .

THE CAT WHO KNEW A CARDINAL: The director of the local Shakespeare production dies in Qwill's orchard—and the stage is set for a puzzling mystery!

THE CAT WHO MOVED A MOUNTAIN: Qwill has a new home in the scenic Potato Mountains. But when a dispute between residents and developers boils over into murder, he has to keep his eyes open to find the culprit!

THE CAT WHO WASN'T THERE: Qwill's on his way to Scotland—to solve another purr-plexing mystery!

THE CAT WHO WENT INTO THE CLOSET: Qwill's moved into a mansion . . . with fifty closets for Koko to investigate! But among the junk, Koko finds a clue—and Qwill's unearthing some surprising skeletons . . .

THE CAT WHO CAME TO BREAKFAST: Peaceful Breakfast Island is turned upside-down by controversy—and murder. Qwill and the cats must find out whodunit . . .

THE CAT WHO BLEW THE WHISTLE: An old steam locomotive has been restored, causing excitement in Moose County. But a murder brings the fun to a screeching halt—and Qwill and Koko are tracking down the culprit . . .

THE CAT WHO SAID CHEESE: The Great Food Explo brings lots of delicious activity to Moose County—as well as a stew of gossip, mystery, and murder . . .

THE CAT WHO TAILED A THIEF: A rash of petty thievery in Pickax puts Qwill and Koko on a killer's elusive trail . . .

THE CAT WHO SANG FOR THE BIRDS
Available in hardcover from G. P. Putnam's Sons

Jove titles by Lilian Jackson Braun

THE CAT WHO COULD READ BACKWARDS
THE CAT WHO ATE DANISH MODERN
THE CAT WHO TURNED ON AND OFF
THE CAT WHO SAW RED
THE CAT WHO PLAYED BRAHMS
THE CAT WHO PLAYED POST OFFICE
THE CAT WHO KNEW SHAKESPEARE
THE CAT WHO SNIFFED GLUE
THE CAT WHO WENT UNDERGROUND
THE CAT WHO TALKED TO GHOSTS
THE CAT WHO LIVED HIGH
THE CAT WHO KNEW A CARDINAL
THE CAT WHO MOVED A MOUNTAIN
THE CAT WHO WASN'T THERE
THE CAT WHO WENT INTO THE CLOSET
THE CAT WHO CAME TO BREAKFAST
THE CAT WHO BLEW THE WHISTLE
THE CAT WHO SAID CHEESE
THE CAT WHO TAILED A THIEF

THE CAT WHO HAD 14 TALES
(*short story collection*)

THE CAT WHO SANG FOR THE BIRDS
in hardcover from G. P. Putnam's Sons

Lilian Jackson Braun

The cat Who Went Under- ground

JOVE BOOKS, NEW YORK

This Jove Book contains the complete
text of the original hardcover edition.
It has been completely reset in a typeface
designed for easy reading, and was printed
from new film.

THE CAT WHO WENT UNDERGROUND

A Jove Book / published by arrangement with
the author

PRINTING HISTORY
G. P. Putnam's Sons edition / March 1989
Published simultaneously in Canada
Jove edition / September 1989

The Penguin Putnam Inc. World Wide Web site address is
http://www.penguinputnam.com

ISBN: 0-515-10123-0

A JOVE BOOK®
Jove Books are published by The Berkley Publishing Group,
a member of Penguin Putnam Inc.,
200 Madison Avenue, New York, New York 10016.
JOVE and the "J" design
are trademarks belonging to Jove Publications, Inc.

PRINTED IN THE UNITED STATES OF AMERICA

20   19   18

ONE

If Jim Qwilleran had read his horoscope in the daily paper on that particular morning, perhaps none of this would have happened. But astrology had never been one of his interests.

As he drank his third cup of coffee in his bachelor apartment over the garage, he glanced at the floor, which was strewn with out-of-town newspapers. He had devoured the national and international news, studied the editorials, scoffed at the viewpoints on the Op-Ed page, and scanned the sports section. As usual he skipped the stock market reports and the comics, and he never thought of looking at the horoscope column.

The advice he failed to read was portentous. The *Daily Fluxion* said, "This is not an auspicious time to change your life-style. Be content with what you have." The *Morning Rampage* said, "You may feel restless and bored, but avoid making impulsive decisions today. You could regret it."

Comfortably unaware of this counsel from the constellations, Qwilleran sprawled in his overscale lounge chair with a coffee mug in his hand, a cat on his lap, and another on the bookshelf nearby. They were an unlikely threesome. The man was a heavyset six feet two, fiftyish, sloppily attired, with graying hair and mournful eyes, and his exceptionally luxuriant moustache needed trimming. His companions, on the other hand, were aristocratic Siamese with elegantly sleek lines and well-brushed coats, who expected pampering as their royal prerogative.

Qwilleran's ragged sweatshirt and cluttered apartment gave no clue to his career credentials or his financial status. He was a veteran journalist with worldwide experience, now retired and living in the small northern town of Pickax, and he had recently inherited millions, or billions, from the Klingenschoen estate; the exact figure had not yet been determined by the battery of accountants employed by the executors.

Qwilleran had never cared for wealth, however, and his needs were simple. He was content to live in an apartment over the Klingenschoen garage, and for breakfast on that particular morning he had been satisfied with coffee and a stale doughnut. His roommates had more discriminating palates. For them he opened a can of Alaska king crab, mixing it with a raw egg yolk and garnishing it with a few crumbles of fine English cheddar.

"Today's special: Crustacean à la tartare fromagère," he announced as he placed the plate on the floor. Two twitching noses hovered over the dish before tasting it, like oenophiles sniffing the bouquet of a rare wine.

After breakfast the Siamese huddled as if waiting for something to happen. Qwilleran finished reading the newspapers, drank two more cups of coffee, and drifted into introspection.

"Okay, you guys," he said as he finally roused himself from his caffeine reverie. "I've made a decision: We're going up to the lake. We're going to spend three months at the log cabin." He made it a policy to discuss matters with the cats. It was more satisfying than talking aloud to himself, and his listeners seemed to enjoy the sound of a human voice making conversational noises in their direction.

Yum Yum, the amiable little female, purred. Koko, the male, uttered a piercing but ambiguous "Yow-w-w!"

"What did you mean by that?" Qwilleran demanded. Receiving only an incomprehensible blue-eyed stare in reply, he smoothed his moustache and went on: "I have three reasons for wanting to get out of town: Pickax is a bore in warm weather; Polly Duncan is away for the summer; and we're out of ice cubes."

For two years he had been living in Pickax—not by choice but in accord with the terms of the

Klingenschoen will—and the old stone buildings and stone-paved streets seemed dull in June. The nearby resort town of Mooseville, on the other hand, was burgeoning with leaf, flower, bird, sunshine, blue sky, rippling wave, lake breeze, and hordes of carefree vacationers.

The second reason for Qwilleran's discontent was more vital. Polly Duncan, the head librarian in Pickax, around whom his life was beginning to revolve, was spending the summer in England on an exchange program, and he was feeling restless and unfulfilled. Although he knew little about the outdoors and cared even less for fishing, he conjectured that a log cabin on a lonely sand dune overlooking a vast blue lake might cure his malaise.

There was a third reason, less sublime but more pertinent: the refrigerator in his apartment was out of order. Qwilleran expected appliances to function without a hitch, and he showed irrational impatience when equipment broke down. Unfortunately the Pickax refrigeration specialist had gone camping in northern Canada, and the only other serviceman in the county was hospitalized with a herniated disc.

Altogether, a summer in Mooseville sounded like an excellent idea to Jim Qwilleran.

"You probably don't remember the cabin," he said to the cats. "We spent a few weeks there a couple of years ago, and you liked it. It has two screened porches. You can watch the birds and squirrels and bugs without getting your feet wet."

The seventy-five-year-old log cabin, with its acres of

woodland and half mile of lake frontage, was among the far-flung holdings Qwilleran had inherited from the Klingenschoen estate, and it was being managed by the executors until the terms of the will could be fulfilled. He had only to express his wishes to the attorneys, and the property-management crew would turn on the power, activate the plumbing system, restore phone service, and remove the dust covers from the furniture.

"You don't need to worry about a thing!" attorney Hasselrich assured him with his boundless optimism. "You'll find the key under the doormat. Just unlock the door, walk into the cabin, and enjoy a relaxing summer."

As circumstances evolved, it was not that easy. The summer vacation started with a dead spider and ended with a dead carpenter, and Jim Qwilleran—respected journalist, richest man in the county, and card-carrying good guy—was suspected of murder.

But in his blissful ignorance, he had taken the attorney at his word. Preparing for the trip to the lakeshore, he packed his small car with a few summer clothes, a box of books, a turkey roaster filled with gravel that served as the cats' commode, a computerized coffeemaker, his typewriter, and the Siamese in their travel coop. This was a wicker picnic hamper outfitted with a down-filled cushion, and Yum Yum hopped into it with alacrity. Koko hung back. He had some covert catly reason for not wanting to go.

"Don't be a wet blanket," Qwilleran chided. "Jump in and let's hit the road."

He should have known that Koko's whims were not

to be taken lightly. The cat seemed to have a sixth sense that detected precarious situations.

When they embarked on their jaunt to Mooseville—it was only thirty miles—the occasion had the excitement of a safari. The skies were sunny, the June breeze was soft, and the temperature was warm enough for Qwilleran to wear shorts and sandals. To avoid tourist traffic he drove north on Sandpit Road instead of the main highway, waving a friendly hand to strangers in pickup trucks and tooting a friendly horn at any farmer on a tractor. Within minutes he had shed the tensions of the City of Stone, for although the population of Pickax was only three thousand, it had the commercial bustle of a county seat. With growing elation he planned his summer. He would do plenty of reading, take long walks on the beach, go canoeing whenever the lake was calm. He also had a writing commitment: two features a week for the Moose County newspaper, to be given thumb position on page two. His column, called "Straight from the Qwill Pen," would be enjoyable to write (the editor was giving him carte blanche) and challenging enough to keep the creative juices percolating.

"Is everybody happy back there?" he called out over his shoulder without, however, hearing any reply from the hamper.

Qwilleran had only one regret about the forthcoming summer: Polly Duncan would not be there to share it with him. Her substitute, a librarian from the English Midlands, had already arrived in Pickax. Young, brash, brisk in her manner, and clipped in her speech, she was far different from Polly, who had a gentle nature and a soft, low musical voice. Polly's figure was matronly, and there were traces of gray in her unstyled hair, but she was stimulating company. Animated discussions enlivened their dinner dates, and weekends at her country hideaway made him feel twenty years younger.

As Qwilleran brooded about the absence of Polly, a car approached from the north, far exceeding the speed limit. He recognized the driver. It was Roger MacGillivray, a young reporter for the county newspaper. Qwilleran presumed wryly that Roger was rushing to the office to file a breaking story on some momentous news event in Mooseville: Someone had caught a whopping big fish, or someone's great-grandmother had celebrated her ninety-fifth birthday. Stop the presses!

Roger was a likable young man, and he had a mother-in-law who was an interesting woman. She spent summers at a cottage half a mile down the beach from the Klingenschoen cabin. Mildred Hanstable taught home economics and art in the Pickax schools, wrote the food page for the Moose County newspaper, and happened to be a superlative cook. It occurred to Qwilleran that he might expect a few dinner invitations in the forthcoming weeks. Mildred had a husband, but he was "away" and no one ever mentioned him.

Soon the potato farms and sheep ranches and sandpits were left behind, and the road plunged through lush evergreen forests. A commotion in the wicker hamper indicated that the Siamese could smell the lake air, still a mile away. Qwilleran himself noticed something different in the atmosphere—an invigorating buoyancy. It was the Mooseville magic! Every summer it attracted droves of tourists from polluted, crime-ridden urban centers in the southern part of the state, which the locals called Down Below.

"It won't be long now," he told his passengers.

The lake burst into view, a body of water so vast that its blue met the blue of the sky at some invisible point. At the side of the road a chamber of commerce sign welcomed visitors to "Mooseville, 400 miles north of everywhere!" Here the highway ran along the shoreline, ascending gradually to the top of Mooseville's famous sand dunes. Qwilleran frowned when he encountered unusual conditions: mud on the pavement, dump trucks coming out of the woods, the whine of chain saws, the grinding din of a backhoe. He regretted the symptoms of lakefront development, while realizing it was inevitable. Next came the rustic arch marking the entrance to the Top o' the Dunes Club, a private community of summer people, Mildred Hanstable included.

Half a mile farther along he turned into a dirt road marked with the letter K on a cedar post. The wicker hamper started to bounce with anticipation. The Siamese knew! It had been two years ago, yet they remembered the scent; they sensed the environment. The private drive meandered through the woods, past wild cherry trees in blossom, through a stand of white birches, up and down over gentle dunes created by lake action eons ago and now heavily wooded with giant oaks and towering, top-heavy pines.

The drive ended in a clearing, and there was the picturesque old cabin, its logs and chinking dark with age, virtually dwarfed by the massive fieldstone chimney.

"Here we are!" Qwilleran announced, opening the top of the hamper. "You stay here while I take a look around."

While the Siamese hopped about inside the car and stood on hind legs to peer out the windows, he walked to the edge of the dune and surveyed the placid lake. Gentle waves lapped the sandy beach at the bottom of the dune with seductive splashes. The breeze was a mere caress. Flocks of tiny yellow birds were flitting in the cherry trees. And here, in this quiet paradise, he was to spend the entire summer!

As Hasselrich had promised, the key was under the mat on the screened porch, and Qwilleran unlocked the door eagerly. The moment he opened it, a blast of frigid air slapped him in the face—the musty breath of a cabin that had been closed for the winter. He shivered involuntarily and retreated to the porch and the warmth of a summer day. Something had gone wrong! Hasselrich had failed him! Tentatively he reached a hand around the door jamb and found a wall switch; the hall light responded, so he knew the cabin had power. And someone had been there to remove the sheets shrouding the living room furniture. Qwilleran retreated hastily to the warm porch to think about this unexpected setback.

From his previous visit he vaguely remembered a

heating device installed unobtrusively on one wall of the living room. Grabbing a jacket from the car and wishing he had not worn shorts and sandals, he once more braved the dank chill. Hurriedly he switched on lights and opened the interior shutters that darkened the place. The wall-heater lurked in a dim corner—a flat metal box with louvers and knobs, and a metal label that had the effrontery to read *Komfort-Heet*.

Qwilleran huffed angrily into his moustache. The thermostat was set for seventy degrees, but the thermometer registered fifty, and to him it felt like a damp thirty. He dialed the thermostat to its highest limit, but there was no rush of heat, not even a reassuring click. He gave the heater a kick, a primitive technique that worked with old steam radiators, but had no effect on the *Komfort-Heet*.

Qwilleran had spent his life in apartments and hotels, where one had only to notify the manager and a dripping faucet would be fixed or a loose doorknob tightened. About space heaters he was totally ignorant. Of one thing he was certain, however: He could not expose the Siamese to this bone-chilling cold. They were indoor cats, accustomed to central heat in winter and sunny windowsills in summer.

There was a fireplace, of course, and there were logs in the wood basket, but he could find no matches. Automatically he felt in his jacket pocket, although he had given up pipe-smoking a year before. He checked the other utilities and found that the plumbing functioned and the telephone produced a dial tone. He gave the space heater another kick and reviled its obstinacy.

At that moment he heard an impatient yowl from the car.

Spitting out a suitable expletive, he looked up a number in the slim phone book that listed Mooseville subscribers.

"Good morning!" chirruped a woman's pleasant voice.

"Mildred, this is Qwill," he said abruptly. "I'm at the cabin. I just drove up with the cats to spend the summer."

"That's ducky!" she said. "You can come to the beach party tomorrow night."

"Forget parties," he snapped. "There's something wrong with the blasted heater! The cabin's like a subterranean cave! What do I do? Is there someone I can call?"

"Perhaps the pilot light's out," she said helpfully. "Did you look to see if the pilot light's out?"

"I don't even know where it is or what it looks like."

"There should be a little access door on the front—"

Qwilleran sneezed. "Just tell me who repairs these things, Mildred. I'm on the verge of double pneumonia."

"Are you on Glinko's list?" she asked.

He was losing patience. "Glinko! Who's Glinko?"

"Didn't anybody tell you about Glinko? You can call him any hour of the day or night, and he'll send a plumber, electrician, or any kind of repairman you need. It's a wonderful convenience for—"

"Okay, what's his number?" he cut in, shivering and stamping his feet.

"Not so fast, Qwill. First you have to go to his shop, sign up, pay a fee, and give him a key to your cabin."

"I don't like the idea of handing out keys indiscriminately," he said with irritation.

"People around here are perfectly honest," she said with a note of gentle reproach. "You've lived Down Below too long. You suspect everyone."

Thanking her briefly, Qwilleran dashed out to the car and dropped the cats into their travel coop again. "Sorry. You're going for another ride," he announced.

They headed for downtown Mooseville, three miles to the west, where the Huggins Hardware Store made duplicate keys.

The proprietor said, "Spending the summer up here, Mr. Q?"

"Only if I can get the chill out of the cabin, Cecil. Where can I find a repairman for a wall-heater?"

"Glinko's got 'em all tied up," said the storekeeper. "See Glinko."

Mildred had said that Glinko's place of business was right behind the post office, and Qwilleran found only one building in that location: a garage—a greasy, shabby garage with a large door standing open. There was a car inside, with its hood raised. Under the hood a pair of spindly legs in old ragged trousers could be seen waving aimlessly, while the torso was buried among the valves, spark plugs, and cylinders. There was no visible head.

"Excuse me," Qwilleran said to the waving feet. "Where can I find Glinko?"

The torso reared up, and the head came into view—a face almost obscured by a wild set of whiskers, a rat's nest of hair under a greasy beret, and a pair of bright, merry eyes. The gnomelike character slid across the fender and landed nimbly on the concrete floor. "Standin' right here," he said with a toothless grin. "Who be you?"

"My name is Qwilleran, and I'm staying at the Klingenschoen cabin near Top o' the Dunes."

The gnome nodded wisely. "That be the place with a K on a post."

"Correct," said Qwilleran. "I have a heating problem. I need a repairman."

"See the wife," said the little man, nodding toward the house in the rear. "She be the one does all that."

Qwilleran grunted his thanks and found his way to the house, picking his way through tall weeds, chunks of concrete, and auto parts. Three other cars were parked in the weedy lot, waiting for Glinko's attention, and they were all in the $40,000 class.

The house was no less dilapidated than the garage. The front steps had caved in, and Qwilleran climbed cautiously through the remaining boards and rapped on the torn screened door. The woman who waddled over to greet him, ample flesh bouncing and tentlike dress billowing, was all smiles and affability.

He introduced himself and said, "I understand you operate a service network."

"Network!" she hooted, her plump cheeks trembling

with merriment. "That's a good one! Wait'll I tell Glinko. Ha ha ha! Come in and join the club. You wanna beer?"

"Thank you, but I have two friends waiting for me in the car," he declined.

She ushered him into a dingy living room where there was nothing to suggest a business operation. "Two hun'erd to join," she stated. "Fifty a year dues, or a hun'erd if you wanna be on the fast track."

Qwilleran thought the fee exorbitant, but he gave his name and the address of the cabin and opted for priority service. "Right now I need a wall-heater repaired in a hurry. How quickly can you dispatch a repairman?"

"Dispatch!" she cried with glee. "That's a good one! Gotta use that! . . . Lemme see . . . In a hurry for a plumber, eh?" She gazed upward as if reading file cards on the water-stained ceiling. "Ralph, he went off to Pickax for a load o' pipe . . . Jerry, he come down with hay fever so bad he can't see to drive . . . Little Joe's workin' out your way, puttin' in a new toilet for the Urbanks. I'll radio out there."

"Do you bill me for the work?" Qwilleran asked.

"Nope. You pay Little Joe when the work's done. But you gotta gimme a key."

He handed over the new key with reluctance. "I'll write you a check for three hundred. Is that right?"

Mrs. Glinko shook her head and grinned. "Gotta have cash."

"In that case I'll have to go over to the bank. Do you want to write down my name and address? It's spelled Q-w-i-l-l-e-r-a-n."

"Got it!" she said, tapping her temple. "I'll *dispatch* Little Joe after dinner. Dispatch! Ha ha ha!"

"Not until after dinner?" he protested.

"We eat dinner. You folks eat lunch. Ha ha ha!"

After picking up some cash at the bank for Mrs. Glinko, Qwilleran drove to a parking lot overlooking the municipal marina. There he released the cats from the hamper. "No point in going home yet," he told them. "We'll give the guy time to fix the heater. Let's hope the Glinko system works."

He bought a hot dog and coffee at the refreshment stand and consumed it behind the wheel, offering the Siamese a few crumbs which they delicately declined. Together they watched the craft rocking at the piers: charter fishing boats, small yachts, and tall-masted sailboats. There was plenty of money rolling into Mooseville, he concluded. Soon the natives would get rich and start spending winters in the South. He wondered where the Glinkos would idle away the winter. Palm Springs? Caneel Bay?

At two o'clock he drove slowly to the cabin, skeptical about Mrs. Glinko's reliability and efficiency. To his relief he found a van parked in the clearing—a rusty, unmarked vehicle with doors flung wide and plumbing gear inside.

The cabin doors were also open, front and back, and warm June air wafted through the building. Little Joe had been smart enough to ventilate the place. Good thinking on his part, Qwilleran had to acknowledge. Why didn't I do that?

The access door on the front of the heater was open,

and in front of it a body lay sprawled on the floor. Qwilleran first noticed the muddy field boots, then the threadbare jeans. By the time his eyes reached the faded red plaid shirt, he knew this was no repairman.

"Hello," he said uncertainly. "Are you the plumber?"

The body rolled over, and a husky young woman with mousy hair stuffed into a feed cap sat up and said soberly, "There was a dead spider in the pilot light. Whole thing's dirty inside. I'm cleanin' it out. Gotta broom? I made a mess on the floor." This was said without expression in her large, flat face and dull gray eyes.

"You surprised me," Qwilleran said. "I was expecting some fellow named Joe."

"I'm Joanna," she said. "My daddy was Joe, so we were Big Joe and Little Joe." She lowered her eyes as she spoke.

"Was he a plumber, too?"

"He was more of a carpenter, but he did all kinds of things."

Noticing the past tense, Qwilleran sensed a family tragedy. "What happened, Joanna?" he asked in a sympathetic tone that was part genuine interest and part professional curiosity. He was thinking that a female plumber would make a good subject for the "Qwill Pen."

"My daddy was killed in an accident." She was still sitting on the floor with her eyes cast down.

"I'm sorry to hear that—very sorry. Was it a traffic accident?"

She shook her head sadly and said in her somber

voice, "A tailgate fell on him—the gate on a dump truck."

"Terrible!" Qwilleran exclaimed. "When did it happen?"

"Coupla months ago."

"You have my sympathy. How old was he?" Joanna appeared to be about twenty-five.

"Forty-three." She turned back to the heater as if wanting to end the painful conversation. She lighted the pilot, closed the door and scrambled to her feet. "Where's the broom?"

Qwilleran watched her sweep, noting that she was very thorough. Joanna was a strong, healthy-looking young person, but she never smiled.

"Be right back," she said as she carried a small toolkit to her van. When she returned, she mumbled, "That'll be thirty-five."

Assuming that she, like Mrs. Glinko, preferred cash, he gave her some bills from his money clip and accepted a receipt marked "Paid—Jo Trupp." He thought the charge was high, but he was grateful to have the heater operating.

Next she handed him a yellow slip of paper. "You gotta sign this," she said without looking at him. "It's for Mrs. Glinko."

It was a voucher indicating that he had paid Jo Trupp for the heater job—that he had paid her twenty-five dollars. Twenty-five? He hesitated over the discrepancy for only a moment before realizing he was dealing with corruption in low places. He would not embarrass the poor girl for ten dollars. Undoubtedly she had to pay Glinko a kickback and liked to skim a little off the top.

Once the plumber's van had disappeared down the long undulating driveway and the indoor climate was within reason, Qwilleran was able to appreciate the cabin: the whitewashed log walls, the open ceiling crisscrossed with log trusses, the oiled wood floors scattered with Indian rugs, two white sofas angled around a fieldstone fireplace, and the incomparable view from the bank of north windows. A mile out on the lake, sailboats were racing. A hundred miles across the water there was Canada.

He carried the wicker hamper indoors and opened the lid slowly. Immediately two dark brown masks with wide, blue eyes and perky ears rose from the interior and swiveled like periscopes. When assured that all was clear, they hopped out: lithe bodies with pale fawn fur accented by slender brown legs, whiplike brown tails, and those inquisitive brown masks. Qwilleran apologized to them for their protracted confinement and the unconscionable delay, but they ignored him and went directly to the fireplace to sniff the spot where a white bearskin rug had warmed the hearth two summers before; bloodied beyond repair at that time, it had since been replaced by an Indian rug. Next, Koko stared up with interest at the moosehead mounted above the mantel, and Yum Yum flattened herself to crawl under the sofa where she had formerly hidden her playthings. Then, within minutes they were both overhead, leaping across the beams, landing on the mantel, swooping down to the sofas, and skidding across the polished floor on handwoven rugs.

Qwilleran brought his luggage indoors and quickly telephoned Mildred Hanstable. "Mildred, I apologize for my bad manners this morning. I'm afraid I was rather curt when I talked with you."

"That's all right, Qwill. I know you were upset. Did it work out all right?"

"Amazingly well! Thanks for the tip. Glinko took care of the matter in no time at all. But I've got to talk to you about that extraordinary couple and their unorthodox way of doing business."

Mildred laughed. "It works, so don't disturb it. Why don't you come over here for dinner tonight? I'll throw together a casserole and a salad and take a pie out of the freezer."

Qwilleran accepted promptly and made a special trip into Mooseville for a bottle of Mildred's favorite brand of Scotch and a bottle of white grape juice for himself. He also laid in a supply of delicacies for the Siamese.

When he returned from town, Koko was in the back hall, busily occupied with a new discovery. The hallway functioned as a mudroom, with a mud-colored rug for wiping feet, hooks for hanging jackets, a cleaning closet, and other utilitarian features. Koko had tunneled under the rug and was squirming and making throaty sounds.

Qwilleran threw back the rug. Underneath it there was a trap door about two feet square, with a recessed metal ring for lifting. The cat eagerly sniffed its perimeter.

Qwilleran had visions of underground plumbing and wiring mysteries, and his curiosity equaled Koko's. "Get out of the way, old boy, and let's have a look," he said. He found a flashlight in the closet and swung back the heavy slab of oak. "It's sand! Nothing but sand!" Koko was teetering on the brink, ready to leap into the hole. "No!" Qwilleran thundered, and the cat winced, retreated, and sauntered away to lick his breast fur nonchalantly.

By the time Qwilleran set out for Mildred's cottage, his companions had been fed and were lounging on the screened porch overlooking the lake. They sat in a patch of sunshine, utterly contented with their lot, and why not? They had consumed a can of red salmon (minus the dark skin) and two smoked oysters. Now they relaxed in leisurely poses that prompted Qwilleran to tiptoe for his camera, but as soon as they saw him peer through the viewfinder, Yum Yum started scratching her ear with an idiot squint in her celestial blue eyes, while Koko rolled over and attended to the base of his tail with one leg pointing toward the firmament.

They were chased off the porch and locked in the cabin before Qwilleran set out on the half-mile walk to Mildred's place. A desolate stretch of beach bordered his own property, lapped by languid waves. Next, an outcropping of rock projected into the water, popularly known as Seagull Point, although one rarely saw a gull unless the lake washed up a dead fish. Beyond Seagull Point a string of a dozen cottages perched on the dune—a jumble of styles: rustic, contemporary, quaint, or simply ugly, like the boatlike structure said to be owned by a retired sea captain.

The last in the row was Mildred's yellow cottage. Beyond that, the dune was being cleared in preparation for new construction. Foundations were in evidence, and framing had been started.

A flight of twenty wooden steps led up the side of the dune to Mildred's terrace with its yellow umbrella table, and as Qwilleran reached the top she met him there, her well-upholstered figure concealed by a loose-fitting yellow beach dress.

"What's going on there?" Qwilleran called out, waving toward the construction site.

"Condominiums," she said ruefully. "I hate to see it happen, but they've offered us clubhouse and pool privileges, so it's not all bad. The lake is too cold for swimming, so . . . why not?"

Handing the bottles to his hostess, he volunteered to tend bar, and Mildred ushered him into the house and pointed out the glassware and ice cubes. Their voices sounded muffled, because the walls were hung with handmade quilts. Traditional and wildly contemporary designs had the initials M.H. stitched into the corners.

"These represent an unbelievable amount of work," Qwilleran said, recognizing an idea for the "Qwill Pen."

"I only appliqué the tops," she said. "My craftworkers do the quilting." Besides teaching school, writing for the local newspaper, and raising money for the hospital, she conducted a not-for-profit project for low-income handworkers.

Qwilleran regarded her with admiration. "You have boundless energy, Mildred. You never stop!"

"So why can't I lose weight?" she said, sidestepping the compliment modestly.

"You're a handsome woman. Don't worry about pounds."

"I like to cook, and I like to eat," she explained, "and my daughter says I don't get enough real exercise. Can you picture me jogging?"

"How is Sharon enjoying motherhood?" Qwilleran asked.

"Well, to tell the truth, she's restless staying home with the baby. She wants to go back to teaching. Roger thinks she should wait another year. What do you think, Qwill?"

"You're asking a childless bachelor, a failed husband, with no known relatives and no opinion! . . . By the way, I saw Roger on my way up from Pickax. He was hightailing it back to the office to file his copy for the weekend edition, no doubt."

Mildred passed a sizzling platter of stuffed mushrooms and rumaki. "I liked your column on the taxidermist, Qwill."

"Thanks. It was an interesting subject, and I learned that mounted animal heads should never be hung over a fireplace; it dries them out. The moosehead at the cabin may have to go to the hospital for a facelift. Also, I'd like to do something with the whitewashed walls. They'd look better if they were natural."

"That would make the interior darker," Mildred warned. "Of course, you could install skylights."

"Don't they leak?"

"Not if you hire a good carpenter."

"Where do I find a good carpenter? Call Glinko, I suppose. Has anyone figured out his racket, Mildred? He has a monopoly, and I suspect price-fixing, restraint of trade, and tax evasion. They don't accept checks, and they don't seem to keep written records."

"It's all in Mrs. Glinko's head," said Mildred. "That woman is a living computer."

"The IRS frowns on living computers."

"But you have to admit it's a wonderful convenience for summer people like us."

"I keep wondering what else they supply besides plumbers and carpenters."

"Now you're being cynical, Qwill. What was wrong with your space heater?"

"A dead spider in the pilot light—or so the plumber said; I'm not sure I believe it. Glinko sent me a *woman* plumber!"

Mildred nodded. "Little Joe."

"She isn't so little. Do you know her?"

"Of course I know her!" Mildred had taught school in the county for more than twenty years, and she knew an entire generation of students as well as their parents. "Her name is Joanna Trupp. Her father was killed in a freak accident this spring."

Qwilleran said, "There's a high percentage of fatal accidents in this county. Either people live to be ninety-five, or they die young—in hunting mishaps, drownings, car crashes, tractor rollovers . . ."

Mildred beckoned him to the dinner table.

"Is Little Joe a competent plumber?" he went on. "I thought of writing a column about her unusual occupation."

"I don't know what it takes to be a competent plumber," Mildred said, "but in school she was always good at working with her hands. Why she decided to get a plumber's license, I haven't the faintest idea. Why would any woman want to fix toilets and drains, and stick her head under the kitchen sink, and crawl under houses? I don't even like to clean the bathroom!"

The casserole was a sauced combination of turkey, homemade noodles, and artichoke hearts, and it put Qwilleran in an excellent frame of mind. The Caesar salad compounded his pleasure. The raspberry pie left him almost numb with contentment.

As Mildred served coffee on the terrace she said, "There's a party on the dunes tomorrow night. Why don't you come as my date and meet some of the summer people? Doc and Dottie Madley are hosting. He's a dentist from Pickax, you know. They come up weekends."

"Who will be there?"

"Probably the Comptons; you've met them, of course . . . The Urbanks are retired; he's a chemist and a golf nut and a bore . . . John and Vicki Bushland have a photo studio in the next county. He's an avid fisherman. Everyone calls him 'Bushy', which is funny because he doesn't have much hair . . . The attorney from Down Below is newly divorced. I don't know whether he'll be coming up this summer . . . There's a young woman renting the Dunfield cottage . . ."

"How about the retired sea captain?"

"Captain Phlogg never mixes, I'm glad to say. He's a stinker in more ways than one."

"I'd like to write a column on that guy, but he's a disagreeable old codger. I've been in his antique shop a couple of times, and it's a farce!"

"He's a fraud," Mildred said in a confidential tone. "He's never been to sea! He was just a ship's carpenter at the old shipyard near Purple Point."

"What is he doing in a social enclave like the Dunes Club?"

"Want to hear the story that's circulating? Phlogg bought lakefront property when it was considered worthless. He scrounged lumber from the shipyard and built the house with his own hands, and now lake frontage is up to two thousand dollars a foot! A word of warning, Qwill—don't ever let your cats out. He has a dog that has a reputation as a cat-killer. The Comptons took him to court when their cat was mauled."

There was a muffled ring from the telephone, and Mildred excused herself. Just inside the sliding doors she could be heard saying, "Hi, Roger! I hear you're babysitting tonight . . . No, what is it? . . . Who? . . . Oh, that's terrible! How did it happen? . . . What will his family do? They have three kids! . . . Well, thanks for letting me know, Roger, but that's really bad news. Maybe we can raise some money for them."

She returned to the terrace with a strained expression. "That was Roger," she said. "There's been a drowning—a young man he went to school with."

"How did it happen?" Qwilleran asked.

"He went fishing and didn't come home. They found his body at the mouth of the river. It'll be in the paper tomorrow."

"Boat accident?"

"No, he was casting from the bank of the river. I feel awful about it. After being out of work all winter, he'd just been hired for the construction gang at the condo development."

Mildred offered more coffee, but Qwilleran declined, saying he wanted to be home before the mosquitoes attacked. The true reason was that he felt a peculiar sensation on his upper lip—a twitch in his moustache that, in some inexplicable way, had always presaged trouble.

He covered the half mile along the beach more briskly than before. For the last few hundred yards he felt compelled to run. Even as he climbed up the dune to the cabin he could hear Koko yowling violently, and when he unlocked the door he smelled gas!

TWO

When Qwilleran returned from Mildred's cottage and smelled the noxious fumes in the cabin, he telephoned the Glinko number.

"Glinko *network!*" a woman's voice said, with emphasis on her new word.

He described the situation quickly with understandable anxiety.

"Ha ha ha!" laughed Mrs. Glinko. "Don't light any matches."

"No advice," he snapped. "Just send someone in a hurry." He had opened doors and windows and had shut the cats up in the toolshed.

In a matter of minutes an emergency truck pulled into the clearing, and the driver strode into the cabin, sniffing critically. Immediately he walked out again, looking up at the roof. Qwilleran followed, also looking up at the roof.

"Bird's nest," said the man. "It happens all the time. See that piece of straw sticking out of the vent? Some bird built its nest up there, and you've got carbon monoxide from the water heater seeping into your house. All you have to do is get up there on a ladder and clean it out."

Qwilleran did as he was told, reflecting that the Glinko network, no matter how corrupt, was not such a bad service after all. Two crises in one day had been handled punctually and responsibly. He found a stepladder in the toolshed, scrambled up on the roof, and extracted a clump of dried grass and eggshells from the vent, feeling proud of his sudden capability and feeling suddenly in tune with country living. Up there on the roof there was an intoxicating exhilaration. He was reluctant to climb down again, but the long June day was coming to an end, the mosquitoes were moving in, and remonstrative yowls were coming from the toolshed.

Settling on the screened porch with the Siamese, he relaxed at last. The yellow birds were swooping back and forth in front of the screens as if taunting the cats, and Koko and Yum Yum dashed to and fro in fruitless pursuit until they fell over in exhaustion, twitching their tails in frustration. So ended the first hectic day of their summer sojourn in Mooseville. It was only a sample of what was to come.

Qwilleran forgot about the drowning of Roger Mac-Gillivray's friend until he bought a newspaper the next morning. He was in Mooseville to have breakfast at the Northern Lights Hotel, and he picked up a paper to read at the table. Headlined on page one was Roger's account:

MOOSEVILLE MAN DROWNS IN RIVER

Buddy Yarrow, 29, of Mooseville Township, drowned while fishing in the Ittibittiwassee River Thursday night. His body was found at the mouth of the river Friday morning. Police had searched throughout the night after his disappearance was reported by his wife, Linda, 28.

According to a spokesperson for the sheriff's department, it appears that Yarrow slipped down the riverbank into the water. There was a mudslide at the location where his tackle box was found, and the river is deep at that point.

Yarrow was a strong swimmer, his wife told police, leading investigators to believe that he hit his head on a rock when he fell. A massive head injury was noted in the coroner's report. Police theorize that the strong current following last week's heavy rain swept the victim, stunned or unconscious, to the mouth of the river, where his body was caught in the willows overhanging the water.

"He always went fishing at that bend in the river," said Linda Yarrow. "He didn't have a boat. He liked to cast from the bank."

Besides his wife, the former Linda Tobin, Yarrow leaves three children: Bobbie, 5; Terry, 3; and Tammy, 6 months. He was a graduate of Moose County schools and was currently employed in the construction of the East Shore Condominiums.

There were pictures of the victim, obviously snapshots from a family album, showing him as a high school youth on the track team, later as a grinning bridegroom, still later as a fisherman squinting into the sun and holding a prize catch.

On page two of the newspaper, in thumb position, was the column "Straight from the Qwill Pen" about a dog named Switch, assistant to an electrician in Purple Point. Switch assisted his master by selecting tools from the toolbox and carrying them up the ladder in his mouth.

Qwilleran noted two typographical errors in his column and three in the drowning story. And his name was misspelled.

He had several ideas for future columns, but the subject that eluded him was the infamous Mooseville antique shop called The Captain's Mess, operated by the bogus Captain Phlogg. The man was virtually impossible to interview, being inattentive, evasive, and rude.

He sold junk and, worse yet, fakes. Yet, The Captain's Mess was a tourist attraction—so bad it was good. It was worth a story.

On Saturday morning—after a fisherman's breakfast of steak, eggs, hashed browns, toast and coffee—Qwilleran devised a new interview approach that would at least command Phlogg's attention. He left the hotel and walked to the ramshackle building off Main Street that was condemned by the county department of building and safety but championed by the Mooseville Chamber of Commerce. He found Captain Phlogg, with the usual stubble of beard and battered naval cap, sitting in a shadowy corner of the shop, smoking an odoriferous pipe and taking swigs from a pint bottle. In the jumble of rusted, mildewed, broken marine artifacts that surrounded the proprietor, only a skilled and patient collector could find anything worth buying. Some of them spent hours sifting through the rubble.

The captain kept an ominous belaying pin by his side, causing Qwilleran to maintain a safe distance as he began, "Good morning, Captain. I'm from the newspaper. I understand you're not a retired sea captain; you're a retired carpenter."

"Whut? Whut?" croaked the captain, evidencing more direct response than he had ever shown before.

"Is it true that you were a carpenter for a ship-builder at Purple Point—before you made a killing in land speculation?"

"Dunno whut yer talkin' about," said the man, vigorously puffing his pipe.

"I believe you live in a house on the dunes that you built with your own hands, using lumber stolen from the shipyard. Is that true?"

"None o' yer business."

"Aren't you the one who has a vicious dog that runs loose illegally?"

The old man snarled some shipyard profanity as he struggled to his feet.

Qwilleran started to back away. "Have you ever been taken to court on account of the dog?"

"Git outa here!" Captain Phlogg reached for the belaying pin.

At that moment a group of giggling tourists entered the shop, and Qwilleran made a swift exit, pleased with the initial results. He planned to goad the man with further annoying questions until he got a story. The chamber of commerce might not approve, but it would make an entertaining column, provided the expletives were deleted.

Returning to the log cabin, Qwilleran was met at the door by an excited Koko, while Yum Yum sat in a compact bundle, observing in dismay. Koko was racing back and forth to attract attention, yowling and yikking, and Qwilleran cast a hasty eye around the interior. Living room, dining alcove, kitchen and bar occupied one large open space, and there was nothing abnormal there. In the bathroom and bunkrooms everything appeared to be intact.

"What's wrong, Koko?" he asked. "Did a stranger come in here?" He worried about Glinko's duplicate key. There was no way of guessing how many persons might have access to that key. "What are you trying to tell me, old boy?"

For answer the cat leaped to the top of the bar and from there to the kitchen counter. Qwilleran investigated closely and, in doing so, stepped in something wet. On the oiled floorboards a spill usually remained on the surface until mopped up, and here was a sizable puddle! The idea of a catly misdemeanor flashed across Qwilleran's mind only briefly; the Siamese were much too fastidious to be accused of such a lapse.

Opening the cabinet door beneath the sink, he found the interior flooded and heard a faint splash. He groaned and reached for the telephone once more.

"Ha ha ha! A drip!" exclaimed the cheerful Mrs. Glinko. "Allright, we'll *dispatch* somebody PDQ."

In fifteen minutes an old-model van with more rust than paint pulled into the clearing—the same plumber's van as before—and Joanna swung out of the driver's seat.

"Got a leak?" she asked in her somber monotone as she plunged her head under the sink. "These pipes are old!"

"The cabin was built seventy-five years ago," Qwilleran informed her.

"There's no shutoff under the sink. How do I get down under?"

He showed her the trap door, and she pulled open the heavy slab with ease and lowered herself into the hole. Koko was extremely interested and had to be shooed away three times. When she emerged with cobwebs on her clothing, she did some professional puttering beneath the sink, went down under the floor again to reopen the valve, and presented her bill. Qwilleran paid thirty-five dollars again and signed a voucher for twenty-five. It made him an accomplice in a minor swindle, but he felt more sympathy for Joanna than for Glinko. He rationalized that the ten-dollar discrepancy might be considered a tip.

"What's under the floor?" he asked her.

"The crawl space. Just sand and pipes and tanks and lots of spiders. It's dusty."

"It can't be very pleasant."

"I ran into a snake once in a crawl space. My daddy ran into a skunk." She glanced about the cabin, her bland face showing little reaction until she spotted Koko and Yum Yum sitting on the sofa. "Pretty cats."

"They're strictly indoor pets and never go out of the house," Qwilleran explained firmly. "If you ever have occasion to come in here when I'm not at home, don't let them run outside! There's a vicious dog in the neighborhood."

"I like animals," she said. "Once I had a porcupine and a woodchuck."

"What are those yellow birds that fly around here?"

"Wild canaries. You have a lot of chipmunks, too. I have some pet chipmunks—and a fox."

"Unusual pets," he commented, wondering if vermin from the wildlife might be tracked into the cabin on her boots.

"I rescued two bear cubs once. Some hunter shot their mother."

"Are you allowed to keep wild animals in captivity?"

"I don't tell anybody," she said with a shrug. "The woodchuck was almost dead when I found him. I fed him with a medicine dropper."

"Where do you keep them?"

"Behind where I live. The cubs died."

"Very interesting," Qwilleran mused. Eventually he might write a column on Joanna the Plumber, but he would avoid mentioning Joanna the Illegal Zookeeper. "Thanks for the prompt service," he said in a tone of farewell.

When she had clomped out of the cabin in her heavy boots, he recalled something different about her appearance. The boots, the jeans, the faded plaid shirt and the feed cap were the same as before, but she was wearing lipstick, and her hair looked clean; it was tied back in a ponytail.

He settled down to work on his column for the midweek edition—about Old Sam, the gravedigger, who had been digging graves with a shovel for sixty years. He had plenty of notes on Old Sam as well as a catchy lead, but there was no adequate place to write. For a desk the cabin offered only the dining table, which was round. Papers had a way of sliding off the curved edges and landing on the floor, where the cats played toboggan on them, skidding across the oiled floorboards in high glee. They also liked to sit on his notes and catch their tails in the carriage of his electric typewriter.

"What I need," Qwilleran said to Yum Yum, who

was trying to steal a felt-tip pen, "is a private study." Even reading was difficult when one had a lapful of cat, and the little female's possessiveness about his person put an end to comfort and concentration. Nevertheless, he made the best of an awkward situation until the column was finished and it was time to dress for the beach party.

As the festive hour approached, the intense sun of an early evening was slanting across the lake, and Qwilleran wore his dark glasses for the walk down the beach to Mildred's cottage. He found her looking radiant in a gauzy cherry-colored shift that floated about her ample figure flatteringly and bared her shoulders, which were plump and enticingly smooth.

"Ooooh!" she cried. "With those sunglasses and that moustache, Qwill, you look so sexy!"

He paid her a guarded compliment in return, but smoothed his moustache smugly.

They walked along the shore to the Madleys' contemporary beach house, where a flight of weathered steps led up the side of the dune to a redwood deck. Guests were gathering there, all wearing dark glasses, which gave them a certain anonymity. They were a colorful crew—in beach dresses, sailing stripes, clamdiggers and halters, raw-hued espadrilles, sandals, Indian prints, Hawaiian shirts, and peasant blouses. Even Lyle Compton, the superintendent of schools, was wearing a daring pair of plaid trousers. There was one simple white dress, and that was on a painfully thin young woman with dark hair clipped close to her head. She was introduced as Russell Simms.

The hostess said to Qwilleran, "You're both new-comers. Russell has just arrived up here, too."

"Are you from Down Below?" he asked.

Russell nodded and gazed at the lake through her sunglasses.

"Russell is renting the Dunfield house," Dottie Madley mentioned as she moved away to greet another arrival.

"Beautiful view," Qwilleran remarked.

Russell ventured a timid yes and continued to look at the water.

"And constantly changing," he went on. "It can be calm today and wildly stormy tomorrow, with raging surf. Is this your first visit to Moose County?"

"Yes," she said.

"Do you plan to stay for the summer?"

"I think so." Her dark glasses never met his dark glasses.

"Russell . . . that's an unusual name for a woman."

"Family name," she murmured as if apologizing.

"What do you plan to do during the summer?"

"I like to . . . read . . . and walk on the beach."

"There's a remarkably good museum in town, if you're interested in shipwrecks, and a remarkably bad antique shop. How did you happen to choose the Dunfield cottage?"

"It was advertised."

"In the *Daily Fluxion*? I used to write for that lively and controversial newspaper."

"No. In the *Morning Rampage*."

Qwilleran's attempts at conversation were foundering, and he was grateful when Dottie introduced another couple and steered Russell away to meet the newly divorced attorney.

Everyone at the party recognized Qwilleran—or, at least, his moustache. When he was living Down Below and writing for the *Fluxion*, his photograph with mournful eyes and drooping moustache appeared at the top of his column regularly. When he suddenly arrived in Pickax as the heir to the Klingenschoen fortune, he was an instant celebrity. When he established the Klingenschoen Memorial Fund to distribute his wealth for the benefit of the community, he became a local hero.

On the Madleys' redwood deck he circulated freely, clinking ice cubes in a glass of ginger ale, teasing Dottie, flattering the chemist's wife, asking Bushy about the fishing, listening sympathetically as a widower described how a helicopter had scattered his wife's ashes over Three Tree Island.

Leo Urbank, the chemist, flaunted his academic degrees, professional connections, and club affiliations like a verbal résumé and asked Qwilleran if he played golf. Upon receiving a negative reply he wandered away.

Bushy, the photographer, invited Qwilleran to go fishing some evening. He was younger than the other men, although losing his hair. Qwilleran had always enjoyed the company of news photographers, and Bushy seemed to fit the pattern: outgoing, likable, self-assured.

The superintendent of schools said to Qwilleran,

"Have you heard from Polly Duncan since she escaped from Moose County?"

Qwilleran knew Lyle Compton well—a tall, thin, saturnine man with a perverse sense of humor and blunt speech. "I received a postcard, Lyle," he replied. "She was met at the airport by the local bigwigs, and they gave her a bunch of flowers."

"That's more than we did for the unfortunate woman who came here. I think Polly's getting the better part of the deal. Since she's so gung ho on Shakespeare, she may decide to stay in England."

Qwilleran's moustache bristled at the suggestion, although he knew that Compton was baiting him. "No chance," he said. "When Polly airs her theory that Shakespeare was really a woman, she'll be deported . . . By the way, do you know anything about that young man who was drowned?"

As superintendent of schools Compton knew everyone in the county, and was always willing to share his information, though taking care to point out that he was not a gossip, just a born educator. "Buddy Yarrow? Yes, he was well-liked at school. Had to struggle to keep his grades up, though. Married the Tobin girl, and they had too many kids too fast. He had a tough time supporting them."

Mildred overheard them. "I'm applying to the Klingenschoen Fund for financial aid for the Yarrows," she said. "I hope you'll put in a good word, Qwill."

Dottie Madley said, "Buddy built our steps down to the beach, and he was very considerate—didn't leave any sawdust or nails lying around. Glinko sent him to us."

"Did someone mention Glinko?" asked Urbank. "We had some plumbing done this week, and Glinko sent us a *lady plumber*!"

"I suppose she fixes everything with a hairpin," said Doc.

Qwilleran concealed a scowl. He had long ago curbed his tendency to make jocular remarks about hairpins and bras.

"Doc!" said Mildred in her sternest classroom voice. "That is an outmoded sexist slur. Go to the powder room and wash your mouth out with soap."

"I'll stop quipping about hairpins," Doc retorted, "when you gals stop calling the john the powder room."

"Objection!" said John Bushland. "Derogatory reference to a minority!"

It was then that Qwilleran made a remark that exploded like a bomb. It was just a casual statement of his summer intentions, but the reaction astonished him.

"Don't do it!" said the host.

"You'll be sorry," his wife warned, and she wasn't smiling.

"Only mistake I ever made in my life," said the attorney. "We tried it last summer, and it broke up our marriage."

"When we did it, my wife almost had a nervous breakdown," said the chemist.

Bushy added seriously, "For the first time in my life I felt like *killing someone*!"

Qwilleran had simply mentioned that he would like to build an addition to the log cabin. Everyone at the party, he now learned, had encountered infuriating or insurmountable obstacles while building an addition or remodeling a kitchen or adding a porch or putting on a new roof.

"What seems to be the problem?" he asked in mild bewilderment.

"All the good contractors are busy with big jobs in the summer," explained Doc Madley. "Right now they're building the condos on the shore, a big motel in Mooseville, senior housing in North Kennebeck, a new wing on the Pickax Hospital, and a couple of schools. For a small job like yours you have to hire an underground builder."

"If you can find one," Urbank added.

"Pardon my ignorance," Qwilleran said, "but what is an underground builder?"

"You have to dig to find one," said Compton by way of definition.

"What about Glinko? I thought his service was the bright and beautiful answer to all problems great and small."

"Glinko can send you someone for an emergency or a day's work, but he doesn't handle building projects."

"Do these underground builders advertise in the phone book?"

"Advertise!" Bushy exclaimed. "They don't even have telephones. Some of them camp out in tents."

"Then how do you track them down?"

"Hang around the bars," someone said.

"Hang around the lumberyard," someone else said. "If you see a guy buying two-by-fours and nails and plywood and *being refused credit*, grab him! That's your man."

"Don't give him a nickel in advance," Compton warned. "Pay him for the hours worked."

"And hope to God he comes back the next day," said Urbank. "We spent one whole summer waiting for a man to finish our job, and then we found out he was in jail in some other county."

"Ours lived in a trailer camp," said Dottie, "and Doc went out there every morning at six o'clock to haul him out of bed."

"If you're interested in bargains," Doc said, "the underground builder is a good bet. He may never finish the job, but he comes cheap."

"And you'll have to watch him every minute, or he'll put the door where the window should be," Bushy warned.

"Hmmm," said Qwilleran, unable to muster any other verbal reaction after the astonishing tirade.

"On the whole," said Compton, "they know their craft, but they're damned casual about it. They don't bother with blueprints. You tell them what you want, draw a picture in the sand with a stick, and wave your hands."

"Of course, if the worst comes to the worst," said Doc, "there's always Mighty Lou."

Everyone laughed, and the discussion died a merciful death as the hostess invited them to the buffet.

The guests pocketed their sunglasses, went indoors, and served themselves cold chicken, potato salad, and carrot straws. Some found small tables. Others balanced plates on their knees. Compton stood up with his plate on the fireplace mantel.

The attorney, sitting next to Qwilleran, said under his breath, "Have you tried talking to that new girl? I'm brilliant in the courtroom, but I couldn't get a blasted word out of that woman!"

Mildred said in her classroom voice, "Did anyone see the visitors last night?"

"What time?" Bushy asked.

"About two in the morning."

"That's when they usually come around," Sue Urbank remarked.

"Let me tell you what happened to me," the photographer said. "I took my boat out last night for some twilight fishing, and I was baiting my hook when I felt something shining over my head. I knew what it was, of course, so I reached for my camera—I never go anywhere without it—but when I looked up again, the thing was gone!"

"What was it?" Qwilleran asked.

"Another UFO," Bushy replied in a matter-of-fact way.

Qwilleran searched the other faces, but no one seemed surprised.

"Ever get a picture of one?" the photographer was asked.

"Never had any luck. They scoot off so fast."

"Have any abductions been reported?" Qwilleran inquired with the smirk of a skeptic.

"Not yet," answered Doc, "but I'm sure Mildred will be the first."

Calmly she retorted, "Doc, I hope all your patients sue you!"

Sue Urbank said, "It's a funny thing. I didn't see a single visitor last summer, but this year they're out there almost every night."

"We can expect abnormal weather—with all that activity over the lake," Dottie predicted.

Qwilleran continued to stare at them with disbelief. Mildred observed his reaction and said, "Shall I phone you, Qwill, some night around two o'clock when they come around?"

"That's kind of you," he said, "but I need all the beauty sleep I can get."

During the small talk Russell Simms was silent, staring at her plate and chewing slowly. Once Qwilleran glanced suddenly in her direction and caught her studying him from the corner of her eye. He preened his moustache.

Urbank said, "Did everyone read their horoscope this morning? Mine said I'd make a wise investment, so I went out and bought a new set of clubs."

"Mine said I should cooperate with my mate," said the attorney. "Unfortunately I don't have one at the moment. Any volunteers?"

Bushy said, "Today's *Fluxion* told me to go out and

have a good time. The *Rampage* told me to stay home and get some work done."

"I don't read horoscopes," Compton announced.

"That's true," said his wife. "I have to read them to him while he's shaving."

"Lyle, I always knew you were a hypocrite," said Doc.

"A hypocritical superintendent is more to be trusted than a painless dentist," said Compton. "Never trust a dentist who doesn't hurt."

"Qwill, what's your sign?" asked Mildred.

"I don't think I have a sign," he said. "When the signs were handed out, I was overlooked."

Three persons asked his birthdate and decided he was a Gemini on the cusp of Taurus. Mildred said it would be an interesting year for Gemini. "You can expect the unexpected," she added.

When coffee was served and guests returned to the deck, Compton wandered down to the beach to smoke a cigar. Qwilleran followed him and said, "Doc is a great kidder."

"He's good at shooting the breeze," Compton said, "but if you want your teeth fixed, you might better go to an auto mechanic."

"How did you react to all that chatter about UFOs and horoscopes?"

"Don't expect any rational conversation from this beach crowd," said the superintendent. "They're all intelligent folks, but they get a little giddy when they come up here. Must be something in the atmosphere."

"I assume Captain Phlogg never comes to any of these parties."

"No, he's an antisocial fellow. He has a big dog that wanders around the dunes like the hound of the Baskervilles, and I've got my shotgun loaded. If I ever catch him doing his business *on my beach*, he's going to get it! Right between the eyes!"

Qwilleran said, "I opened a can of worms when I mentioned building an addition."

"You don't really intend to do it, do you?"

"I'm badly in need of more space. The cabin is okay for weekends or a brief vacation, but it's inadequate for the whole summer. Did you ever hire an underground builder?"

"About two months ago," said Compton. "He poured a slab for a two-car garage and roughed it in, and then he never came back. I've done everything but hire a private detective. He was one of the itinerants who come up here during the resort season, you know, and the only way I could get hold of him was to leave a message at the Shipwreck Tavern. They haven't seen him for five weeks, and we're sitting there with a half-built garage. Can't get anyone else to finish the damn thing."

"This is not very encouraging," Qwilleran said.

"You have to live through it to believe it."

"Someone mentioned Mighty Lou . . ."

"Forget him! You may have seem him swaggering around town—a weight lifter who thinks he's a builder. He has a fortune in tools, but he doesn't know which end of the nail to hit."

"How does he make a living?"

"He doesn't need to make a living. His family used to own all the sandpits in the county."

There was a spectacular sunset—a ball of fire sinking into the lake and turning it blood red. Then the mosquitoes swooped in, and the guests went indoors to play cards. Qwilleran suggested to Mildred that they leave.

"Let's go home and make a sundae," she said. "I'm still hungry. Do you realize there were thirteen of us at that party? That's unlucky."

"We'll all get food poisoning from the potato salad," Qwilleran predicted cheerfully. "Did you get a chance to talk to the young woman in the white dress? Her first name is Russell. She acts like a sleepwalker."

"I don't know what she's all about," Mildred said. "Did you see her eyes when she took off her sunglasses? Weird!"

"Maybe she landed from one of your extraterrestrial aircraft."

"You don't believe in the visitors," Mildred reproached him. "But just wait till you see one!" When they got to Mildred's she served homemade French vanilla ice cream with strawberries and a sprinkling of something crunchy. "What do you think of the topping?"

"It looks like dry catfood," he said, "but it's good!"

"It's my homemade cereal—wonderful in the morning with milk and sliced bananas. What do you eat for breakfast, Qwill?"

"I haven't eaten cereal since I was twelve years old."

"Then I'm going to give you some to take home."
Mildred was always mothering her friends with homemade food. "Now tell me about the addition you want
to build."

"Nothing very large—just a room for sleeping and
writing, and a lavatory, and an apartment for the cats.
Could you make a rough diagram? Something I could
show the builder?"

"That will be easy," she said. "I'll make elevations,
too. You'll never be able to match the log walls, but
you can use board-and-batten and stain it to harmo-
nize with the logs."

She made sketches, and they discussed details, and
he stayed longer than he had intended. When he finally
left for home, Mildred gave him a plastic tub of cereal
and lent him a flashlight for the beach. "Watch out for
the rocks at Seagull Point," she warned as she sprayed
him with mosquito repellent. "And watch out for visitors!" she added mischievously.

Walking back to the cabin, he was confident he
could line up a reputable builder without resorting to
workmen on the fringe. He had contacts in Pickax; the
Klingenschoen money was at his disposal; and he had
done many favors for individuals and organizations.
He could foresee no problem.

Arriving at the cabin, he scrambled up the side of the
dune, walked around the building and let himself in
the back door. "I'm home!" he called out. "Where's
the welcoming committee? . . . Damn!" He tripped
over a crumpled rug that was supposed to cover the
trap door.

Switching on lights, he searched for the Siamese. As soon as he saw Yum Yum sitting on the sofa in her worried pose, he knew something was amiss, and then he noticed the shower of confetti on the hearth rug. An entire page of the newspaper had been torn to bits! Completely destroyed was the story on page one about the drowning of Buddy Yarrow, and that included Qwilleran's own column on the reverse side—the story about Switch, the electrician's dog.

"Where the devil are you?" Qwilleran shouted. There was a slight movement overhead, and his gaze moved slowly up the face of the stone fireplace to the high mantel—a huge timber hewn from a twenty-foot pine log. Koko was not on the mantel or on the cross-beams. He was on the moosehead, sitting tall between the antlers and radiating satisfaction in every whisker.

"Don't sit there looking smart!" Qwilleran barked at him. "Whatever you're trying to tell me, your mode of communication is not appreciated. Furthermore, you rolled up that rug in the hall and I tripped over it! I could have broken my neck!"

Koko squeezed his eyes and looked angelic.

"You devil!" Qwilleran said as he collected the bits of paper, wondering why Koko had done what he did.

THREE

If Qwilleran had read his horoscope Monday morning, he could have saved a few phone calls. Most vacationers consulted their stars in the *Morning Rampage*, which was flown to Mooseville daily from Down Below. On Monday morning the *Rampage* had this to say to Gemini readers: "Listen to the advice of associates. Don't insist on doing things your own way."

Qwilleran never read the horoscopes, however. First he telephoned XYZ Enterprises in Pickax, and Don Exbridge said, "I wish we could accommodate you, Qwill, but we're having labor trouble, and it'll be a miracle if we can meet our contract deadlines. We're in

danger of losing a whole lot of money." Then he called
Moose County Construction, second largest contractor
in the area, and was assured they would be glad to do
the work for him—next summer. Finally, the owner of
Kennebeck Building Industries declared it would be a
privilege and a pleasure to build an addition to the
Klingenschoen log cabin—after Labor Day.

Qwilleran wanted the new wing in July, not September, and his disappointment was aggravated by two
other developments. First, a cluster of insect bites had
suddenly appeared on his left buttock, and they were
driving him crazy despite applications of an expensive
preparation recommended by the Mooseville druggist.
And that was not all: The kitchen sink was leaking
again!

Irately he made another emergency call to Glinko
and then stormed out of the house in frustration and
annoyance, hoping the lonely half-mile stretch of sand
between the cabin and the dune cottages would restore
his perspective.

As he walked he began to realize that he had lived
contentedly with very little money during his entire
adult life; now that unlimited funds were available, he
was reacting like a spoiled child. He sat down on a log
tossed up on the beach by a recent storm, sitting carefully to avoid the cluster of bites. The lake rippled
gently, and the water lapped the shore with soothing
splashes. Sandpipers ran up and down the beach. Gulls
were squawking.

An unusual number of gulls filled the sky to the east,
wheeling and diving and screaming. Something special

was happening beyond the clump of rocks and willows known as Seagull Point. He walked slowly toward the promontory lest he disturb their fun, and when he reached the willows he saw a woman on the beach, a drab figure in fawncolored slacks and sweater. She was standing at the water's edge, taking food from her sweater pockets and tossing it to the hysterical birds. He recognized Russell's dark clipped hair and her dreamlike movements. The gulls were going berserk, skreeking and chattering, fighting each other for scraps in midair, swooping in and taking the food from her fingers. And she was talking to them in a language he could not interpret. He watched the spectacle until her pockets were empty and she walked slowly east toward the cottages.

As Qwilleran sauntered back toward the cabin his pique was somewhat soothed by the tranquility of the beach and the performance of the gulls. Climbing the slope of the dune was an awkward exercise. In the fine dry sand he climbed three steps upward and slid two steps backward. Avalanches of sand cascaded down to the beach. Other beach-dwellers had installed steps to combat the erosion. He really would need to find a carpenter . . .

A familiar van stood in the clearing, and Joanna was in the kitchen repairing the second leak under the sink.

"How did it happen so soon after you fixed it?" he demanded with a hint of accusation.

"You need new pipe. This old stuff is no good."

"Then why didn't you tell me? Why didn't you install some new pipe?"

"I just did," she said simply, lying on the floor, propped on one elbow, with her head under the sink.

When Qwilleran saw the bill, he said, "What kind of pipe am I buying? Gold-plated?"

"It's plastic," she said in her humorless way. "Could I have a drink of water?"

He handed her a glass. "Help yourself. I think you know where it is."

"You gonna be here all summer?" She was wearing lipstick again—a purplish red.

"That's my intention," he said with pointed brevity, thinking she might be planning to pay daily social visits.

She looked around the cabin, staring at the Indian throw rugs with their splashes of red. "Pretty rugs."

A raucous voice was coming from her van. "I believe your short-wave radio wants your attention," he said.

After she had driven off in her van to the next job, Qwilleran began to suspect the entire Glinko method of doing business. When Joanna fixed the sink the first time, could she have left a fitting loose so that it would start dripping again? Was this a Glinko technique? Did Mrs. Glinko train her people, like a north-country Fagin?

Suspicious, frustrated, and disgruntled, he needed the therapy of a long lunch hour at the Press Club with half a dozen fellow journalists, but there was no Press Club within four hundred miles of Moose County. There was, however, his old friend Arch Riker. He made a call to the newspaper office in Pickax.

After years without an adequate newspaper, Moose

County now had a publication of professional caliber that reached the reading public twice a week, answering their need for local news and local advertising. It was called the *Moose County Something*, a name that had started as a joke and had persisted. Editor and publisher of the *Something* was Qwilleran's lifelong friend from Down Below. He telephoned Arch Riker. "Are you free for dinner tonight, Arch? It's been a long time."

"Sure has!" said Riker. Because of his approaching marriage and the pressures of launching a new publication he had not been available for bachelor dinners for many weeks. "I'm free, and I'm hungry. What did you have in mind?"

"I've moved up to the cabin for the summer. Why don't you meet me here, and we'll go to the Northern Lights Hotel. They have spaghetti on Mondays . . . How's your lovely fiancée?"

"Lovely, hell! We broke it off this weekend," Riker growled into the phone. "I'll see you at six o'clock . . . Wait a minute! Where's your cabin? I've never been there."

"Take the main highway north to the lake, then left for three miles until you see a K on a cedar post."

The editor's car pulled into the clearing shortly after six, and Qwilleran went out to meet his paunchy, red-faced, middle-aged friend.

"Man, this is my idea of the perfect summer place!" Riker exclaimed as he admired the weathered logs, hundred-foot pine trees, and endless expanse of water.

"Come in and mix yourself a martini," Qwilleran said. "We'll relax on the porch for a while."

The editor entered the cabin in a state of awe and envy as he saw the massive stone fireplace, the open ceiling trussed with logs, the moosehead over the mantel, and the bar top made from a single slab of pine. "You're one lucky dog!"

He mixed his drink with the concentration of a research chemist while Qwilleran leaned on the bar, watching the process, knowing enough not to interrupt. Then, "What happened between you and Amanda?" he asked with the genuine concern of an old friend.

"She's the most cantankerous, opinionated, obstinate, unpredictable woman I've ever met," Riker said. "Enough is enough!"

Qwilleran nodded. He knew Amanda Goodwinter. "Too bad. She's losing a good man. Do you ever hear from Rosie?"

"She writes to the kids, and they keep me informed. Rosie married again, and they say she has to support him."

"Rosie lost a good guy, too. How do you feel about living up here? Have you adjusted?"

Riker gave his martini a trial sip, winced, and nodded approval. "Yes, I'm glad to be here. I was relieved to cut loose from the *Fluxion*, and after the divorce I wanted to get out of the city. I never thought I'd like living in the hinterland, so far from everywhere, but my attitude is changing. My viewpoint is changing."

"In what way?"

"Remember our front-page story about the chicken coop fire last week? It destroyed 150,000 chickens. When I was working Down Below I would have written a flippant headline about the world's largest chicken barbecue, assuming the place was fully insured and no particular loss." He took another sip of his martini. "Instead, I empathized with the farmer. I've never met Doug Cottle, but I've driven past his farm— the neat house, well-kept barnyard, huge facility for chickens. And when it happened, I felt real agony over the loss of his property and the fate of all those birds trapped in a burning building. I could imagine his dreams and years of work going up in flames in the middle of the night! . . . Ironic, isn't it? I've edited copy for hundreds of fires Down Below, and I never felt that way before. Am I getting old?"

They carried their drinks to the lakeside porch, where the armchairs were made of three-inch logs hammered together by some anonymous carpenter at some date unknown.

"Sit down, Arch. They're more comfortable than they look."

Riker slid cautiously into a hollowed-out seat and breathed a deep sigh of contentment. "Beautiful view! I'll bet you get some spectacular sunsets. You have a lot of goldfinches."

"What do you know about birds, Arch?"

"When you raise a family you learn a lot of things you didn't want to know."

"My plumber said they're wild canaries."

"Your plumber didn't have three kids working on

merit badges in ornithology. What do you hear from Polly, Qwill? Does she like England?"

"I've had a couple of postcards. They've asked her to give talks to civic groups."

"I suppose you'll be seeing a lot of Mildred while Polly's away."

Qwilleran's moustache bristled. "If you're thinking what I think you're thinking, the answer is no! Mildred lives half a mile down the beach; we both write for the newspaper; her son-in-law is one of my best friends; she's a great cook. But that doesn't mean I intend to jeopardize my relationship with Polly. And, for what it's worth, Mildred has a husband."

"Okay, okay!" said Riker, throwing up his hands in surrender. He and Qwilleran had grown up together in Chicago, and their friendship had survived fistfights in grade school, arguments in high school, competition in college, and bickering ever since.

Qwilleran said, "Now that you've broken up with Amanda, there's no reason why you couldn't take Mildred out to dinner yourself, Arch. On a scale of one to ten I'd give your ex-fiancée a two and Mildred a nine."

"Not bad!"

"And I'd rate you six-plus."

Riker threw him a sour look. "Don't forget I'm your boss."

"Don't forget I'm your financial backer." The *Moose County Something* had been made possible by a loan from the Klingenschoen Fund, engineered by Qwilleran behind the scenes. "And if you don't start spelling my name right in my column, the interest rate is going up."

"I apologize. We gave the typesetter twenty lashes and an hour to get out of town." Riker looked around the porch. "Where's that supercat? Has he read any minds lately? Predicted any crimes? Sniffed out any dead bodies?"

"Mostly he's too busy being a cat—laundering his tail, chattering at squirrels, eating spiders—all that kind of stuff. But yesterday he tore up the front page of your newspaper, Arch. That should tell you something about the *Something*. He may be protesting the number of typos."

Koko was a legend among newsmen Down Below—the only cat in the history of journalism to be an honorary member of the Press Club. In addition to feline curiosity and Siamese intelligence he possessed an intuition that could put him on the scent of a crime. With a sniff here and a scratch there he could dig up information that astounded humans who had to rely on brainpower alone.

"He would have made a great investigative reporter," Riker said. "We always had cats at home, but never any to compare with Koko. I think it has something to do with his whiskers. He has a magnificent set of whiskers."

"Yes," Qwilleran agreed quietly, stroking his ample moustache.

Riker leaned forward suddenly and squinted at a small mound of sawdust on the porch floor. "You've got carpenter ants!"

"Carpenter *what*?"

"Ants that chew their way through old wood. You'd better get a fumigator out here."

Qwilleran groaned. He envisioned another call to Glinko.

Riker misunderstood the reaction. "Well, you don't want the porch to fall down around your ears, do you? You should get a carpenter out here to examine the logs."

Qwilleran groaned again. "Let me tell you about the joys of living in a seventy-five-year-old log cabin—the perfect summer place, as you call it." He explained the Glinko system, described the couple who operated it, and recounted the visits of Joanna Trupp. "Three visits from a plumber in four days!"

"Sounds to me as if she goes for your moustache," Riker said. "You know how women react to that brush on your lip! Are you going to take her to lunch?"

Qwilleran ignored that quip. "It sounds to me as if the whole Glinko network is a racket. I'll know more at the end of the summer. If my suspicions are correct, the *Something* should run an exposé!"

"Put Koko on the investigation," the editor said with a grin.

"I'm serious, Arch! The whole operation stinks!"

"Oh, come on, Qwill! You're making a mountain out of a molehill. You'd suspect your own grandmother."

Qwilleran shifted his position uncomfortably.

"What's the matter? You're doing a lot of wriggling

tonight. I think the porch posts aren't the only place you've got ants."

"They're insect bites that itch like hell," Qwilleran said testily. "About a dozen bites in one spot, and they don't go away."

His friend nodded wisely. "Spider bites. Our kids used to get them at summer camp. They last about a week."

At that moment Koko swaggered onto the porch with a show of authority and stared pointedly at Qwilleran.

"Excuse me while I feed the cats," he said. "Mix yourself another drink, Arch, and then we'll go into town for dinner."

The resort town of Mooseville was two miles long and two blocks wide, strung out along the shoreline at the foot of the sandbluffs.

"One of these days," Riker predicted, "some horny buck will chase a sexy doe across the top of that hill, and all that sand will come sliding down. We'll have another Pompeii. I only hope it's on our deadline."

At the village limits the lakeshore highway became Main Street, with the municipal docks, a marina, and the Northern Lights Hotel on the north side. Across the street were civic buildings and business establishments built entirely of logs, or concrete poured to resemble logs. Post office, town hall, bank and stores acted out the charade, and only the Shipwreck Tavern deviated from civic policy. The town's noisiest and most popular bar occupied what appeared to be the wooden hull of a beached ship.

Qwilleran said, "We'll stop at the tavern for a quickie and then go over to the hotel to eat."

The interior of the bar emulated the hold of an old sailing vessel with sloping bulkheads and massive timbers, but instead of creaking hull, slapping waves, and singing whales, the sound effects were of television, jukebox, video games, and shouting, laughing patrons.

"*Like the pressroom at the Fluxion!*" Riker yelled. "*Who are they?*"

"*Tourists! Summer people! Locals!*" Qwilleran shouted back.

A busy waitress with a talent for lip-reading took their order: one martini straight-up with an anchovy olive, and one club soda with a lemon twist. When the bartender received the order, he waved in the direction of their table. Only Qwilleran ever ordered club soda with a twist.

Excusing himself, Qwilleran ambled over to the crowded bar to wedge in a few words with the man who was pulling beer. What followed was a pantomime of frowns, head-shaking, shrugs, and other gestures of helplessness.

"*What was that?*" Riker shouted.

"*Tell you later.*"

A whiskered old man in a battered naval cap lurched into the tavern and climbed on a stool; the nearby barflies moved away.

"*Who's that?*"

"Antique dealer!" Qwilleran pointed out another colorful ancient in overalls—red-cheeked, bright-eyed, nimble as a monkey. *"Gravedigger!"*

They were soon blasted out of the Shipwreck Tavern and across the street to the hotel, where the dining room was so quiet, Riker complained, that it hurt his ears. Plastic covers on the tables and paper bibs on the customers identified it as spaghetti night.

"Now I'll explain," said Qwilleran. "That perfect summer place of mine that you admire so much is too small for everyday living. I want to build a small addition. I've talked to Hasselrich, and it's approved by the estate, but now comes the problem: finding a builder."

"That shouldn't be difficult," said Riker. "The county has some big contractors."

"Unfortunately they're tied up with major projects in the warm months, and they won't take a small job. The summer people have to resort to itinerant carpenters who drive into town in rusty crates and live in tents."

"Are they licensed?"

"They get away without a license because they're a necessary evil. The township looks the other way."

"I never heard of such a thing!"

"There are plenty of things you never heard of, Arch, until you came to Moose County. It's like living on another planet . . . Speaking of planets, do you hear any talk about UFOs?"

"Occasionally from the wire services, but that's old stuff."

"I mean—have you heard reports of recent activity over the lake?"

"No," said the editor with amused interest. "Are there rumors?"

"The summer people discuss visitors from outer space the way you talk about the Chicago Cubs. Why don't you assign Roger to do a story?"

"Why don't you do the story yourself? It's your lead."

"I'm a nonbeliever. You and I know it's some kind of meteorological phenomenon, but Roger swears it's interplanetary, and Mildred acts as if she's on first-name terms with the crews."

The salad was crisp, the garlic bread was crusty, and the spaghetti was al dente. "It's the best thing they do," Qwilleran said. "All the locals come on Mondays. They let the tourists have the gray pork chops and gray baked potatoes and gray broccoli on the other nights."

A young couple at a nearby table waved to Qwilleran, and when Riker said he had to go back to the office, Qwilleran went over to speak with Nick and Lori Bamba. "Who's baby-sitting tonight?" he asked.

"My mother-in-law," said Lori. "Thank God for mothers-in-law. I've given up trying to get you to do it, Qwill."

"Pull up a chair," Nick invited. "Have dessert with us."

Lori was Qwilleran's part-time secretary. Working out of her house, she answered his mail with one hand and held the formula bottle with the other. "Your mail has doubled since you started writing the 'Qwill Pen,' " she said. "I can hardly keep up with it."

"Start typing with two hands," he suggested.

"How are the cats?"

"They're fine. We've moved up to the cabin for the summer, and I want to build an addition. Know where I can find a good builder?"

Lori and Nick exchanged significant glances. "Clem Cottle?" Nick suggested.

"Perfect! Clem needs the work."

"And he's not so busy on the farm since the fire . . . Qwill, we're talking about Doug Cottle's son," said Nick. "They're the ones had the big chicken coop fire."

Lori said, "Clem's getting married, and he could use some extra money."

"Is this guy any good?" Qwilleran asked.

"Very good, very reliable," Nick said. "When would you want him to start? I'll phone him right away. We're in the same softball league."

"For starters I'd like him to build a flight of steps down to the beach."

"Sure, he can do that with one hand!"

Nick excused himself and went to the phone, and Lori said to Qwilleran, "I wish Nick could find another job that would use his skills and experience—and still allow us to live here—and still pay a decent salary. Being an engineer at the state prison isn't the most elevating occupation. He sees so much that's sordid and just plain wrong."

"But he has a built-in verve that keeps him riding on top. He's always up."

"That's his public posture," Lori said. "I see him at home . . . Here he comes."

"Clem's interested," Nick said. "He wants to talk to you."

The voice on the phone had the chesty resonance of a man who has spent his life on a farm—and on a softball field. "Hello, Mr. Qwilleran. I hear you want a carpenter."

"Yes, I have several jobs in mind, but the most urgent is a set of steps down to the beach before my cabin slides down into the lake. Do you know the kind I mean?"

"Sure, I helped Buddy Yarrow build those a couple of years ago for some people at the Dune Club. I know what lumber to order without any waste."

"When could you start?"

"How about tomorrow?"

"I couldn't ask better than that. Do you know where to find me?"

"It's the drive with a K on a post. I've passed it a million times."

"See you tomorrow then." Qwilleran tamped his moustache with satisfaction and returned to the Bambas' table. "I'm indebted to you kids," he said, and picked up their dinner check.

When Qwilleran returned home, the Siamese greeted him with a look of hungry eagerness, and he scouted for a small treat that they might enjoy. Mildred's tub of homemade cereal was still unopened. "This may look like catfood," he explained, "but it's breakfast cereal for humans." (They normally objected to anything produced especially for cats.) They gobbled it up. Then he sprawled on the sofa with a news magazine, while Yum Yum snuggled on his lap and Koko perched on the sofaback, both waiting to hear him read aloud about the trade deficit and the latest hostile takeover.

At midnight it was time to lock the doors and close the interior shutters. Daybreak came early in June, and unless the louvered shutters were closed, the pink light of sunrise illuminated the cabin and gave the cats the erroneous idea that it was time for breakfast.

The lakeshore could be very dark and very quiet on a calm, moonless night, and Qwilleran slept soundly until two-thirty. At that hour a sound of some kind roused him from sleep. It was alarming enough to cause him to sit up and listen warily. Again he heard it: a deep, continuous, rumbling moan that rose louder and angrier and ended in a high-pitched shriek. Recognizing Koko's Tarzan act, reserved for stray cats, Qwilleran shouted "Quiet!"

He lay down again. Then he became aware of intermittent flashes of light. He swung out of bed and hurried into the living room. A greenish light so powerful that it filtered through the louvered shutters was coloring the white walls, white sofas, and even Koko's pale fur with a ghastly tint. The cat was on the arm of the sofa, his back humped, his tail bushed, his ears back, his eyes staring at the front window.

Qwilleran threw open the shutters and was blinded

by a dazzling, pulsating light. He rushed to the front
door, struggled with the lock, dashed out on the porch
shouting *"Hey, you out there!"*

But the light had disappeared, and there was not a
sound, although a breeze sprang up and swished
through the cherry trees. He groped his way back indoors, still blind from the intensity of the flashes.

It was a joke, Qwilleran decided, as he regained his
vision, and as Koko's tail resumed its normal shape,
and as Yum Yum came crawling out from under the
sofa. It was that photographer from the Dune Club, he
decided. He had been flashing his strobe lights to play
a trick on a nonbeliever, and no doubt Mildred was the
one who gave him the idea.

FOUR

The whining of an electric saw and the sharp blows of a hammer interrupted Qwilleran's sleep on Tuesday morning. He looked at his bedside clock with one eye open; it was only six-thirty. He was a late riser by preference, but he realized that the carpenter was on the job and the beach steps were being built. He pulled on a warmup suit and went out to the top of the dune.

There was a light blue pickup in the clearing—one of five thousand of that color in Moose County according to his private estimate. This one was distinguished by a cartoon on the cab door: a screeching, wing-flapping chicken. On the door handle hung a

softball jacket: red with white lettering that spelled out
COTTLE ROOSTERS. Lumber was stacked in the clearing,
and a table-saw was set up. The carpenter himself was
halfway down the sandbank working at top speed,
driving home each nail with three economical strokes
of the hammer. *Bang bang bang.*

"Morning," said Qwilleran sleepily when the hammering stopped.

The young man looked up from his work. "Hope I
didn't wake you up."

"Not at all," said Qwilleran with amiable sarcasm.
"I always get up at six o'clock and run a few miles before breakfast."

The humor was lost on the carpenter. "That's good
for you," he said. "Oh, I forgot—I'm Clem Cottle."
He scrambled up the sandbank, holding out a cal-
loused hand.

He was one of five thousand big, healthy, young
blond fellows in Moose County—again a private estimate. "Your face looks familiar," Qwilleran said.

"Sometimes I help out behind the bar at the Shipwreck." Clem wasted no time on conversation, but
returned to building the steps.

"What kind of wood are you using?" The lumber
had a greenish tint like the bilious light that had seeped
into the cabin in the middle of the night.

"It's treated so it doesn't have to be painted. Everybody's using this now." *Bang bang bang.*

As one who could smash a finger with the first blow,
Qwilleran watched the carpenter with admiration. Every nail went in straight, in the right place, with an

economy of movement. "You're a real pro! Where did you learn to do that?"

"My dad taught me everything." *Bang bang bang.* "I'm building a house for myself. I'm getting married in October."

"I was sorry to hear about the fire. That must have been a devastating experience."

Clem stopped hammering and looked up at Qwilleran. "I hope I never have to live through anything like that again," he said grimly. "I woke up in the middle of the night and thought my room was on fire. The walls were red! The sky was red! The volunteers came out from Mooseville and some other towns, but it was too late."

"What will your father do now?"

Clem shrugged. "Start all over again."

"Would you care for a cup of coffee or a soft drink?"

"No, thanks. Too early for a break yet." *Bang bang bang.*

Qwilleran prepared coffee for himself and astounded the Siamese by serving their breakfast two hours ahead of schedule—a can of boned chicken topped with a spoonful of jellied consommé. Unable to believe their rare good fortune, they pranced in exultant circles, yikking and yowling.

"You deserve this," he told them. "You've had a disturbing vacation so far . . . leaks, plumbers, crazy lights in the night, and now that noisy carpenter!" He watched them devour their food. They seemed to enjoy an audience; there were times when Yum Yum refused to eat unless he stood by, and it gave him pleasure to observe them crouching over the plate with business-like tails flat on the floor, ears and whiskers swept back, heads jerking and snapping as they maneuvered the food in their mouths. When he offered them a few nuggets of Mildred's cereal for dessert, Koko rose on his hind legs in anticipation.

Qwilleran was so intent on studying his companions that the telephone startled him. It was Mildred's excited voice on the phone. "Qwill, have you heard the news?"

"I haven't turned on the radio," he said. "What happened? Did a flying saucer splash down in front of the Northern Lights Hotel? Probably needed a few repairs at Glinko's garage."

"You're being funny this morning, Qwill! Well, listen to this: Roger called me a couple of minutes ago. Captain Phlogg was found dead in his shop!"

"Poor fool finally drank himself to death. The chamber of commerce will be distraught. Who found the body?"

"A Mooseville officer making the rounds at midnight. He saw a light inside the shop and the door open. The captain was slumped in his chair. But here's the chief reason I'm calling," she said. "His dog has been howling all night. Do you think I should go over and feed it?"

"Do you want to lose an arm? I suggest you call the sheriff. I wonder if the old guy has any relatives around here."

"Not according to Roger. I wonder what will happen."

"The state will bury him and search for heirs and assets. Do you think he had money stashed away? You never know about miserly eccentrics . . . Well, anyway, Mildred, you'd better call the sheriff about the dog. It's good of you to be concerned."

Qwilleran hung up the receiver gently, thinking warm thoughts about his kind, considerate neighbor . . . and wondering why he had received no long letter from Polly Duncan.

On the dune, where construction was nearing completion, he said to Clem, "Would you be interested in building an addition to this cabin?"

Clem appraised the weathered logs. "You'd never match that old logwork."

"I'm aware of that, but I'd settle for board-and-batten with the proper stain."

"And the old foundation is fieldstone. The last stone mason died two years ago. You'd have to have concrete block under the new part."

"No objection."

"How would you connect the old and the new?"

Qwilleran showed him the sketches, with the new wing right-angled to the cabin, and a door cut through into the back hall. Clem took them to his truck, figured costs, and presented an estimate in writing.

He said, "You're outside the village limits, so you won't need a permit. I mean, you're supposed to have one, but nobody ever does. So I could start digging for the footings tomorrow and pour them the next day. They'll set over the weekend."

"I'll give you a deposit."

"Forget it! I've got credit at the lumberyard. The Cottles have been here since 1872."

"One question," Qwilleran said. "Do you know anything about carpenter ants? They're getting into the porch posts."

"Just get a bug bomb and spray 'em good," Clem advised.

After the blue truck with the frantic chicken on the door had pulled away, Qwilleran recalled the transaction with satisfaction. The bill for the steps had been reasonable, and Clem had accepted a check with no hemming and hawing about cash. The young man was not only honest and skilled but remarkably industrious. He worked on his father's farm, moonlighted at the Shipwreck Tavern, and was building himself a house. Now Qwilleran was inclined to discount the alarmist gossip about building problems. Lyle Compton had called the dune-dwellers a giddy bunch, and their chitchat about UFOs and horoscopes confirmed that opinion. It had been a mistake to believe their cocktail conversation about underground builders.

On the whole he was feeling so elated about the latest turn of events that he agreed to act as a judge for the Fourth of July parade when someone called him from the county building in Pickax. It was a civic chore he ordinarily would have sidestepped, but the caller was a woman with a voice like Polly Duncan's. She said that the countywide parade would be held in

Mooseville and Mildred Hanstable had agreed to be a judge, with a third yet to be announced. She said that Qwilleran's name on the panel of judges would add greatly to the prestige of the event. She added that she always read "Straight from the Qwill Pen" and it was the best thing in the paper. Grooming his moustache modestly, Qwilleran agreed to help judge the floats on the Fourth of July.

For lunch he went into town to the Northern Lights Hotel, and as he walked through the lobby he recognized something out of the corner of his eye. It was the picture of a young man. The hotel had a quaint custom of announcing social news on a glorified bulletin board in the lobby. A gilt frame and some ribbons and artificial flowers were intended to glamorize the display. Qwilleran usually walked past quickly with averted eyes, but this time he stopped for a closer look. A photo of a young couple was displayed with a neatly printed card reading, "Mr. and Mrs. Warren Wimsey announce the engagement of their daughter, Maryellen, to Clem Cottle, son of Mr. and Mrs. Douglas Cottle, all of Black Creek. An October wedding is planned." Clem was stiffly posed in a collar and tie. The girl looked wholesome and intelligent and country-pretty.

Wimsey! The name was familiar to Qwilleran. There were dozens of Wimseys, Goodwinters, Trevelyans, and Cuttlebrinks in the slim directory of Moose County telephone subscribers. Families had a tendency to stay in the area for generations, and the annual family reunions were attended by a hundred members of the clan, or even more. In the cities where Qwilleran had lived and worked, such family get-togethers were unheard of, and he thought, Ah! Another idea for the "Qwill Pen."

After lunch he walked to Huggins Hardware to buy insect spray as Clem had suggested. It was a brilliant summer day, and Main Street was teeming with tourists, always distinguishable from the locals by their clothing, speech, and attitude. The young vacationers were as boisterous and as naked as the law would allow. The middle-aged tourists from the city stared at the natives with amused superiority. Busloads of white-haired day-trippers followed tour guides in and out of the shipwreck museum and gazed obediently at a certain spot in the lake where, they were told, a shipful of gold bullion had sunk a hundred years ago and was still there! Qwilleran made another mental note for his column.

The hardware merchant was taking advantage of the traffic by displaying minnow pails, beach balls, bicycles, and life preservers on the sidewalk.

Qwilleran, in his present elevated mood, had a taste for adventure. "How much for a lightweight ten-speed, Cecil?" he asked.

"Where do you plan to ride, Mr. Q? The traffic is murder on the highway this summer. You'd be better off to get a trail bike and stick to the dirt roads. Much safer!"

"They look like the clunkers I pedaled when I was delivering newspapers."

"Just take one out and try it, Mr. Q. You won't be disappointed. Head for the riverbank," Cecil Huggins advised. "Go out Sandpit Road half a mile and then get off the asphalt onto Dumpy Road till it dead-ends at Hogback. If you cut across the fields to the river, there's a dandy trail there. Be careful of mudslides. That's where Buddy Yarrow slipped in."

The seat and handlebars were adjusted to Qwilleran's six feet two, and he set out on Cecil's proposed route. He had to admit that the bike negotiated the uneven terrain in exhilarating fashion. Leaping over ruts and roots and washouts, he felt like an intrepid twelve-year-old, and there were no trucks, no electric signs, no whiffs of carbon monoxide.

Dumpy Road was a benighted colony of substandard housing, but it led to the bank of the Ittibittiwassee, which bubbled into eddying bays and babbled on the pebbles like Tennyson's brook. To Qwilleran all was enchantment: the splash and gurgle of the rapids; the willows weeping over the water's edge; the wildflowers, birds, and scurrying animals that he could not identify, never having bothered to learn about nature. He envied the country-smart locals who rescued bear cubs and built their own houses. They were descendents of the pioneers who had settled this north country, chopping down trees to build their log cabins and picking wild herbs to make their own medicines. Qwilleran wondered what they did about spider bites in the old days. Much of his biking was done standing up on the pedals.

Around each bend there was another surprise: a deer having a drink; a solitary fisherman in waders; something sleek, brown and flat-tailed, swimming and div-

ing. There was one discordant note: Ahead he could
see a jumble of junk marring the natural beauty of the
riverbank—a series of boxlike structures built of
chickenwire and scrap lumber. He dismounted and
wheeled his bike cautiously closer. They were ramshackle cages. In one of them an animal was sleeping,
rolled up in a ball; it looked like a fox. In another en-
closure some tiny creatures with striped backs were
chasing each other and climbing over a wheel that ro-
tated. An old bathtub sunk in the ground was filled
with rainwater, and ducks waddled in and out of their
pool.

It was obviously Joanna's zoo, and Qwilleran hoped
she was not there. Her house—no better than a large
box with windows, perched on concrete blocks—
fronted on the dirt road called Hogback, and it was
surrounded by plumbing fixtures. Broken or rusted
sinks, toilets, oil tanks, and water heaters were dotted
about the yard like tombstones in a plumbing graveyard. To add to the funereal effect there was a row of
wooden crosses marking small graves.

He was contemplating these crosses when a van ca-
reened down Hogback Road in a cloud of dust. It
jerked to a stop, and Joanna jumped out.

"I was biking on the riverbank and saw your interesting zoo," he explained, unhappy to be caught
prowling about her property.

"Didja see my chipmunks?" she asked with more
spirit than she usually mustered. "I built 'em an exercise wheel."

"What do you feed them?" he asked in a lame attempt to show intelligent interest.

"Sunflower seeds and acorns. You should see 'em sit up and eat and wash their face. Wanna hold one? They like being stroked."

"No, thanks," he said. "Anything that eats acorns probably has very sharp teeth. What happens to them in winter?"

"I give 'em straw, and they sleep a lot."

"Those crosses—are they graves?"

"That's where I buried the bear cubs. The woodchuck, too. And some chipmunks."

Appraising the yardful of retired fixtures, he asked, "What made you decide to be a plumber, Joanna?"

"My daddy showed me how to do all that kind of stuff, so I took a test and got my license." She saw Qwilleran looking at her house. "Someday I'm gonna get somebody to build me a real house, when I get enough money. Wanna beer?"

"No, thanks. I borrowed this bike, and if I don't return it soon, the sheriff will come gunning for me. What's the quickest way back to Mooseville?"

She pointed down Hogback Road, and he rode off through the dirt ruts at top speed, gripping the handlebars, concentrating on his balance, certain that she was watching, hoping he would not take an embarrassing header.

The following days were eventful for both Qwilleran and the Siamese. Clem Cottle and his younger brother staked out the new east wing and went to work with shovels, digging like madmen, then building wooden forms. The next morning the cement mixer truck rumbled into the clearing, and the two young men ran back and forth trundling wheelbarrows filled with wet concrete. Yum Yum hid under the sofa, and even brave Koko retired discreetly under a bunk in the guestroom, slinking out to peek once in a while.

Qwilleran went for another ride on his new bike, this time taking a back road to an abandoned nineteenth-century cemetery that he had visited two years before. To his surprise the vandalized tombstones had been restored, the weeds were under control, and there was hardly a beer can to be seen. A new sign announced: PIONEER CEMETERY. NO PICNICS. He suspected the preservation program had been instigated by the tireless Mildred Hanstable, and he telephoned her when he returned home.

"Hi, Qwill!" she said in her exuberant style. "I saw you out riding on one of those funny-looking bikes."

"I am now a demon on wheels," he replied. "The terror of the countryside. I visited the old cemetery. Who's been cleaning it up?"

"The student history clubs. They're restoring all the abandoned cemeteries and cataloguing the family graveyards around the county. The early settlers used to bury their dead on their own land, you know, and the sites are protected by law, but first they have to know where they are."

Another idea for the "Qwill Pen," he thought. "I understand you're one of the judges for the parade. How about dinner afterward? At the Fish Tank."

"I'd love it!" she said. "Their navy grog is fabulous, and I always need a stiff drink after a Moose County parade. How did you like the cereal?"

"It's delicious," he said, speaking for the others. "Great wonders come out of your kitchen, Mildred. And another great wonder: I've found a carpenter without resorting to the underground."

"Who?"

"Clem Cottle from Black Creek."

"You're lucky!" Mildred said. "Clem is a good carpenter and a fine young man. He's marrying Maryellen Wimsey, and she used to be in my art classes. She's a lovely girl."

During the next few days Maryellen drove into the clearing daily at noon in a small yellow car, bringing a hot lunch and staying long enough to pick up stray nails and stack the scraps of wood in tidy heaps.

Clem reported for work every morning at six-thirty—sometimes with his younger brother, but more often alone. He laid the foundation blocks, installed the basic drainage, put in the joists and subfloor, and started the framing.

There were other visitors besides Maryellen. Dune-dwellers who had never cared to walk on the beach suddenly began to take exercise. Attracted by the sounds of industry or compelled by curiosity or driven by envy, they strolled casually past the cabin, waved to Qwilleran on the porch, and climbed the new wooden steps to check the carpenter's progress. Mildred Hanstable and Sue Urbank were the first visitors, applauding Qwilleran's good fortune in finding a decent builder. Mildred brought him another tub of cereal.

Leo Urbank robbed valuable time from his golf game to inspect the new structure, predicting that it would never be completed. "Take it from me," he warned. "They're hot at the beginning, but they drop out halfway through."

The Comptons were unexpected callers. Lisa Compton was a jogger who regularly pounded the shoreline in a green warmup suit, but her husband considered the beach solely as a place to smoke a cigar. Yet, there he was, plodding through the sand and climbing the steps.

"When the guy finishes your place," he said, "maybe he could come over and work on our garage."

"I'll line him up for you," Qwilleran said. "I suppose you know Clem Cottle."

"Oh, sure," said the superintendent. "We had thirteen Cottles going through the school system at one time. Clem was the brightest. Too bad he didn't go to college for more than two years. But they were all conscientious—all good stock. I wish I could say the same for all the old families. There's a lot of inbreeding in a tight community like this."

One evening John and Vicki Bushland sauntered down the beach to take pictures of the sunset, and Qwilleran invited them to view the spectacle from the screened porch, minus mosquitoes. "Where's your studio?" he asked them.

"In Lockmaster. It's been there for eighty years."

"I'm not familiar with that town."

"It's sixty miles southwest of here—a county seat like Pickax, only bigger," Bushy said.

"What kind of work do you do?"

"The usual: portraits, weddings, club groups. When my grandfather started the business he photographed a lot of funerals. At the cemetery they'd open the coffin and prop it up on end, with the mourners gathered around the corpse. You can still see those gruesome group pictures in family albums. He was a great guy, my grandfather. He took two kinds of pictures—what he called vertical-up-and-down and horizontal-sideways."

Qwilleran asked, "Do you shoot animals?"

"A few. Some people want their kids taken with the family pooch."

"How about cats?"

"Lockmaster isn't big on cats," said the photographer. "Mostly dogs and horses."

"But cats make wonderful models," said Vicki. "They never strike a pose that isn't photogenic."

Qwilleran huffed lightly into his moustache. "I dispute that. Every time I think I'm getting a good snapshot, my cats yawn or turn into pretzels, and nothing is less picturesque than a cat's gullet or his backside."

Knowing they were being discussed, the Siamese sauntered onto the porch and posed as a couple—Yum Yum sprawled in a languid posture with chin on paw and ears tilted forward; Koko sitting tall with tail curved gracefully around haunches.

"See what I mean?" cried Vicki.

"Look at those highlights!" said Bushy as he raised

the camera to his eye, but before he could snap the picture, both cats dissolved in a blur of fur and were gone. Challenged, he said, "I'd like to get those two characters in my studio and work with them. Could you bring them down to Lockmaster?"

"I don't see why not," Qwilleran said. "They're good travelers."

"You could bring them down some evening when the studio's closed, and I could spend time with them. Just give me a ring." He gave Qwilleran his business card. "I'd like to enter them in a calendar competition."

Not all the visitors were dune-dwellers during those exciting days of construction activity. One afternoon Joanna's van pulled into the clearing.

"Whatcha doin' over there?" she asked.

"Building an addition to the cabin," Qwilleran said. She stared at it wordlessly for a while. "No more leaks?" she said finally.

"So far, so good."

"Did you find my lipstick?"

"I beg your pardon?" Qwilleran said.

"My lipstick. I thought maybe it rolled out of my pocket when I was here."

"I haven't seen it," he said, noting that her face had the original washed-out appearance.

"It could be under the house."

"Feel free to have a look, but don't let Koko go down there."

Joanna went indoors, and the trap door slammed

twice. She returned, looking disappointed. "I'll hafta buy another."

After she had left, Qwilleran wondered why she had waited so long to ask about her missing lipstick. Was it simply an excuse to pay a social call? He felt sorry for the girl—so plain, and with so few advantages. But he was not going to take her to lunch! He had lunched his doctor and his interior designer, but Joanna was getting a ten-dollar tip for every plumbing job; she could buy her own lunch.

By July third the roof trusses had been erected, and the roof boards were in place. Clem had been working fast. "Trying to get it under cover before it rains," he explained when he collected his tools on Thursday night.

"Are you taking a long holiday weekend?" Qwilleran asked him.

"Can't afford to. I'll be here bright and early Saturday, but tomorrow I'll be in the parade. The boss at the Shipwreck came up with a good idea, and I said I'd do it."

"Are you riding on a float?"

"Nothing like that," said the young man with a wide grin. "I'm just gonna walk down the middle of the street. Then after the parade there's a softball game—Roosters against the state prison team. If you like ballgames, you oughta come and see us play."

Qwilleran liked the young carpenter, and he gave him a parting salute as the Frantic Chicken drove away. It was prophetic. That was the last time he ever saw Clem Cottle.

FIVE

The Fourth of July dawned with the sunshine of a flag-waving holiday, and Qwilleran was in good spirits, despite some soreness following his last bike ride. The east wing with its roof boards in place was beginning to look like a habitation.

"Well, chums, we're on our way!" he told the Siamese. "You'll have your own apartment in a few weeks. What would you like for breakfast? Turkey from the deli? Or cocktail shrimp from a can?"

Koko was not present to cast his vote, but Yum Yum was rubbing against Qwilleran's ankles in anticipation and curling her tail lovingly around his leg, and he knew she preferred turkey. He began to mince slices of white meat.

"What's that noise?" He set down the knife and looked up. "Did you hear a tapping noise? . . . There it is again!"

Tap tap tap.

With a sudden drop in his holiday mood he envisioned another leak or mechanical breakdown. "There it goes again!" Possibilities flashed through his mind: the electric pump; the water heater; the refrigerator. It would mean another emergency call to that laughing hyena in Mooseville.

Tap tap tap.

Qwilleran followed the sound. It led him past the mudroom, past the bathroom, and into the guestroom. The tapping had stopped, but Koko was sitting on the windowsill overlooking the building site, and the morning sun made glistening shafts of every whisker, every alert hair over his eyes.

"Did you hear that, Koko?"

The cat turned his head to look at Qwilleran, and at that moment his brown tail slapped the windowsill three times. *Tap tap tap.*

Qwilleran uttered a sigh of relief. "Okay, Thumper, come and get your breakfast, and please don't play tricks like that."

The parade was scheduled to start at two o'clock, and he dressed in what he considered appropriate garb: white pants and open-neck shirt with a blue blazer. He was sure the judges would be required to wear some absurd badge of office, and he was prepared for the worst. Mildred, when he picked her up at her cottage, was wearing one of her fluttery sundresses in a blue-and-white stripe.

"Keep your fingers crossed," she said, as she stepped into his car.

"What should I deduce from that cryptic remark?"

"Maybe you didn't see the parade last year."

"I did not. I'm not a parade-goer by choice."

"Well, I went with Sharon and Roger last year, and I was appalled! It was nothing but a candy-grab! Politicians rode in new-model cars, throwing candy to the crowd. Beauty queens rode in convertibles, throwing candy to the crowd. The used-car dealer rode in a three-year-old car *with a price tag*! And he was throwing candy to the crowd. There were no floats and no marching bands—just sound trucks blaring pop music, and commercial vehicles advertising the Mooseville video arcade and the Friday night fish fry in North Kennebeck. But worst of all, there was not a single flag in the parade! This was Independence Day, and there was not an American flag to be seen!"

"How did the crowd react to all of this?"

"All that free candy? Are you kidding? They loved it!"

"I'd say you had reason to be disturbed," Qwilleran said.

"Disturbed! I was *furious*! When the holiday weekend was over, I got on my horse and went into battle. You don't know me, Qwill, when I get mad! That was before the *Something* started publication, so I couldn't write an irate letter to the editor, but I wrote to every elected and appointed official, every civic leader, every chamber of commerce, every citizens' group, and every school principal in the county. I spouted off at meetings of the county commissioners and the village councils. I really made myself a public nuisance. You know, Qwill, every veterans' organization and fraternal lodge has a big flag and a color guard. The two high schools and three junior highs have marching bands. Their uniforms don't fit, and they hit some wrong notes, but they march, and they beat drums, and they blow trumpets. Where were they on Independence Day? That's what I wanted to know."

"What happened after your outburst?"

"We'll soon find out. They appointed a county committee to organize this year's parade, and—wisely, perhaps—I wasn't asked to serve. Apparently they laid ambitious plans, but you know what happens when a committee takes charge. Sometimes nothing!"

The sidewalks in Mooseville were already crowded with parade-goers, and the parking lots were filled. Police had barricaded several blocks of Main Street, detouring traffic, but Qwilleran found a place to park near Glinko's garage. He and Mildred pushed their way through the crowds to a reviewing stand built in front of the town hall. A committeewoman wearing a tri-color bandoleer guided them to the judges' table, and gave them scorecards and straw boaters with tri-color hatbands. Mildred wore hers straight-on, and Qwilleran said she looked saucy. He tipped his at a rakish angle, and Mildred said he looked dashing, especially with that big moustache.

"The floats," the committeewoman explained, "are to be rated on originality, execution, and message, using the suggested point system."

The third judge had not arrived. Mildred guessed it would be an announcer from WPKX. Qwilleran thought it might be the superintendent of schools; Lyle Compton was always the most visible official in the county.

"He says it's part of his job," Mildred confided, "but I think he's getting ready to run for the state legislature."

"My carpenter is going to be in the parade," Qwilleran said. "It's some kind of stunt sponsored by the Shipwreck Tavern."

"I hope the parade won't be so commercial this year."

Their conversation was interrupted by the arrival of the third judge, who was creating a commotion as she complained about the steps, fell over the folding chairs, and upset the tripods that held the public-address speakers.

"Who wants to drive thirty miles for a parade?" she grumbled. "It should have been held in the county seat!"

The committeewoman tried to explain. "It was thought that Mooseville is the center of population on a big holiday, Miss Goodwinter. All the tourists are here."

"Tourists, bah! Why don't they stay home? Let them go to their own parade and leave some parking spaces for the citizens. I had to walk three blocks!"

It was Amanda Goodwinter, Pickax interior designer, city council member, and former fiancée of Arch Riker. She was wearing her usual colorless, shapeless clothing with a man's golf hat jammed over her spiky gray hair. "I don't know why I'm here!" she added grouchily. "I hate parades! And I'm not going to wear that silly straw hat!" She banged the boater down on the table and looked at the scorecard. "Originality, execution, and *message*? What does that mean? A parade is a parade. Why does it have to have a *message*?" Scowling and fussing, she settled herself in a folding chair. "Five minutes of this will give me a backache."

"Good afternoon, Amanda," said Qwilleran graciously.

"What are you doing here? You're as big a fool as I am!"

The beat of drums could be heard in the distance, and voices below the reviewing stand drifted up to the judges' table:

Excited youngster: "I think they're coming!"

Police officer: "Back on the curb, sonny."

Child: "Are they gonna throw candy?"

Mother: "Don't forget to salute the flag, the way your teacher said."

Old Man: "The band's getting ready to play."

Screaming child: "He took my sucker!"

Another screaming child: "Lift me up! I can't see!"

With a stirring flourish one of the high school bands swung into "The Stars and Stripes Forever," the sun glinting on their brass instruments two blocks away. A sheriff's car with flashing rooflights led the way at four miles an hour. Then there was a breathless wait as heads turned and necks craned.

The wait was long enough to solemnify the marching of the color guard—a tall, beefy flag-bearer flanked by two men and two women in uniform, arms swinging and eyes straight ahead. As if on cue a breeze sprang up when they reached the reviewing stand, and the stars and stripes rippled over the heads of the stern-faced marchers.

When the guard of honor had passed and the officials on the reviewing stand had resumed their seats, tears were rolling down Mildred's face. "This really gets to me," she said in a choked voice.

"Congratulations!" Qwilleran said. "You won your battle."

"Not yet. I'm waiting for the candy."

There was no candy. Before the afternoon was over the onlookers had seen a grand marshal on a proud-stepping horse with nodding plumes and glittering harness brasses; seven color guards from organizations around the county; four student bands, plus Scottish pipers from Lockmaster, sixty miles away; ten floats, two drill teams, three fire trucks sounding their sirens; and fourteen dogs from the St. Bernard Club, pulling their owners on leashes.

Each municipality in Moose County sponsored a float. Pickax honored the men who had worked the mines in the nineteenth century: Moving silently past the viewers was a tableau of grimy miners wearing candles in their hats and carrying pickaxes, coils of rope, and sledgehammers.

Sawdust City, once the hub of the lumbering industry, staged a lumbercamp scene on a flatbed truck—with a cook flipping flapjacks, loggers brawling over a card game, and someone in a bear costume stealing the flapjacks.

Then came the Mooseville entry—a flatbed crowded with sportsmen and outdoor-lovers; fishermen with rods and reels, boaters with binoculars and lifejackets, golfers with their clubs, and campers grilling hot dogs. Presiding over them all was the reigning queen of the annual Fishhook Festival, her formal ballgown fashioned of camouflage fabric and her crown of deer antlers.

"Confused! Cluttered!" Amanda growled. "No organization!"

"But it's graphic," Mildred said.

"It projects a message," Qwilleran added.

"It's a mess!" Amanda insisted.

The lakeside town of Brrr, so named because it was the coldest spot in the county during the winter months, presented a plastic snow scene with a papier-mâché igloo and papier-mâché polar bear. Lounging in the synthetic snowdrifts were male and female sunbathers in bikinis. Judging by the whistles, this float was the popular favorite.

"No taste!" Amanda objected. "But what do you expect of that godforsaken town?"

Even the dreary little village of Chipmunk managed to enter a float. Known as the moonshine capital of the county during Prohibition, and notorious for the lethal nature of its white lightning, Chipmunk had resurrected a homemade still and displayed it on a flatbed draped in black. The visual punch line was the scattering of bodies on the truck, lifeless or comatose.

"Now *that one* shows some wit!" Amanda said, "and if you want a message, that says it all."

The judges agreed, and first prize went to the muchmaligned village of Chipmunk.

Relegated to the end of the two-hour parade were the commercial exhibits with their advertising slogans. A tow truck pulling a wrecked car was sponsored by Buster's Collision Service, "Where We Meet by Accident."

The Pickax Auto Repair and Radiator Shop advertised "A Good Place to Take a Leak."

Then a solitary man walked down the middle of Main Street, leading a donkey. There was laughter from the crowd.

"Can't see what it says!" Amanda complained.

Qwilleran read her the lettering on the animal's saddle blanket. "Get Your Donkey over to the Shipwreck Tavern."

Amanda snorted.

The last flatbed in the parade was sponsored by Trevelyan Plumbing and Heating—an arrangement of oldfashioned bathroom fixtures, with Grandpa Trevelyan sitting in the footed bathtub smoking a corncob pipe. The banner read, "If It Wasn't for Your Plumber, You'd Have No Place to Go."

The parade was over. The watchers swarmed across the parade route. Only then did Qwilleran realize that Clem Cottle had not marched. The man leading the donkey was the regular daytime bartender from the Shipwreck Tavern.

"Fabulous parade!" Mildred said. "They didn't throw a single piece of candy! And I love those Scottish pipers! Don't they have wonderful legs? You'd look good in kilts, Qwill."

"They did a good job of pacing the units," he said. "No long waits and no pileup and no overlapping bands."

"Whole thing was too long," Amanda groused.

Mildred said, "Mighty Lou made the grandest grand marshal I've ever seen. He has all those expensive leather clothes with silver nailheads, you know, and that was his own horse. Wasn't it a beauty?"

Qwilleran and Mildred raced the crowds to the Fish Tank and had an early dinner. It was a new restaurant in an old waterfront warehouse on the fishing wharves, and the old timbers creaked with the movement of the lake. They ordered the Fish Tank's famous clam chowder and broiled whitefish—from a waiter named Harvey who had once been in Mildred's art class.

"How's everything at the Top o' the Dunes?" Qwilleran asked her.

"Well, the animal-rescue people picked up Captain Phlogg's dog right away ... And Doc and Dottie are buying a boat, which they'll berth at the marina in Brrr ... And the Urbanks (don't repeat this) are splitting up, I happen to know. They got along fine until they retired, but that's the way it goes. Frankly, I don't know how Sue could stand him all these years."

"How about your next-door neighbor?"

"Russell? I've tried to be neighborly, but she doesn't respond. She's a strange one."

"I've seen her on the beach, feeding the gulls," Qwilleran said. "She talks to them."

"She's lonely. Why don't you talk to her, Qwill? You're always so sympathetic, and she might warm up to an older man."

"Sorry, Mildred. I've had enough complications with younger women. Even my plumber is getting a little too friendly."

"In what way?"

"She's started wearing lipstick and washing her hair. I recognize the early warning signals."

"Did you read your horoscope this morning?"

"You know I don't buy that nonsense, Mildred."

"Well, for your information, the *Morning Rampage* said your charisma will make you very popular with the opposite sex, and romance is just around the corner."

Qwilleran huffed into his moustache. "I'd be happier if they'd give practical advice, such as 'Don't order fish in a restaurant today; you could choke to death.' My whitefish is full of bones."

"Send it back!" Mildred said. "Don't eat it! Mine is filleted to perfection."

Qwilleran summoned the waiter and voiced his complaint.

"All fish has bones," the waiter said.

"But not all waiters have brains," Mildred snapped. "Harvey, take that plate out to the kitchen and bring Mr. Qwilleran a decent filet of whitefish—and no excuses!"

The waiter scuttled away with the plate.

Qwilleran asked, "How long does your authority over these kids continue? Harvey is at least twenty-five. Is there a statute of limitations?"

"Anyone who goes through my classes gets me for life," she stated flatly.

"There must be advantages and disadvantages in knowing everyone. How long do I have to live in Moose County before I know the entire population?"

"It's too late for you, Qwill. You have to be born here, grow up here, and teach school for a couple of decades."

There was a flurry of activity at the entrance as the parade's grand marshal entered and was seated at a table by himself, still glittering with silver nailheads.

"I wonder why he's alone," Qwilleran said.

"He's a loner," said Mildred.

But the waiter, serving the fresh plate of whitefish, said with a wicked grin, "Because they won't let his horse in."

Mildred reached across the table and rapped his knuckles with the handle of her table knife. "That was uncalled for, Harvey. Don't expect a tip!" To Qwilleran she added, "Mighty Lou is one of our town characters—colorful and harmless. If you were thinking of writing a column about him, don't! Let sleeping dogs lie."

"I was considering a column on family reunions. Are they closed sessions, or could a reporter barge in?"

"They'd be thrilled to have someone from the newspaper! They really would!"

"What do they do at these affairs?"

"They have a business meeting and elect officers for

the coming year, but mostly they just visit and eat and play games."

"There was an announcement in the paper that the Wimsey family is having a reunion this Sunday on someone's farm."

"They're the largest family in the county, next to the Goodwinters," Mildred said. "Do you know Cecil Huggins at the hardware store? He's related to the Wimseys by marriage. Just tell Cecil you'd like to cover the reunion. And when you get there, look up Emma Wimsey. She's real old but still sharp, and she has the most wonderful cat story to tell! When she told me, I got shivers!"

When the waiter brought the dessert menu he said, "I'm sorry if I made a boo-boo, Mrs. Hanstable. It just slipped out."

"Your apology does you credit, Harvey. You're back in my good graces." To Qwilleran she said, "Why don't we go home for dessert? I could build a parfait with homemade orange ice and fresh raspberries."

They set out for the Dune Club, but not until Qwilleran had ordered a freshly boiled lobster tail to take home to the cats. On the way, Mildred made a critical appraisal of his posture at the wheel. "Do you have a stiff neck or something, Qwill?"

"Just some soreness in my shoulders—from biking, I suppose. I'm using a different set of muscles, or else I jarred something loose when I bounced over an exposed tree root."

"Take off your shirt," she ordered when they arrived

at her yellow cottage. "I have a wonderful Swiss oil that Sharon got for me, and I'll give you a rub."

As she rubbed in all the right places, his thoughts flew across the Atlantic to Polly Duncan. In England the Fourth of July would be only "4 July," and Polly would have worked all day at the library, stopping for tea and seedcake at four o'clock. Perhaps she went to an early theater performance after work and then had fish-and-chips with a new friend. (What kind of new friend? he wondered.) And now she would be home in her flat, watching the telly and drinking cocoa—and writing him another postcard.

"Now you can put your shirt on," Mildred said. "The oil won't stain. It's wonderful stuff."

After the parfait Qwilleran admitted that he felt better, outwardly and inwardly, but he declined to stay longer, saying that he had to feed the cats before they started chewing the table leg. On the way back to the cabin he reflected on Mildred's charitable nature and her spunk. Singlehanded she had turned the Fourth of July celebration around—from a travesty to a spectacular success. The firm way she handled the whitefish situation; her concern for the lonely girl next door; her initiative in raising money for Buddy Yarrow's family; everything she did was admirable. And she was a superb cook! He could forgive her silliness about horoscopes and UFOs.

When Qwilleran let himself into the cabin, the rug over the trapdoor was askew as usual. He straightened it automatically and greeted the Siamese, who knew he was carrying something edible, aquatic, and expensive.

"How was your day?" he asked them. "Any excitement? Any phone calls?"

Yum Yum rubbed against his ankles, and Koko pranced in figure eights while he diced the lobster meat. After the feast all three of them went to the lakeside porch, where Koko emulated an Egyptian sculpture and Yum Yum languished in her seductive Cleopatra pose. Stealthily Qwilleran went indoors for his camera, but as soon as he returned, Yum Yum crossed her eyes and scratched her ear, and Koko assumed a grotesque position to wash a spot on his belly that appeared to be perfectly clean.

It was still daylight, and somewhere along the shore the gulls were squawking again. Qwilleran went down the wooden steps and walked toward the clamor. Scores of soaring wings were wheeling over Seagull Point. Moving in slowly, he photographed the performance without disturbing the woman who was feeding them. Then he sat on a boulder until she tossed the last morsel of food.

"Good show!" he applauded. "Fantastic aerial ballet. I snapped some pictures."

"Oh," said Russell, walking hesitantly toward him.

"Pull up a rock and sit down." He indicated a boulder a few feet from his own seat, and Russell sat down dutifully. "Did you go to the parade today?"

"I don't like crowds," she said sadly, addressing the lake.

"You missed an exceptional spectacle." He picked up a stone and flung it into the water. "Are you enjoying your vacation?"

She nodded without enthusiasm.

"I hope you've been to the museum."

"It was interesting," she said.

Clenching his teeth, he waited for an inspiration . . . The subject of food, he remembered, was a foolproof ice-breaker in difficult social situations. He said, "Have you discovered any good restaurants in town?"

After a pause she said, "I never go to restaurants."

"Do you prefer to cook?"

"I don't eat much."

That explained her pencil-thin figure and perhaps her low-energy level. He found a few flat stones and skipped them across the surface of the lake. Then he tried a desperate quip. "Read any good books lately?"

"Nothing special," she said.

"There's a small library in Mooseville, and also a woman who operates a paperback book exchange, in case you run out of reading material."

There was no comment from the other rock, and he skipped a few more stones.

"How do you like the Dunfield cottage?"

Russell squirmed on the rock. "I don't know."

"What's the trouble?"

"I feel uncomfortable." She appeared to shrink.

"If anything worries you," he said, "feel free to talk it over with your neighbor, Mildred Hanstable. She's a kind and understanding woman. And if you need help of any kind, call Mildred or me."

"You're a nice man," said Russell suddenly.

"Well, thank you!" he said. "But you really don't know me. I turn down the corners of pages in books.

I sometimes split an infinitive. And once I wore brown shoes with a black suit."

She almost smiled, but not quite. Waving a hand toward the log cabin, she said, "You're building something."

"I'm building an addition. Walk over and look at it some day. All our neighbors are interested in the process."

Russell stood up. "I have to go before it gets dark."

Without further civilities she walked toward the east, and Qwilleran ambled into the setting sun, wondering about this reticent young woman who never really looked at him. Obviously no one had told her the history of the Dunfield cottage, and yet she felt uncomfortable there. In a way she was like Koko; she could sense a sinister influence.

Back at the cabin Qwilleran detected mischief. Yum Yum was darting insanely about the living room while Koko looked on with magisterial calm from the top of the moosehead. Yum Yum seemed to have something small and gray in her mouth.

"Drop it!" Qwilleran shouted, and this was her cue to take flight. Around and around the cabin she flew with the thing in her mouth, while Qwilleran pursued with the grace of a Neanderthal, using all his wits to intercept her and being outwitted at every pass. Tired at last, she hopped on the dining table and dropped the dead mouse in his typewriter.

"Thank you!" he said. "Thank you very much!"

SIX

To the disappointment of holiday weekenders it rained on Saturday—rained hard. The bare roofboards on the east wing provided little protection from the downpour, which funneled between the boards and descended in sheets to drench the exposed subfloor. Qwilleran hardly expected Clem to work, and yet the carpenter failed to telephone. Previously he had been punctilious about reporting any change of plan, a businesslike practice that Qwilleran appreciated.

"That young man has a good head on his shoulders," he said to the Siamese. "He's bound to be a success. In a few years from now—if he quits the chicken business and sticks with contracting—he'll be giving XYZ Enterprises some competition."

Koko merely maneuvered his tail in reply. *Tap tap tap.* Much of the morning he spent in the window overlooking the building site. Nothing was happening, but he was waiting. *Tap tap tap.* The cat had always shown an interest in human occupations. He watched Joanna do plumbing repairs, and in Pickax he had supervised Pete Parrott's paperhanging and Mr. O'Dell's window washing and carpet cleaning, as well as Qwilleran's pecking on the typewriter. Koko regarded each operation studiously, like an alert apprentice learning the trade. Now it appeared that he wanted to be a carpenter.

Qwilleran's first order of business on Saturday was to dial the phone number that he knew so well. "This is Qwilleran at the K cabin on the east shore."

"Ha ha ha! Don't need to tell me," laughed Mrs. Glinko. "Whatcha done now?"

He wanted to say, Dammit, do you think I sit around all day thinking of things to destroy? But she was so relentlessly cheerful and so conscientiously accommodating that he could not be angry with her. He explained, "It's like this, Mrs. Glinko. I'm afraid mice are getting into this seventy-five-year-old cabin. Is there anyone who could advise me how to stop the invasion?" One mouse hardly constituted an invasion, but he thought it wise to dramatize the urgency of the situation.

"Allrighty. I'll dispatch Young Jake," she said. "He'll know what to do. He goes to college. Ha ha ha!"

Young Jake arrived promptly—another of the big blonds indigenous to Moose County, driving another of the ubiquitous blue pickups. "We're having a little trouble here?" he asked with the kindly manner of an old country doctor.

Qwilleran explained the episode of the previous evening. "That's the first mouse I've seen, but it might be only the reconnaissance detail."

"Has your cat been showing interest in any particular part of the cabin?"

"She's spent a lot of time watching the stove and refrigerator in the last couple of days. I thought she was dropping broad hints about the meal service."

"We'll have a look," said Jake. "How do I get into the crawl space?" When shown the trapdoor he handed Qwilleran a flashlight. "I'll scout around down below, and you shine the light in the corners of the rooms and behind the appliances where pipes or cables come into the house. If I see a pinpoint of light, I'll close the crack with a sealant. Those little rascals can squeeze through even a hairline crack."

Jake dropped through the trapdoor with practiced ease and proceeded to shout orders. "Move east. That's right . . . Hold it! . . . All tight here. Move on . . . Hold it! . . . False alarm. Move on. Cables coming up. Not too fast! Hold it! . . . Ah! This is it! Hold steady!"

When the job was done, the expert emerged from the hole, draped with cobwebs. "The mice had an open invitation where the power lines come into the house," he said. "Excuse me. I'll step outside to brush myself off."

"You seem to know what you're doing," Qwilleran said when he returned and presented his bill.

"The job's guaranteed. If you have a problem, I'll come back. No extra charge."

"Fair enough. Is this your specialty?"

"No, I'm a general practitioner, but I've had plenty of cases like this at the beach cottages. I work during summer vacation."

"If you're Young Jake, I presume there's an Old Jake," Qwilleran said.

"My father. Maybe you know him. Dr. Armbruster, surgeon at the Pickax hospital. I'm in pre-med myself. I'm going into surgery."

Another idea for the "Qwill Pen," Qwilleran thought as the GP drove away. He released the Siamese from the guestroom where they had been confined while the trapdoor was open. "Thank you for your quiet and courteous cooperation," he said. "You've earned a treat. Cereal!" Yum Yum bounded to the kitchen, and Koko pranced on his hind legs.

When the rain stopped around noon, Qwilleran half expected to see the Frantic Chicken pulling into the clearing; Clem never wasted an hour, never missed an opportunity to earn a dollar for his forthcoming marriage to Maryellen. She was a fine young woman, and she was getting a good man.

There was no action on Saturday afternoon, however, and no phone call. Now everything would have to wait until Monday.

* * *

On Sunday the sun was shining, the temperature was pleasant, and Qwilleran dressed with the anticipation of a cub reporter assigned to a good story; in more than twenty-five years of newspapering he had never lost that element of challenge and expectation, though it were only a family reunion. There are no dull stories, he told himself—only dull reporters.

He sang in the shower, he soaped lavishly, and then the water suddenly ran cold. It was more than a shock to his wet body; it was a vexation to his equanimity. Wrapped in a bathtowel, he padded to the mudroom, where the water heater shared a closet with the washer-dryer combination. The heater gave no clue to its failure; it was neither dripping nor clanking nor blowing off steam. The cylindrical tank was silent and baffling.

Cursing the ill-advised timing of the mishap, Qwilleran called Glinko once more.

"You again!" Mrs. Glinko said in great glee. "What's buggin' you this time?"

"The water heater."

"Allrighty. I'll try to find Little Joe. Maybe she's at church. Ha ha ha!"

"I'm going out on assignment for the newspaper," Qwilleran said, "but you have the key, and she knows where everything is."

Unhappy about this latest emergency but resigned to the eccentricities of old plumbing, he said goodbye to the Siamese, cautioning them to behave well, and drove to the Wimsey centennial farm on Sandpit Road.

He had seen it before—a vast complex of barns, sheds, coops, fences and acreage, with a plaque stating that it had been in the same family for a hundred years. It included a large oldfashioned stone farmhouse with flowerbeds and kitchen garden, a spacious front lawn with ancient lilac bushes, and a farmyard with parking space for the thirty or more cars that were piling in for the reunion.

Long rows of picnic tables were set up, and families arrived with hampers, coolers, and folding lawn chairs.

Cecil Huggins was watching for Qwilleran and he introduced him to the elected officers of the family. "What do you want us to do?" they asked.

"Whatever you normally do," Qwilleran said. "Forget I'm here."

"Well, dive in and get some grub when the dinner bell rings," they said, "and if you like to pitch horseshoes, there's always a coupla games going, down by the corn crib."

There were all ages in attendance: infants in arms, tots in strollers, oldsters in wheelchairs, pregnant women, children playing with Frisbees, beer-drinking husbands, and older men pitching horseshoes. Qwilleran noticed that men were inclined to talk to men, women talked to women, and mothers of small children talked to mothers of small children, while the elderly sat on lawn chairs under a large spreading tree and talked to each other. Yet, when the dinner bell rang, the entire clan came together in one lively, noisy mix of ages and sexes. Qwilleran counted a hundred and eleven persons, and he imagined that the genealogical tree of this family would resemble the circuitry of a computer.

There were a few celebrities in the crowd. A young serviceman, home on furlough after completing basic training, was welcomed like a brigadier general. Homage was paid to a new baby as if he were the firstborn of a crown prince. A couple who had recently announced their engagement were showered with effusive sentiments. Qwilleran expected to see Clem and his fiancée accorded the same star treatment, but they were not in evidence.

Wandering from group to group, listening and observing, he began to speculate that life might have cheated him. He saw cousins and second cousins and third cousins jabbering about family affairs and so happy to see each other. His only "family" consisted of an alienated ex-wife in Connecticut, some hostile in-laws in New Jersey, and two Siamese cats.

Cecil Huggins asked Qwilleran how he was enjoying his new bike and suggested some back roads to explore. "Try MacGregor Road," said the merchant. "There's a mighty pretty stretch after the pavement ends."

Qwilleran was well aware of that pretty stretch; Polly Duncan's hideaway was on MacGregor Road.

"And then, if you're feeling ambitious," Cecil said, "someday you might try the Old Brrr Road. It was abandoned after they built the lakeshore highway in the twenties, and it's all gone back to nature. Totally! My grandfather used to have a general store on Brrr Road at what they called Huggins Corners. Not a stick of it left! But it was a thriving emporium in its day. I guess that's how I got into the hardware business. Storekeeping is in my blood."

Mrs. Huggins joggled her husband's elbow. "Tell Mr. Q about Grandpa and the loaf of bread."

"Yes, that's a good one!" Cecil laughed. "I should write some of these down. You see . . . Grandma used to bake bread to sell in the store, and Grandpa always lined up the fresh loaves on the counter near the door, where customers could smell 'em as soon as they walked in. The bread was right next to the 'chawin' terbaccer' and the penny candy. Don't tell me they didn't know about merchandising in those days . . . Well, there was an old geezer who used to come in to swipe crackers out of the barrel—or a dill pickle when he thought no one was looking."

"He had a pile of money buried in his backyard," Mrs. Huggins said, "but he hated to spend a penny."

"That's right. Josh Cummins, his name was. And on his way out of the store after a game of checkers with his cronies around the stove, he'd always pick up a loaf of bread—the one nearest the door—and never pay for it. It griped Grandpa more and more every time, but he didn't want to collar the old guy and accuse him. You don't do that in a small town. So he thought of a scheme. He told Grandma to bake a loaf of bread with a dirty sock in it."

"And I guess socks really got dirty in those days," put in Mrs. Huggins.

"So Grandma baked the bread, and Grandpa put that loaf nearest the door when Josh was about to leave the store," Cecil said. "And sure enough, the old guy picked it up and walked out . . . Never stole another loaf!"

"They never found the money buried in his backyard," said Mrs. Huggins.

"That's right," said her husband, "and they never will. It's paved over now, for the high school parking lot. And they never found what old Mr. Klingenschoen buried on his property at the lake. All kinds of valuables, they say—back in the 1920s—just before he died, when he was a little tetched in the head. You ought to start digging, Mr. Q."

"Sorry, Cecil. I don't want to pay any more income tax."

"There goes the dinner bell!" said Mrs. Huggins, as someone tugged at a rope and clanged a large cast-iron farm bell mounted on a high post.

The long tables were loaded with fried chicken, baked beans, and Cornish pasties; ham sandwiches, deviled eggs, potato salad, homemade pickles, and gelatine molds of every color; chocolate cakes, berry pies, and molasses cookies.

When the dinner bell rang a second time, there was a brief business meeting, and prizes were awarded to the oldest person in attendance, the youngest, and the family traveling the farthest distance. Then they all scattered—the elderly back to their chairs under the tree, the young ones to a field for softball, a few men to the front porch for a big league broadcast, and the young mothers to the farmhouse where they bedded down their tots for naps.

Qwilleran sauntered among the crowd, eavesdropping, as they talked about fishing, crops, television, funerals, babies, recipes, accidents, surgery, and the good old days.

Two women were arguing about the right way to make Cornish pasties. "My grandfather," said one, "went to the Buckshot Mine every day with a pasty in his lunch bucket, and my grandmother made pasties every day of her life. I have her recipe, and I know for a fact that she never used anything but meat and potatoes and a little onion."

The other said, "Well, in my family a pasty wasn't a pasty unless it had a little turnip."

"Never!" said the first. "My grandmother would sooner poison the well!"

Among the elderly men reminiscences were flying like the bees buzzing around the lilacs. A white-haired man wearing a blue ribbon labeled "Oldest" ventured to say, "When I started comin' to these shindigs, there was always a lineup at the outhouse, or the Cousin John as they used to call it. Now they rent a coupla them portable things. Times sure has changed."

One of his listeners said, "How about banks? Used to be you could go see the banker at home after supper, and he'd walk downtown with you and open up the bank if you was strapped for cash. Didn't have any of them time locks and alarms and cameras and such."

Eventually Qwilleran found Maryellen Wimsey among a group of young women. "Where's Clem?" he asked.

"He couldn't be here," she said simply.

"He's not ill, I hope. He didn't report for work yesterday, and he wasn't in the parade on Friday."

"He's out of town," the girl said, her gaze wavering.

"Will he be back tomorrow? I'm expecting him at the cabin. We've got to get the shingles on that roof."

"I hope so," she said uncertainly.

Qwilleran glanced at the group under the big tree. "Do you know which one is Emma Wimsey?"

"Yes," said Maryellen brightly, as if glad to change the subject. "She's in a wheelchair. She's the one with a blue sweater."

As he approached the congregation of oldsters he was hailed by an exuberant woman wearing a yellow blazer with a "We Care" emblem. "Mr. Qwilleran, you probably don't remember me. I'm Irma Hasselrich."

"Of course," he said. "You're the attorney's daughter, and you're a volunteer at the Senior Care Facility in Pickax."

Among the casually dressed picnickers she was conspicuous for her well-styled hair, her careful makeup, and the good cut of her clothes. Ms. Hasselrich was not young, but she was strikingly attractive.

"Oh, aren't you wonderful to remember!" she exclaimed. "You came to the facility last year to interview one of the ladies."

"A farmwife, as I recall. Mrs. Woolsmith, I believe her name was. How is she?"

"The dear soul passed on," said Ms. Hasselrich sweetly. "She was ninety-five and had nearly all her own teeth."

"And what brings you here today?" Qwilleran asked.

"I chauffeured three of our residents in the lift-van. I brought Abner Huggins, who won the prize for the oldest, and Emma Huggins Wimsey, eighty-nine, and Clara Wimsey Ward, eighty-two."

"I'd like to meet Emma Wimsey. They say she has an interesting story to tell. I'd like to get it on tape."

"She'll be delighted!" said the volunteer. "She used to teach school, and you'll find her very articulate. Her heart is weak now, but her memory is good . . . Emma! Emma, dear! You have a visitor!"

"Who is it? Who is it?" cried a faltering voice in great expectation.

"A reporter from the newspaper. I think he wants to hear your story about Punkin."

"Oh, dear! I've never been written up in the paper except when I married Horace. Do I look all right?"

"You look lovely . . . Emma, this is Mr. Qwilleran."

Emma Wimsey was a frail woman with thinning white hair, whose cheeks had been lovingly blushed, probably by Ms. Hasselrich. Though she appeared fragile, she was very much alive, and on her sweater was an enamel pin in the shape of a cat with a long curved tail. "Pleased to meet you," she said.

Qwilleran took her tiny hand warmly. "Mrs. Wimsey, it is my pleasure," he said. He had a courtly manner with persons over seventy, and it always pleased them.

Ms. Hasselrich suggested wheeling the chair to a quiet place, and they found a shady spot on the far side of the lilacs. "Are you warm enough, dear?" asked the volunteer.

Qwilleran brought lawn chairs and set up his tape recorder. "Why did you call your cat Punkin, Mrs. Wimsey?" he began.

"She was orange, and she came to me on Halloween. I was six years old. We were such good friends! We had a secret game that we played . . ." Her voice faded away, wistfully.

"What was your secret game, Mrs. Wimsey?"

"Well, after my mother put me to bed every night and closed the bedroom door, Punkin would come and scratch under the door, as if she was trying to get in. I'd jump out of bed and grab her paw. She'd pull it away and stick another paw under the door. Oh, we had such fun, and we never got caught!"

"How long did this secret game continue?" Qwilleran asked. "I mean, for how many years?"

"All the time I was growing up. Let me see . . . Punkin died before I went away to teachers college. Normal school, they called it then. Schoolteaching was the most respectable work a respectable young lady could do in those days. My grandfather had the first sawmill in Sawdust City, and we were supposed to be very respectable." Her eyes twinkled.

The volunteer said, "Emma, dear, tell Mr. Qwilleran about the fire at the college."

"Yes, the fire. I lived in a dormitory and studied hard and forgot all about Punkin's game. Then one night I suddenly woke up because I heard scratching under the door! For a minute I thought I was back home and Punkin wanted to play. But Punkin was dead! Then I smelled smoke. I ran down the hall shouting, 'Fire! Fire!' and pounding on everybody's door." She stopped to recall it in her mind's eye.

"Did you all escape safely?"

"Yes, and the firemen came and put the fire out."

"Did you tell anyone how you happened to wake up?"

"Oh, no! They would have laughed at me. But another time I heard the scratching again."

"When was that?"

"After I married Horace. We lived on a farm and had five children, four of them boys . . ." Her concentration wavered as nostalgia swept over her face. She was smiling to herself.

Ms. Hasselrich said gently, "Tell Mr. Qwilleran about the windstorm, dear."

"It was a tornado!"

"Yes, dear. Tell what happened."

"Well, one night while I was carrying my fourth child, I woke up and thought I heard scratching under the door, the way Punkin used to do. I sat up and listened, and the wind was howling something fierce! I woke up Horace, and he jumped out of bed and said, 'Get the children down in the cellar!' It was a real tornado, and it blew the roof off our farmhouse. But we were all safe in the cellar." There was a long pause, and her eyes glazed.

Qwilleran asked, "Was that the last time you heard scratching under the door?" He waited patiently until she collected her thoughts.

"No," she said. "There was one more time, after Horace died and the children were all gone. I sold the farm and bought a little house in the town—Black Creek, it was. I lived alone, you see, and one night that scratching noise woke me up again. I listened hard, and I could hear someone moving around in the kitchen. So I got out of bed and tiptoed to the door, and I could see a flashlight! I don't remember if I was scared or not. I don't think I was."

"What did you do?"

"I closed the bedroom door very softly and called the police on my bedroom phone. My sons made me have a bedroom phone. I'd never had one before."

"Who was it in the kitchen?"

"A burglar. They caught him. That was the last time I ever heard the scratching." Emma turned to the volunteer. "Wasn't that the last time?"

"Yes, dear," said Ms. Hasselrich, "that was the last time you heard the scratching."

"Thank you, Mrs. Wimsey," said Qwilleran. "That's a remarkable story. How do you explain it?"

"It was the Lord's work," said the little woman, her eyes shining. "The Lord works in mysterious ways."

Emma Wimsey's story haunted him as he drove back to the cabin. As a journalist he was conditioned to scoff at supernatural tales, but as the daily companion of a Siamese who could sense danger and sometimes transmit such information, he had second thoughts. There was something in this north country—a kind of primeval force—that unsettled one's educated beliefs.

When he reached the cabin, he unlocked the door

and called out, "Where's the gang? I've brought fried chicken right from the farm!"

Yum Yum came running.

"Where's your sidekick?" he asked her with a glance at the moosehead. "Where are you, Koko? Fried chicken!"

He expected to hear yikking and yowling, or at least a thump as Koko jumped down from a high place, but there was no audible response.

"Cereal!" That was their new buzzword.

Still there was no reply. Suddenly concerned, Qwilleran checked the bunkrooms, searched under bunks, opened closets and kitchen cabinets, opened the shower door—all with mounting anxiety.

As a chilling thought crossed his mind, he felt tension in his throat and a flush spreading over his face. Joanna had been there to fix the water heater, *and she had let Koko get out*!

He tested the hot-water faucet. Yes, she had been there.

"Oh, God!" he groaned as he rushed from the cabin.

SEVEN

Koko was lost!

Qwilleran ran from the cabin, calling his name. He looked up in the trees. He searched the toolshed. He combed the woods. He plunged down the steps to the beach, calling . . . calling . . .

Then in panic he ran back to the cabin and grabbed the phone book. Hands trembling, he looked up Joanna Trupp on Hogback Road. She was not listed. He might have guessed as much. He dialed the Glinko number, thinking they could radio her.

The Glinko telephone rang once . . . twice . . . but before they could answer, Qwilleran heard a distant yowl. He slammed down the receiver and rushed out doors again.

"Koko!" he bellowed and then listened. There was no answer. Again he searched the grounds, fearing that the cat might be injured—mauled by a dog or wild animal—lying helplessly in the brush, too weak to cry out. How could he be found in these acres of woods?

Again he called Koko's name and listened to the answering silence. Had he imagined Koko's yowl, just as Emma Wimsey had imagined the scratching?

Defeated, he returned to the cabin, aware that his heart was pumping fast. He sat down on the sofa and put his head in his hands . . . Did he hear a faint yowl? It seemed to come from the fireplace! He tried to look up the chimney, but the damper was jammed. He looked in the woodbox. On a wild hunch he ran to the toolshed and brought the ladder, climbed up on the roof and looked down the chimney. There was no cap on the flue, no screening. A small animal could fall down and be trapped! If Koko had run out of the house and then found himself locked out, he might climb a tree, drop onto the roof and try to enter the house by way of the chimney. It would be good thinking—up to a point. How would Koko know the damper was closed—and jammed?

Qwilleran slid down the ladder, ripping his hands and tearing his trousers. He ran into the cabin, stuck his head in the fireplace and shouted up the chimney.

There was a distant answer, but this time it came from the opposite end of the cabin.

Qwilleran made a dash for the guestroom. "Koko!"

Once more he heard the ghostly reply. It was driving him mad, and Yum Yum was racing about the cabin and shrieking hysterically.

"Shut up!" he yelled at her.

Calm down, he told himself. Think carefully. Listen unemotionally. He's got to be here—somewhere. "Koko!"

This time the answer came from the rear of the cabin. He rushed to the mudroom, kicked the rug aside and hoisted the heavy trap door.

"YOW!" said Koko as he jumped out of the hole and shook the cobwebs from his fur.

Qwilleran let the door drop with a crash. "How long have you been down there?" he demanded.

"Yow!" said Koko, batting the cobwebs from his whiskers. He walked calmly to his water bowl in a corner of the kitchen and took a long drink.

Qwilleran washed and bandaged his hands. "Don't ever do that to me again!" he said sternly. Now it was clear what had happened: Joanna had gone down under the cabin to deal with the defective water heater; Koko followed without her knowledge and was probably exploring some remote corner when she closed the trap door, locking him in the crawl space. Then she replaced the rug and left the premises. Koko had been down there for how long? An hour? Two hours? Three hours? It would teach him a lesson!

Qwilleran apologized to Yum Yum for shouting at her and then chopped the fried chicken for them, although his right hand was still shaking and he gripped the knife with difficulty. After placing the plate of chicken on the floor, he went for a walk on the beach to calm himself.

The loneliness of the shore, the gentle lapping of the water, the vast expanse of lake and sky ... all these natural tranquilizers worked together to quiet his nerves. *Nerves?* He had never in his entire life exhibited nervous symptoms. And yet, his hands had been trembling when he consulted the phone book; they were still shaking when he chopped the chicken. During his career as a crime reporter he had faced life-threatening crises without flinching. Of course, he had been younger then. Now he was fiftyish, and it had been two years since his last physical examination. Perhaps he had been drinking too much coffee. Polly Duncan had urged him to cut down. Every woman he had known in recent years had nagged him about his health. Every woman except Mildred, that is. They hovered about his life like a Greek chorus, chanting, "Eat right ... Get more exercise ... Quit smoking!" He had given up his pipe. He had bought a bicycle. He ate broiled fish. And now Polly was campaigning to limit his caffeine.

Slowly he ambled along the beach, breathing deeply, stopping at intervals to gaze across the placid lake. Even before he reached Seagull Point he saw Russell walking toward him, wearing sunglasses and her usual drab attire.

"Hi!" he said. "Where are your feathered friends today?"

"I fed them early," she said.

"Just taking a walk?"

She nodded.

"I'm walking to lower my blood pressure," he told her. "I've just had a traumatic experience."

The Cat Who Went Underground 125

She looked at his bandaged hands. "You're hurt."

"That's nothing, but it's part of the story. You see, I thought my cat was lost in the woods. I have two cats, and they're not supposed to go out. In fact, they *never* go out. When I came home and found one of them missing, I don't mind telling you that I panicked! My cats mean a great deal to me. Actually, they're all the family I have. I worried about roving dogs, wild animals, hawks, even kidnappers. It turned out that the plumber came in my absence and opened the trap door to the crawl space. Koko went down under the floor and was trapped. He's the male. The female is Yum Yum. They're Siamese. Would you like to meet them?"

He realized he was babbling like a simpleton, but it helped him to talk about the distressing experience.

After a moment's hesitation Russell answered his question with a timid yes. He continued to talk all the way to the cabin.

She accepted a chair on the lake porch, sitting on the edge of it.

"Would you care for a ginger ale?" he asked.

"No, thank you."

"The cats are around somewhere," Qwilleran said. "They'll come out when they hear us talking about them. They're incredibly vain, and they like to be admired. Yum Yum is a lapcat, very affectionate, with all kinds of catly traits. Koko is something else, though! He's a remarkable animal with a keen intuition about people, situations, and events . . . I wonder where they are. Excuse me a moment."

He found the Siamese in deep slumber on the

guestroom bunk—Koko evidently exhausted after his ordeal in the crawl space, Yum Yum glad to curl up in companionable proximity, and both of them stuffed with fried chicken. Picking them up in two hands, he carried them to the porch, one under each arm, their legs and heads and tails drooping, their bodies a dead weight. He set them down gently on the porch rug.

Yum Yum shook herself awake and looked at Russell with mild curiosity, then speculated on the laces in her canvas shoes. Koko, on the other hand, froze in the spot where he had been deposited, bushed his tail, and chattered at the visitor with the hostility he usually reserved for squirrels and stray cats.

"Koko! Watch your manners!" Qwilleran scolded.

"They're interesting," Russell said.

The tail gradually resumed its normal shape, and Koko walked back into the cabin with one or two backward glances at the stranger.

In embarrassment Qwilleran said quickly, "Would you like to see the new addition?"

They walked around to the back of the cabin. "Big chimney," Russell remarked as they passed the huge block of fieldstone. "Another porch," she commented when she saw the one in the rear.

"It's handy to have porches fore and aft. One is always cool, and one is always sheltered."

"Tall trees," she said, looking up at the hundred-foot pines.

"Very old," he said, nodding and looking wise.

As they stood in front of the east wing, he explained the floor plan, discussed the method of connecting it to the original cabin, and described the proposed exterior of board-and-batten.

Russell observed everything in silence, nodding noncommittally, and when he had completed the prospectus, she said in a hollow voice, "I hope . . . they . . . get it finished."

As soon as Russell had headed down the steps to the beach, Qwilleran felt an urge to talk with Mildred Hanstable. "Thank you for steering me to Emma Wimsey," he said. "That's a good cat story, and it makes one think. I'll have to fix it up a little, but I think the readers will like it."

"And how about the reunion? Did you find it worthwhile?"

"Quite! It's enlightening to see how the other half lives. While I was there I felt envious, but now that I'm home, I find the idea of all those relatives somewhat suffocating."

"How long were you there?"

"About three hours, and when I reached the cabin, I got a real shock. I thought I'd lost Koko."

"What!"

"The plumber had let him get down into the crawl space, and I had some uneasy moments until I found him."

"How dreadful, Qwill! I know how you feel about those kitties."

"After that, I had a visit from your next-door neighbor. We spent a half hour together, and she said all of fifteen words in that time."

"I'm glad to hear she's loosening up," Mildred said.

"Who is this woman?" he demanded. "Where did she come from? Why is she here? She seems to be in her late twenties, but she dresses like 1935. Apparently she can afford a thousand dollars a month for a cottage."

"Maybe she's a poor girl who inherited some money from an old uncle."

"And inherited the wardrobe from an old aunt. When Koko met her he reacted as if she'd come from outer space. I think he knows more than we do ... And another curious thing about that girl, Mildred: She detects something unsavory about the Dunfield house. Did you tell her what happened there?"

"Not a word!"

"And when I showed her the new addition, she said she *hopes it gets finished*! I'm beginning to worry."

"What is there to worry about?" Mildred said. "You have a splendid young man working for you."

"That's what I worry about. He's too good to be true." Qwilleran combed his moustache with his finger-tips. "Clem didn't march in the parade Friday; he didn't show up for work yesterday; he didn't attend the reunion with his fiancée today. Maryellen's excuse was that Clem was out of town, but she wasn't very convincing."

"Oh, Qwill! You're always so suspicious. It's not un-thinkable that a person would go out of town on a big holiday weekend."

Qwilleran huffed into his moustache, mumbled something about hoping for the best, and said goodnight. He refrained from mentioning that Koko had been tapping his tail in a significant way for the last three days.

EIGHT

Qwilleran had become accustomed to six-thirty reveille on weekday mornings, sounded by the rumble of Clem's truck, the whine of the table saw, and the staccato blows of the hammer. On Monday he slept until eight o'clock, however, and only the weight of two cats on his chest caused him to open his eyes.

His doubts about the carpenter's whereabouts proved to be well-founded; Clem did not appear. Qwilleran kept glancing at his watch and smoothing his moustache anxiously. Finally he telephoned the Cottle farmhouse.

A weary-voiced woman answered—Clem's mother, he assumed.

"Hello, Mrs. Cottle? This is Jim Qwilleran. I'd like to speak with Clem, if he's there."

There was a breathless pause. "You want . . . to talk to . . . Clem?"

"Gimme that phone," said a gruff male voice. *"Who is this?"*

"Mr. Cottle? This is Jim Qwilleran. Clem is doing some construction work for me, and he didn't show up on Saturday. I'm wondering when I can expect him."

"He's out of town," the man snapped.

"Do you know when he'll be back?"

"Don't know. I'll tell him to call you." The chicken farmer hung up.

Here was a situation that called for the moral support of caffeine, and Qwilleran made himself a cup of coffee—weaker than usual, in the wake of his nervous shakes the night before. How long should he wait for Clem to return? Would Clem ever return? An uneasy sensation on his upper lip was intensifying. When should he start hunting for a substitute? Would anyone want to finish a job started by another builder? Where would he find anyone to equal Clem? And then the burning question: What had happened to Clem Cottle?

The Siamese had finished their three-hour morning nap and had not yet settled down for their four-hour afternoon siesta. It was their Mischief Hour. Yum Yum was batting a pencil she had stolen from the writing table, and Koko was parading around with a sweat sock that Qwilleran used for biking.

"What shall I do, Koko?" he asked. "You have a lot of good ideas. Tell me what to do."

Koko ignored him pointedly as he staggered about the cabin, dusting the floorboards with the sock dragging between his forelegs.

"Are you telling me the house is dirty?" Qwilleran noted the fluffballs in the corners and the dust on almost everything. "Well, maybe it is." He ran the dustmop around the edges and flicked a duster half-heartedly over several tabletops.

The sock brought to mind Cecil's story about Grandpa Huggins and the loaf of bread. They had a sly wit, those early settlers. Grandpa's General Store had completely disappeared. Not a stick of it left, Cecil had said. It had been on the Brrr Road at Huggins Corners. The county was dotted with ghostly memories of villages and hamlets that had vanished without a trace, and they held a singular fascination for Qwilleran. He retrieved his sock, found its mate, changed into shorts and T-shirt, and set out on his bike to find the site of Grandpa Huggins's General Store.

Only a trail bike or a vehicle with four-wheel drive could negotiate the sandy furrows of the Old Brrr Road, and there was not enough traffic to keep the weeds from growing in the ruts. Yet, this had once been the only thoroughfare between Mooseville and Brrr, traversed by wagons, carriages, doctors on horseback, and pedestrians who thought nothing of walking ten miles to exchange a catch of fish for a few dozen eggs. Here and there one could see the remains of a collapsed barn or a stone chimney rising from a field of weeds. A crude bridge crossing the Ittibittiwassee River was nothing more than a collection of rattling planks.

Qwilleran passed a clearing with a circle of charred ashes in the center. Hunters had made camp here, or Scouts had pitched tents. He saw the rear end of a blue truck ahead, parked off the road with the front end in a shallow ditch. A varmint hunter, he surmised, but when he biked abreast of the pickup, he saw the frantic chicken painted on the door.

He threw down his bike and approached the truck warily, fearful of what he might find. The windows were open, and the cab was empty, but the key was in the ignition—not an unusual circumstance in the north country. When he flipped the key, the motor turned over, so the truck was not out of gas. But where was the driver? Qwilleran touched his moustache tentatively. Clem was not "out of town" as his father and fiancée had insisted.

After making this mystifying discovery, Qwilleran lost all interest in Grandpa Huggins's General Store. He turned the bike around and headed back to the dunes, thinking what a coincidence it was—and how fortunate it was—that Koko had stolen his sock. All that remained now was to determine an appropriate course of action.

As he pedaled up the snaking drive to the cabin, a small yellow car was leaving the clearing. He dropped his bike and walked to the driver's window. "Looking for me, Maryellen?"

"I wanted to talk to you," she said in a small voice.

"Back up," he said, "and come into the cabin."

He wheeled the bike to the toolshed and met her at the door to the back porch. "Let's sit out here. It's a little breezy on the lakeside. May I get you a drink?"

"No, thanks," she said, studying her hands clenched in her lap.

"What's the problem?" Qwilleran asked, although he could guess.

"I'm worried about Clem."

"So am I, but yesterday you told me he was out of town."

"That's what Mr. Cottle told me to say."

"What's his line of reasoning?"

"He says a young man has to have a last fling before he settles down. He says he did it himself when he was Clem's age. But Mrs. Cottle doesn't think that's what happened to Clem, and neither do I. It's not like him to go away without letting us know—not like him at all! He's too thoughtful to do that."

"From my brief acquaintance with him, I'm inclined to agree, but why did you come to me?"

"I didn't know who else to go to. I don't want to upset my parents. Dad has a heart condition, and Mom goes to pieces easily. Clem always said you were an important man in the county, so that's why I came." She looked at him appealingly.

"You're not going to like what I have to say, Maryellen, but . . . I've just been biking on the Old Brrr Road, and I saw Clem's truck."

Her face and neck flushed a bright red.

"It's not wrecked," he went on. "The keys are in the

ignition, and it's not out of gas. It's just parked off the road, halfway in the ditch. Would he have any reason for using the old road?"

She shook her head slowly. "He's not a hunter. Only hunters go back in there." Her eyes grew wide. "What do you think it means?"

"It means that Clem's father should stop kidding himself and report the disappearance to the sheriff."

In Qwilleran's early days as a newsman, when he covered the police beat for newspapers Down Below, he had a good rapport with the law-enforcement agencies, and he could always discuss cases with fellow journalists at the Press Club. In Moose County he had no such connections. There was Arch Riker, of course, but his old friend only kidded him about his suspicions. And there was Andrew Brodie, but the Pickax police chief dried up when the case was outside his jurisdiction, and the Cottle farm in Black Creek was on the sheriff's turf.

Under the circumstances, Qwilleran's only contact was Mildred's son-in-law, who covered the police beat for the *Moose County Something*. Having quit a teaching job to join the paper, Roger MacGillivray was hardly a seasoned reporter, but he was a willing listener, and he had enthusiasm.

Qwilleran telephoned Roger at the office. "Could you shirk your parental duties for one night," he asked the new father, "and meet me somewhere for dinner?"

"Right! Sharon owes me one. I baby-sat twice last

week while she went out," said Roger. "Want to meet me in Brrr for a boozeburger?"

"Sure," Qwilleran said, "or we could try that new restaurant if you like red-hot food."

"I'm willing to give it a try. I have some red-hot news for you."

The new restaurant was called the Hot Spot, and it advertised in the *Something* as "the cool place to go for hot cuisine." It occupied a former firehall in Brrr, with thirty tables jammed into space that once housed two firetrucks. The original brick walls and stamped metal ceiling had been retained, and there was nothing to absorb sound except the sweating bodies that swarmed into the place for Mexican, Cajun and East Indian dishes.

"Noisy, isn't it?" Qwilleran observed as he and Roger stood in line for a table.

"Noisy is what people like," Roger said. "It makes them think they're having a good time."

A flustered host seated them at a small table squeezed between two others of the same limited dimensions. On one side were a pair of underclad beach-combers, shouting at each other in order to be heard. On the other side were two shrill-voiced women in resort clothes.

"This is not the place for exchanging confidences," Qwilleran said.

"Let's just eat and get out," Roger suggested. "Then we can have pie and coffee at the Black Bear and do some talking."

Waiters scurried about, bumping the chairs of the

closely packed diners and colliding with each other. Qwilleran felt something splash on the back of his neck and dabbed at it with a napkin; it was red.

A harried waiter came to take their orders.

"Enchiladas!" Qwilleran said loudly.

"How hot d'you want the sauce?"

"Industrial strength!"

"Cajun pork chops!" Roger shouted.

After ordering they stared at each other dumbly, defeated by the high-decibel din. Qwilleran saw—seated across the table—a pale, slender, eager young man whose neatly clipped black beard and trimmed black hair accentuated his white complexion. Roger saw a robust fifty-year-old whose luxuriant salt-and-pepper moustache was known throughout Moose County and in several cities Down Below.

Although they found it difficult to communicate, nearby voices came through with amazing clarity. A woman's strident voice said, "My cat is always throwing up hairballs as big as my thumb."

Qwilleran frowned. "How's Sharon?" he shouted to Roger.

"Itching to go back to work!"

"How old is Junior?"

"Six months, two weeks, three days!"

Qwilleran became aware of a large bare foot, probably size fifteen, rising from the floor alongside him, as the beachcomber at the next table said to his companion, "Look at this toenail. D'you think I'll lose it? It turned black after I dropped the anchor on it."

The shrill voice on the other side was saying, "Her

husband's in the hospital. They cut him from ear to ear and took out a tumor as big as a brussels sprout."

At that moment two dinner plates were banged down on the table without warning. Qwilleran sniffed his and said, "This isn't Mexican food. This is Indian curry."

"I ordered pork chops," said Roger, "but this is some kind of omelette."

"Let's get out of here!" Qwilleran seized both plates and carried them to the entrance, where he handed them to the astonished host. "Warm these up and serve them to somebody else," he said. "Come on, Roger, let's go to the Black Bear."

The Black Bear Café in the century-old Hotel Booze was famous for its boozeburgers and homemade pies. The atmosphere was dingy and the furniture sleazy, but one could converse. Qwilleran and Roger seated themselves cautiously in two rickety chairs and were greeted by Gary Pratt, the shaggy black-bearded proprietor. He had a stevedore's shoulders and a sailor's tan.

"Looks like you've been out on your boat," Qwilleran remarked.

"Every Sunday!" said the big man in a surprisingly high-pitched voice.

"Is the Hot Spot cutting into your business?"

"All my customers went there once, when the place first opened, but they've all come back. What'll you have?"

"Boozeburger and a beer for me," said Roger.

"Boozeburger and coffee," Qwilleran said. "Okay, Roger, let's have your hot news."

"Do you know Three Tree Island?"

"Only by name. It's out in the lake in front of my place, I believe, but not visible from shore."

"It's several miles out—just a flat, sandy beach with a hump in the middle and a clump of trees. It belongs to a guy who owns some charter fishing boats, and he has a dock and fishing shack out there. Fishermen tie up to do a little drinking and clean their catch. Kids go sunning on the sand and use the shack for God-knows-what."

"So what's the news? He's decided to build condominiums?"

"The news is—and I got it from the pilot of the sheriff's helicopter—that there's been a UFO landing on the beach!"

Qwilleran regarded Roger with scornful disbelief. "He's putting you on."

"He's serious. I know the guy well. He spotted a large burned patch on the island—perfectly round."

"Some kids had a bonfire," Qwilleran said.

"Too big for that."

"What does the sheriff say?"

"The pilot hasn't made an official report. It might affect his credibility in the department."

"What are you leading up to?"

"I thought we could get a Geiger counter or something and go out there, and I'd write a story for the paper. Bushy has a boat, and he's game."

Qwilleran was temporarily speechless. In his early

days, however, as a reporter he had followed wilder leads than this one. Roger was young. He should not be discouraged.

"Would you like to come with us?" the younger man asked.

Qwilleran smoothed his moustache thoughtfully. Although he placed no stock in the rumor, he hated to be left out of the investigation. "I wouldn't mind going along for the ride."

"As a disinterested third party you could corroborate our findings, and it would add weight to the story."

"Don't trap me into endorsing any harebrained adventure tale, m'boy. What's Bushy's reaction?"

"He's ready to go! I just wanted to get some input from you."

A waitress served the boozeburgers, six inches in diameter, four inches high, and famous throughout the county. The two men munched in silence for a while. This mountain of food required the utmost concentration and several paper napkins, and it so happened that the Black Bear charged a nickel for a paper napkin, not of the best quality.

"Everything okay?" asked Gary Pratt, prowling around the dining area like the black bear that he resembled.

"Next time I'm bringing my own paper napkins," said Qwilleran. "What's the pie today?"

"Chocolate meringue, but it's going fast. Want to order a couple of pieces?"

"It all depends on how you're cutting the pie—with

an inch-rule or a micrometer. I know your game, Gary. What you lose on the burgers, you make up on the pie and the paper napkins."

"For a couple of healthy guys like you," Gary said, "I'd suggest two slices apiece, and I won't charge for the napkins."

"It's a deal!"

Gary shuffled away, cackling his high-pitched laugh.

By the time the four slices of pie were served to the two men, it was Qwilleran's turn to launch a rumor of his own. He said, "Instead of chasing UFOs, Roger, you should be investigating a rash of criminal activity in Mooseville."

Roger gulped and set down his fork.

NINE

"How's the pie?" asked the proprietor, making his rounds.

"Best I ever tasted, Gary," said Qwilleran. "Is your grandmother still making your pies?"

"No, the old lady died, but my aunt has her recipes."

"It's rich but not cloying, creamy but not viscid."

"I should raise the price," Gary said as he walked away to ring up a sale on the antique brass cash register.

Qwilleran said to Roger, "There's something satisfying about the sound of an old cash register: the thump of the key, the ring of the sale, the scrape of the drawer popping out . . . How come you're not eating your pie?"

"You threw me a curve," said Roger, who had been staring into space. "What kind of criminal activity do you mean? Is something going on that I don't know about?" Like most natives of the county he considered it his privilege to know everything that was happening, and as a reporter he considered it his duty to know it first.

"It's happening right in front of your eyes. If you're going to be a journalist, you've got to start thinking as well as reporting."

"Gosh! Give me a clue!"

"I ran into a similar case in Rio fifteen years ago, but you expect that sort of thing in South America; you don't expect it in Mooseville." Qwilleran was purposely prolonging the suspense.

Roger stared at him expectantly, with his fork poised in midair.

"I seriously suspect," said Qwilleran, taking time to groom his moustache, "that someone in the Mooseville area has put a curse on carpenters."

Roger relaxed. "What's the joke, Qwill? Give me the punch line."

"It's no joke. Carpenters are dying and disappearing at an ungodly rate. Anyone who believes in UFOs should be able to accept the age-old mystique of the curse—an evil spirit exerting influence in an otherwise healthy community."

Roger put down his fork. These statements were coming from a veteran journalist whom he admired and respected. "Where do you get your statistics, Qwill?"

"It's common knowledge. We've had two accidents, one death from so-called natural causes, and a couple of disappearances. And it's all happened in the last two months. Joe Trupp appears to have been the first."

"Everybody knows the tailgate of a truck fell on him," Roger said. "It was an open-and-shut case of accidental death. That's what the coroner ruled."

"That's the beauty of a curse. Everything looks so natural, so normal, so accidental. Then there was the underground builder who was putting up Lyle Compton's garage. He vanished completely, and all efforts to trace him have failed."

"Well, you know those itinerants," said Roger. "They come and go. Half the time I suspect they're fugitives, and when the law starts to catch up with them, they take off!"

"Then how about Buddy Yarrow, drowned in a fishing accident? He was neither an itinerant nor a fugitive. He was a family man and highly respected craftsman. Also an experienced fisherman. Also a strong swimmer."

"Yeah, I know," Roger said with regret. "I knew Buddy well. But the coroner ruled that he slipped on the muddy bank of the river—after that big rain we had—and hit his head on a rock."

"And how about Captain Phlogg," Qwilleran persisted. "He masqueraded as a sea captain, but actually he was a ship's *carpenter*."

"We all knew he'd drink himself to death sooner or later."

"Roger, if you're not going to eat your chocolate pie, push it over this way."

The young man applied himself to the dessert, consuming it but not necessarily enjoying it. "That's four victims," he said. "Are there more?"

"I suspect the fifth is Clem Cottle."

"Clem Cottle! What happened to him? Nothing has been reported."

Qwilleran finished his second piece of pie before continuing. "I don't know what happened to him. He'd been building a new wing on the cabin for me and doing a great job. When he left Thursday night he told me he'd be marching in the parade the next day. He also said he'd be on the job Saturday. Now listen to this: He wasn't in the parade, and he didn't work Saturday, nor did he attend the Wimsey reunion with his fiancée yesterday. Again this morning he failed to show up, so I called his folks. His father said Clem was out of town, and he had no idea when he'd be back."

"There's nothing unusual about that, is there?"

"Only that Maryellen was looking worried and Mrs. Cottle was sobbing when she answered the phone."

"Do you suppose he got in some kind of trouble?"

"Wait a minute. Here's the clincher: This afternoon I went biking on the Old Brrr Road, and I found Clem's truck, headed into a ditch. There was no sign of a crash; it was simply parked there—abandoned—with the key in the ignition!"

"What did you do?"

"I told Maryellen it was time for the family to notify the authorities. So we may not be dealing with a curse in the old sense of the word, but you have to admit that something bizarre is happening in Mooseville. The town has a few peculiar characters. I won't mention any names. You know them as well as I do. Perhaps better. You've lived here all your life."

"Jeez!" said Roger in a daze. "You wouldn't think anything like that could happen in Mooseville."

"Think about it," Qwilleran said. "Keep your eyes open when you cover your beat. Don't believe everything you hear. Cogitate beyond the obvious . . . And finish your pie. I'll get the check."

After Roger had left for home, Qwilleran thought, That'll give the kid something to ponder while he's baby-sitting. It'll take his mind off UFOs.

He moved over to the bar where Gary was filling drink orders.

"Squunk water and a twist?" asked the barkeeper. Mineral water from a flowing well at Squunk Corners was Qwilleran's regular drink at the Black Bear. Gary trucked demijohns to the well and filled them without charge, then retailed the precious stuff in his bar at an incalculable markup.

Qwilleran said to him, "Considering what you make on Squunk water and paper napkins, you could afford to buy new chairs—or at least glue the old ones."

"The place would lose all its character. The boaters especially like the shabby atmosphere."

"Do you ever sail out to Three Tree Island, Gary?"

"Nah! What's there? Nothing but a stinkin' fish shack. The beach is okay for sunning, but I get all the sun I need on deck. And the water's too cold for swimming. That's the only thing wrong with this lake. Don't fall overboard, or you're an instant ice cube."

"Do you ever see any UFOs over the lake?"

"Oh, sure. All the time. They like us. I don't know why."

A few stools down the bar a man in a silk designer shirt and alligator Loafers joined the conversation. "I've seen seventeen this year." Among the come-as-you-are crowd he was highly conspicuous.

Gary said, "Mighty Lou is the official scorekeeper for extraterrestrial activity. Do you know Mighty Lou?"

Qwilleran turned and nodded at the man who had ridden in the parade as grand marshal. The man ignored the introduction but said, "I write them down in a book."

Gary moved away to serve a customer, and Qwilleran went to the men's room. When they resumed their conversation, Qwilleran said to the barkeeper, "Do you happen to know a good carpenter who would take on a small job? I've been building an addition to my cabin, but the guy let me down."

"They're hard to find in summer. They sign on with the big firms."

"I'd even consider an underground builder."

"Funny you should mention it," said Gary. "Iggy's back in town. He came in last night."

"Iggy?" Qwilleran repeated. "Can you recommend him?"

"He's a good craftsman, I guess, but he's lazy. You have to keep on his tail."

"Does he have a job lined up?"

"I doubt it. He just got in on his broomstick last night."

"Is he that bad?"

"Nah, I'm kidding. Want me to send him out to your place? He'll probably come in the bar later tonight. Write down your address."

Qwilleran wrote the information on a bar check. "Ask him to come early tomorrow morning."

"I'll try, but I doubt whether 'early' is in his vocabulary."

"Can you tell me anything about him?" Qwilleran asked.

"For one thing, he's the skinniest guy I ever saw— with a nicotine habit that won't stop. But he's strong as an ox! Can't understand it. He hardly ever eats."

"But he drinks?"

"He does his share of boozing, but the thing of it is, he's just lazy. And wait till you see his truck! I swear the only thing that holds the body onto the chassis is the brake pedal." Gary got a signal from a customer down the bar and moved away.

Mighty Lou settled his tab and threw a large bill on the bar for a tip. Then he approached Qwilleran with a chesty air of importance. "You need a builder?" he asked. "I can handle a few small jobs between contracts. Here's my card." He handed over a business card with engraved lettering on good stock: MIGHTY LOU, CONTRACTOR. There was a telephone number but no address.

"Thank you," said Qwilleran, putting the card in his wallet. "I may get in touch." He looked questioningly at Gary as the big man left the restaurant.

The barkeeper shrugged in a gesture of sympathy. "Harmless," he said. "Another Squunk?"

"No, thanks. I'm driving." As Qwilleran left the restaurant, he was hailed by diners at one of the tables. Lyle and Lisa Compton were lingering over coffee.

"Sit down and have a cup," said the superintendent. Qwilleran lowered himself carefully into one of the wobbly chairs. "You're just the people I wanted to see! What was the name of the fellow who was building your garage?"

"Mert," said Compton. "He never told me his last name, and I was afraid to ask. These underground characters are very suspicious. They value their privacy."

"I'm hiring a guy named Iggy."

"What happened to Clem Cottle?" asked Lisa. "We were counting on him to do our garage when he finished with you."

"Clem . . . uh . . . hasn't come around lately, and I'm not going to fool around any longer. I'm going underground and hoping for the best."

"Let me give you some advice," said Lyle. "Don't give this Iggy fellow any money in advance. Have the lumberyard bill you directly for supplies. And keep a record of the hours he works."

"Also," said Lisa, "don't irritate him or he'll walk off the job."

"And one more thing," said the superintendent. "There's a law in the county against using an unlicensed builder unless he's related to you. So let it be known that Iggy is a close relative."

Qwilleran returned to the cabin, where he was greeted vociferously by the Siamese. "Guess who's coming tomorrow?" he said without enthusiasm. "Cousin Iggy."

TEN

On Tuesday morning Qwilleran was awakened by the bouncing of his mattress and the pummeling of his body. The Siamese were having a morning scrimmage on his bed and on his person. He hoisted himself out of bed and stretched, wincing as certain muscles reminded him of the bike ride on the Old Brrr Road.

"This is the day we're supposed to meet our new builder," he said to the cats as he coated some sardines with cheese sauce and garnished them with vitamin drops and crumbled egg yolks. "Let's hope he shows up. Keep your whiskers crossed."

"Yow," said Koko, tapping his tail on the floor three times.

In preparation Qwilleran called the lumberyard and alerted them that a fellow named Iggy would be picking up building materials, which should be charged directly to the Klingenschoen office in Pickax.

"Old horse-face? Is he back again?" said the man on the phone with a laugh. "Lotsa luck!"

The Siamese tossed off their breakfast and looked hopefully at Qwilleran for a chaser.

"Oh, all right," he said and gave them a few crumbles of Mildred's cereal. Thus far they had consumed onesixteenth of a tub of the stuff. "You have one-and-fifteen-sixteenths of a tub left," he told them.

At nine o'clock there was no sign of the builder. At ten o'clock Qwilleran was getting fidgety. When he heard the quiet rumble of a vehicle making its way up the winding, hilly drive, he went to the clearing to wait for it, although he knew it was hardly the sound of a truck held together by the brake pedal. He was quite right; the car that drove into the clearing was Mildred's little white compact.

She rolled down the window. "I'm on my way to a hair appointment and can't stay, but I brought you some more cereal." She handed him a plastic tub. "I toasted a new batch this morning."

"Thank you," he said, with more enthusiasm than he actually felt. He thought, I'll have to get another cat. The stock on hand was now two-and-fifteen-sixteenths of a tub. "Sure you won't come in for a cup of coffee?"

"Not today, thanks. But tell me—is there any more news about Clem Cottle? Roger called last night and said he's been reported missing. It'll be in tomorrow's paper."

"I haven't heard anything further." When the Moose County grapevine is functioning, he thought, who needs a newspaper?

"What will you do about your new addition, Qwill?"

"I've hired an underground builder. He's due here this morning."

Mildred said, "I don't know whether to say this or not, because I know you're skeptical about such things, but I've been wondering . . ." She bit her lip. "I really feel terrible about Clem's disappearance, you know. He had such a promising future. Sharon used to date him when they were in high school."

"What have you been wondering, Mildred?"

"Well, I have a friend who might throw some light on the mystery."

"Does your friend have evidence?"

"No, she's a clairvoyant. Sometimes she gets messages from the spirit world."

"Oh," said Qwilleran.

"Mrs. Ascott is quite old, and she lives in Lockmaster, but if I could get her to come up here for a brief visit, she might be able to tell us something." Mildred waited for an encouraging sign from Qwilleran. Receiving none, she went on. "Mrs. Ascott came up earlier this year for my grandchild's christening—she's godmother, you see—and while she was here I invited a few friends to meet her, and she was kind enough to answer questions ... How do you feel about it, Qwill?"

"You do whatever you think is ... uh ... worthwhile, Mildred."

"Would you be available Saturday evening?"

"Me? What would you want me to do?"

"Just attend the meeting, and if you feel like asking a question, do so. Sharon and Roger will be there. They're quite enthusiastic about Mrs. Ascott's powers."

Uh-huh, Qwilleran thought. And about UFOs. And about horoscopes. And about tarot cards.

"It might be an idea for the 'Qwill Pen'," Mildred said.

"All right," he said. "I'll go as an observer. Who'll be there?"

"Just some people from the Dunes. Now I must dash off for my appointment."

It was almost noon when Qwilleran heard what sounded like rifle shots in the woods, or a small cannon. The blasts became louder and the onslaught came closer until a ramshackle truck chugged into the clearing and stopped with one final backfire and a rattle of loose parts.

"Good morning," said Qwilleran pleasantly as he sauntered over to the vehicle, a rusty pickup with camper top.

Out stepped an emaciated man in a dirty T-shirt and torn jeans. What jarred Qwilleran was the man's teeth—the largest set, real or false, that he had ever seen. Thirty-two jumbo-size teeth grinned as the man approached, with a cigarette in hand, appraising the property as if he considered buying it.

Qwilleran's first thought was: They can't be real. His second thought was: They're not even *his*! "Are you Iggy?" he asked in the same hospitable tone.

"That's what they CALL ME!" the man said. He gestured toward the skeleton of a structure adjoining the cabin. "That the job you WANT DONE?" He had a peculiar speech pattern, starting almost inaudibly and ending in a shout.

"That's the job," Qwilleran said. "It's ready for shingles, and I hope you can get them on before it rains again. You have to pick them up from the lumberyard. The previous builder ordered them to match the ones on the main cabin."

"Can't match them old suckers," Iggy said. "Shingles CHANGE COLOR!"

"The people at the lumberyard understand the problem, and they're giving us the best match they can."

Iggy stood there with his thin body curved in a concave slump, one hand in a hip pocket, a cigarette in the other, and a seeming reluctance to leave.

"Gotta have some GREEN STUFF," he said, lipping the cigarette and rubbing his fingers together.

"The shingles will be billed directly to me, and I'll pay you for your labor at the end of each work day."

Still Iggy lingered.

"Is there any question?" Qwilleran asked.

"Got any CIGARETTES?"

"Sorry, I don't smoke."

"Can't work without SMOKE IN MY EYES," he said with a squinting grin.

Qwilleran handed him a few dollar bills. "Better get on your horse. The lumberyard closes for lunch from noon to one o'clock."

"See ya LATER."

How much later was a question that Qwilleran would have been wise to ask. As soon as the truck had spluttered down the drive with explosive reports every thirty seconds, he thawed a frozen deli sandwich in the microwave and gulped it down in order to finish by the time Iggy returned with the load of shingles. After all, the lumberyard was only two miles away, on Sand-pit Road. As it evolved, there was no need to hurry. It was three hours before Iggy's truck returned, gasping and choking and backfiring.

"Couldn't find the sucker of a LUMBERYARD," he explained with his horsy grin that stretched the skin over the bones of his face. He started to unload bundles of shingles, and Qwilleran marveled at the weight the scrawny fellow could lift.

He went indoors to work at the typewriter and had barely inserted a sheet of paper around the platen when Iggy appeared in the doorway with a toothy question. "Where's the NAILS?"

"Didn't you pick up nails when you picked up the shingles?" Qwilleran asked in astonishment.

"You didn't say nothin' ABOUT NAILS."

"Then beat it back to the lumberyard before they close. They open at six in the morning and close at four in the afternoon."

"Won't get *this sucker* up at no six o'clock in THE MORNING," Iggy said with his leathery grimace.

"Go! Go!" Qwilleran ordered. And he returned to his typewriter, growling at the cats who were sitting placidly on his notes without a worry in their sleek heads.

In two minutes the set of teeth appeared in the doorway again. "Gotta LADDER?"

Qwilleran drew a deep breath and counted to ten. "Don't you have a ladder in your truck? I never heard of a carpenter without a ladder."

"The sucker's too big to TOTE AROUND!"

"There's a stepladder in the toolshed."

"Need an EXTENSION LADDER!"

"Then buy one at the lumberyard and tell them to put it on my bill, and hurry before they close. Let's get some slight amount of work done today!" He was feeling snappish.

Trying to resume his writing, Qwilleran concentrated with difficulty until the truck returned, fracturing the silence with its ear-splitting racket. After that, reassuring noises could be heard on the roof. *Bang bang bang.* At least the man knew how to use a hammer.

After a while, consumed with curiosity, Qwilleran went outdoors to inspect the carpenter's progress. What he saw sent him sprinting to the building site, shouting and waving his arms. "Wrong color! Wrong color!" The shingles were bright blue.

"The suckers was on sale," Iggy called down from the roof. "You can PAINT 'EM!" *Bang bang bang.*

"Stop! I don't want to paint them. I want the right

color! They're supposed to be brown. I'll phone the lumberyard ... No, it's too late. They're closed ... Take them off! Take them off! I'll phone the yard in the morning."

So ended the first day. Qwilleran computed the man's time: half an hour of work, five hours of travel back and forth.

"This is going to be worse than I thought," he told the cats, who sensed his discomposure and remained sympathetically quiet. "I've paid him for five and a half hours, and we have nothing to SHOW FOR IT! Dammit! I'm talking like Iggy."

When the carpenter reported for work on Wednesday morning—or, rather, when he arrived and observed the ritual of smoking several leisurely cigarettes—Qwilleran told him to return all unopened bundles of blue shingles to the lumberyard and bring the brown ones previously ordered. Iggy was quite agreeable. He flashed his teeth and nodded to everything, then smoked another cigarette.

The lumberyard was five minutes away, even in a junk vehicle like Iggy's spastic truck, but it was two hours before the man returned with the correct shingles. "Got a HAMMER?" he asked.

"A hammer! What happened to yours?" Qwilleran demanded. "You were using it yesterday."

"Had to hock the sucker FOR BREAKFAST."

Qwilleran huffed into his moustache with impatience. There was a hammer in the mudroom closet, but the idea of lending his own hammer to a carpenter hired to do carpentry was something he found offensive. "Here, take this money," he said. "Get your hammer out of hock."

It was a matter of two more hours before Iggy returned, grinning and puffing smoke, and after an inexplicable delay he tackled the shingles. *Bang bang bang.* Qwilleran listened with one ear as he tried to concentrate on his writing at the dining table. The carpenter had an eccentric habit of talking to himself as he worked.

All the time he was pounding he was mumbling, "Get in there, you sucker! . . . Whoa! Not there. Wrong place . . . Attaboy! Now y'got it . . . Need another nail . . . Where's that shingle?"

There were also long stretches of silence during which he lighted up and inhaled deeply and enjoyed the landscape from his perch on the roof. During each interruption Koko's tail went *tap tap tap.*

"Cut it out!" Qwilleran yelled at him. "You're making me NERVOUS!"

To escape from the exasperating performance Qwilleran went into Mooseville for lunch, picking up the midweek issue of the *Moose County Something* and noting that rain was predicted. Making his usual stop at the post office he found two items of interest—one of them a postcard from Polly Duncan.

Dear Qwill—Very busy meeting people, giving talks, seeing the beautiful countryside. "This other Eden . . . This precious stone set in the silver sea . . . This blessed plot . . . This England."

But I think wistfully of your quiet summer in
Mooseville. Love—Polly

Qwilleran huffed into his moustache. He had hoped
for a long letter, not a postcard, with less Shakespeare
and more personal news and a few endearments, but it
was better than no word at all. Also in his post-office
box was the following note:

Dear Mr. Qwilleran,
   I'm writing you in behalf of Mrs. Emma
Wimsey who so much appreciated your time and
kind attention on Sunday. You were so gracious!
It's safe to say that your visit was one of the
highlights of her long life. She talks about you
constantly.

Sincerely,
Irma Hasselrich, MCSCF
Chief Canary

He read this note twice. In the middle of a day that
was less than satisfactory, Ms. Hasselrich's flattery
made him feel good. The acronym he could decipher:
Moose County Senior Care Facility. But what was a
Chief Canary?

When Qwilleran returned to the cabin, the roof was
half-shingled, but Iggy was not on the site and not in
his truck. Iggy, he soon discovered, was on the
screened porch, asleep on the redwood chaise. He had
removed his shoes and covered his face with a piece of

shingle-wrapping. He had holes in his socks. He was snoring gently.

Qwilleran kicked the man's feet. "Up! Up! What do you think this is? A summer resort? I'm not paying you to sleep! Let's get that roof shingled before it rains!"

Iggy sat up, grinned, and felt for his cigarettes.

Now Qwilleran was as grouchy as he had been before going to lunch. He returned to his writing table and started a fretful letter to Polly. A "quiet summer," she had said. He'd give her an enlightening rundown on his "quiet summer." Then his eye fell on Irma Hasselrich's note. He read it once more and telephoned the Senior Care Facility in Pickax. Ms. Hasselrich answered from the reception desk.

"This is Jim Qwilleran," he said. "I've just received your thoughtful note, and it brightened an otherwise frustrating day. But I'd like to ask a question: What is the function of a Chief Canary?"

She trilled a tuneful laugh and said, "Our volunteers wear yellow smocks when they're on duty, and they're called canaries—a cheerful image, don't you think? I'm president of the volunteers this year, and so I'm entitled to wear a yellow blazer—as chief canary." She had the kind of voice he liked in a woman—cultivated, well-modulated, melodic. He remembered the yellow blazer she had worn at the reunion, and how well it had looked with her shining dark hair and shining dark eyes and artful makeup. She was a goodlooking woman, and she had her father's upbeat personality. Qwilleran had lunched with Hasselrich several times; he thought he would like to have dinner with his daughter. She was the right age—not too young but still youthful.

He said, "Tell Mrs. Wimsey that her story about Punkin will be in the paper this weekend."

"How wonderful! Thank you so much for alerting us."

Qwilleran went back to work in a more productive mood and maintained his equanimity until four o'clock, when Iggy wanted to quit for the day.

"Get back on that roof!" Qwilleran barked. "You don't get a nickel until those shingles are on. I don't care if you have to pawn your truck to buy your dinner! Finish that roof! It's going to rain tonight."

It was eight o'clock when Iggy drove the last nail and collected his earnings. "Before you go," Qwilleran said, "let me show you the sketches of the addition." He explained where the doorway would be cut in the existing cabin wall—to connect the old and the new. He explained that the cut-through would be left until the very last—for several reasons. He explained the choice of exterior siding and the style of window. "The lumberyard has the dimensions and will have the siding ready for you tomorrow morning. Don't come here first. Go to the lumberyard. Pick up the siding *and the nails* and bring them here."

The unflappable Iggy drove off, waving a friendly farewell, and Qwilleran strolled about the premises in peace, trying to imagine the finished wing, climbing between the studs to experience the orientation of rooms, gazing through the openings that would be windows, picturing the view. There was only one annoyance; the backyard was littered with cigarette butts, and rain would turn them into a soggy pudding. He found a sack and filled it with the unsavory litter. He had smoked pipe tobacco himself until recently, and he voiced no objection if his friends smoked, but Iggy's non-stop habit represented sloth and delay, for which he was paying by the hour. As a journalist he had always done ninety minutes' work for an hour's pay, and he deplored Iggy's laxity, even though the Klingenschoen estate was paying for it.

On Thursday morning he handed the carpenter a coffee can and said, "For every butt that lands on the ground instead of in this can, I deduct a dime from your pay." He realized he risked alienating the man and losing his services, but Iggy was always tractable. He would merely grin with those extraordinary teeth and light another cigarette.

Despite weather predictions, the rain held off, and the exterior siding went up slowly, at the rate of three boards per cigarette, with plenty of conversation at the same time: "Where's that sucker? . . . Get in there! . . . Gimme the hammer. Where's the hammer? . . . There we go! Right size . . . Need another nail . . . That'll fix the sucker."

Before installing a board, Iggy would stand back, look up at the studding, then saw the proper length and nail it in place. Smaller lengths he measured with his foot or the spread of his hand.

Qwilleran said, "Don't you ever measure?"

"Don't need to measure," the carpenter said with his ivory grin. "I just EYEBALL THE SUCKER!"

With mixed amazement and disapproval Qwilleran went indoors to make a cup of coffee, but when he plugged his computerized coffeemaker into the wall outlet, sparks flew! The radio went dead. The refrigerator stopped humming. Without a moment's hesitation he reached for the phone and called Glinko for an electrician.

"Allrighty," said Mrs. Glinko. "I'll dispatch Mad Mac. He's out on the east shore, puttin' in circuit breakers for somebody—another one of you rich people. Ha ha ha!"

"This rich person would also like a chimney sweep," Qwilleran said. "There's something wrong with the fireplace."

"Allrighty. I'll dispatch Little Harry if he ain't busy."

Mooseville natives were fond of honorifics, which were bestowed on certain persons by consensus: Old Sam, Big Joe, Crazy Marvin, Mighty Lou, Fat William, and so on.

Little Harry was a young man of slight build who wore a tall silk topper, the traditional badge of his profession, somewhat incongruous with his smudged T-shirt and jeans. He quickly discovered why the damper was jammed; a raccoon had built a nest in the chimney.

"The chimney top should be screened," he said. "It looks like you had a screen up there, but something knocked it off. And I don't see a fire extinguisher anywhere. You should have a fire extinguisher. You wouldn't want to burn down a nice old cabin like this, would you?" he asked patronizingly. "What kind of wood do you burn?"

"I haven't burned any wood," Qwilleran said. "I couldn't get the damper open. That's why you're here."

"My job is to educate, not just to clean chimneys," said the young man haughtily. "If you burn green wood, it builds up creosote and you can have a chimney fire. Hot ashes are another common cause of fire. What do you use to take out ashes, and where do you dump them?"

"I haven't taken out any ashes, because I haven't burned any wood, because I couldn't get the damper open!" said Qwilleran, raising his voice. "If you'll come back next week, when I'm not so busy, I'll be glad to sign up for Basic Fireplace Technique 101. But now, if you'll excuse me . . ."

He was in a vile mood by the time the electrician arrived. Mad Mac—a hulking individual with bulging biceps and no neck—found a loose connection in the wall outlet and pronounced the entire wiring system obsolete.

"Y'oughta have the whole house checked. A mouse or chipmunk gets in, chews on the wires, and you have a fire. These old logs—they're dry as tinder, burn like matchsticks. Whole place can go up quicker'n you can spit."

He lumbered about the cabin like a bulldozer, checking exposed wires, knocking over furniture, frightening the Siamese. "You got cats," he observed as they flew about the rafters. "With this kind of wirin' they could electrocute themselves."

Qwilleran clenched his teeth and kept his mouth shut. Just before leaving, the electrician said, "Who's the carpenter out there? One of them hoboes? Don't know why you summer people hire them bums. I was wirin' a garage for some folks down the shore, and the damn carpenter stole my tools and took off! I ain't got no use for carpenters. Plumbers, they're okay, but carpenters! If I was president, I'd have 'em all shot at sunrise!"

Shortly afterward it started to rain, and Iggy had an excuse to quit for the day. His teeth flashed a thank-you when Qwilleran paid up, and he headed toward the rattling gypsy wagon that served as a truck.

"Wait a minute!" Qwilleran yelled. "You didn't put the boards under cover!"

"Won't do the suckers NO HARM," said Iggy.

"Nevertheless, I want the siding INSIDE!"

Iggy finished his cigarette, flipped the butt on the ground, and carried the lumber into the new wing.

"Koko, you and I are the only sane ones left," Qwilleran said when the carpenter's truck had coughed and exploded its way down the drive. "And it won't be long before I go off the deep end."

Koko was prowling irrationally, as he did before a violent storm, and his instincts were on target. High winds soon lashed the lake into a fury. Trees bent to the ground, and even the tall pines swayed alarmingly. The cabin windows were drenched with rain, July hail pelted the roof, and sheets of water blew through the new addition, only half of which was sided. Then a black cloud looming over the dune dumped bolts of lightning and volleys of thunder. The entire cabin shuddered, and . . . the submersible pump stopped pumping.

So, it was back to the telephone. "Mrs. Glinko, this is Qwilleran."

"Don't tell me! Somethin' blew out!"

"Whatever. All I know is—we're not getting any water."

"Drink beer. Ha ha ha."

"No jokes, please."

"Allrighty. Keep your hair on. We'll dispatch somebody."

As Qwilleran was scurrying about with bath towels, mopping up the horizontal downpour that forced its way through closed doors and windows, Arch Riker phoned from Pickax and asked casually, "Getting any rain up there?"

"Rain! We're inundated!" Qwilleran said. "The lake's rising! Tree branches are dropping like bombs! And the pump has conked out. The plumber's on the way over here. We've already had the electrician and the chimney sweep today ... I don't know, Arch. I've had it with country living. I'm ready to throw in the towel."

"How's your building project progressing?"

"In slow motion. It's a long story. I could cheerfully murder the guy who's working on it now."

"Can you stand some good news?" asked the editor. "The whole staff thinks your copy for the weekend edition is great stuff—especially the story about the old lady and her cat. It's better than fiction. Why don't you do more memoirs?"

"I knew I'd wind up on the geriatric beat," Qwilleran said sourly.

"It was your choice," Riker reminded him. "You could

have been an investigative reporter Down Below, but you opted for Pickax and the Klingenschoen bucks."

"Why don't you get the Historical Society to do oral histories for you?"

"Because you do 'em better."

"Well, I can't talk now, Arch. Here comes the plumber."

Joanna swaggered into the cabin in her heavy boots. "Your pump get hit?"

"I don't know. You're the plumber. All I know is—there's no water."

"Prob'ly burned out the motor." She kicked aside the mudrug, swung open the heavy trapdoor as if it were a cereal boxtop, and disappeared into the crawl space. Minutes later she emerged from the lower depths, covered with cobwebs. "Gotta go and get something," she said. She drove away mysteriously, returned with whatever it was, sank down under the floor once more, and soon shouted, "Try the tap!"

Water gushed from the faucet, and Qwilleran was grateful. Unlike Iggy, Joanna had done the work with no stalling, no mistakes, no excuses, no mumbling, no cigarette butts. Then she surprised him by saying, "I haven't seen Clem lately. He did the drains under the new place. Want me to do the finish plumbing?"

"It sounds like a good idea, but I have a different builder now. I'll mention it to him when he comes tomorrow," Qwilleran said. But Iggy did not report the next day . . . nor the next . . . nor the next.

ELEVEN

A day without Iggy should have blessed the cabin with tranquility, but Qwilleran felt only anxiety when the carpenter failed to appear on Friday morning. Where was he? Why had he not returned? Would he *ever* return? The skeleton of the east wing was rain-soaked and forlorn. Qwilleran spent the morning glancing frequently at his watch and listening for the explosive arrival of Iggy's truck, but he found the woods surrounding the cabin disappointingly quiet except for peeps amd chirps, buzzing and chattering, as birds, insects, and small animals went about their daily business, whatever it might be; Qwilleran did not pretend to know.

Following the storm of the night before, the wind had subsided and the lake was settling down. The woods still had the verdant aroma of a rain forest; trees were dripping, the ground was scattered with fallen tree branches, but the sun was making an effort to shine through a milky sky.

Qwilleran was in no mood to write. He passed the time by picking up the storm's debris—piling large branches behind the toolshed and breaking twigs into suitable lengths for fireplace kindling. The carpenter had left scraps of shingles strewn about the property, and Qwilleran stacked them in neat piles along with their discarded wrappers. Every time a heavy truck rumbled down the distant highway he stopped to listen, regretting that he had spoken harshly to Iggy.

In midday, before he had taken time to drive into Mooseville, he was surprised to receive a phone call from Nick Bamba. "Say, Qwill, do you know you're blockaded?"

"Blockaded! What do you mean?"

"I just drove past your place, and there's a big tree down across your driveway. Also, the K sign has blown away."

"That explains it!"

"Explains what?"

"It's like this," Qwilleran said. "I was expecting a workman, but he didn't show up today. It's obvious now that his truck couldn't get through."

"But wouldn't he call you?"

"Not this one! He wouldn't have the common sense, or he wouldn't have the coins to put in the phone box. And without the K on the post, I doubt whether he could even find the driveway. It took him half a day to find the lumberyard, and they have a sign that's ten feet high. So thanks for telling me about the tree, Nick."

"That's okay, Qwill. Here's Lori. She wants to talk to you."

Lori Bamba was not only Qwilleran's part-time secretary; she was his advisor in matters pertaining to cats. She had three of her own, and Koko and Yum Yum knew it. Whenever she telephoned, Koko sensed who was on the line. Now he jumped on the bar and purred throatily.

"Hello, Lori," said Qwilleran. "Koko wants to say a few words."

He held the receiver to the cat's head, and there were yowls and musical yiks and cadenzas that Lori seemed to understand.

"Okay, that's enough," Qwilleran said, pushing Koko away. "What's on your mind, Lori?"

"I just wanted you to know I'm taking a vacation and won't be able to do any typing for about ten days. Do you want me to find a substitute?"

"No need. If there's anything urgent, I'll handle it myself. Everything else can wait till you get back. Where are you going?"

"I'm flying Down Below so the baby can meet his two sets of grandparents. They've never seen him. Nick will drive down later to pick us up, and we'll do some camping on the way home."

"Isn't the baby rather young for tents and ants and canned beans?"

Lori laughed. "We have an RV—not a big one—just enough for camping in comfort. You can borrow it if you ever want to go camping with Koko and Yum Yum."

"I appreciate the offer, and I'll mention it to them, but I don't think they'd care for roughing it." Koko knew he was being discussed and started pushing the receiver away from Qwilleran's ear. "Have a good trip, Lori, and let me speak to Nick again."

Koko lost interest when Lori's husband came on the line.

Qwilleran said, "You've heard the news about Clem Cottle?"

"I couldn't believe it!" said Nick. "What do you think happened?"

"Nobody knows. He built my steps to the beach, and I was grateful to you for recommending him. Then he started on my new addition. Did he play ball on the Fourth of July?"

"No, now that you mention it. The Roosters lost to us, twelve to three. He's their best pitcher."

"It appears that he hasn't been seen since he left my place Thursday night. Of course, we don't know what the police have found, if anything. Let me know if you hear." Nick's status at the state prison made him a good source of scuttlebutt. "And thank you again, Nick, for telling me about the tree."

Qwilleran lost no time in calling Glinko. "Please dispatch a crew to remove a fallen tree," he requested. "It's a big one, blocking my driveway."

"Ha ha ha! That'll keep you home tonight," said the cheerful Mrs. Glinko. "What d'you want 'em to do with it? Chop it up for firewood? That'll cost extra."

"Tell them to take it away," Qwilleran said. "Immediately."

Fallen trees, vanishing builders, raccoons in the chimney, leaking sinks, birds' nests in the vents, spider bites on the seat! He was beginning to yearn for his dull apartment in Pickax.

The next morning he walked down the long drive to the highway and was pleased to see that the Glinko crew had spirited away the fallen tree. He drove into town for breakfast and bought a large letter K at the hardware store.

The hardware merchant said, "I read in the paper about Clem Cottle. They said he was last seen building something for you."

"That's true. You can't believe everything you read in the paper, but they get some of it right."

"He was engaged to marry one of the Wimsey girls, you know. I can't imagine what happened."

"The police are investigating, Cecil. They probably know more than they're telling."

The hardware man frowned. "It makes me wonder if it's connected with that big fire on Doug Cottle's farm."

"In what way?"

"I haven't figured it out yet, but it bothers me. The

chicken operation was fully insured, I happen to know. Clem and his father weren't getting along together. My wife got that from her sister; it's her daughter that was going to marry Clem . . . I don't know. I keep trying to put two and two together, and I come up with six-and-a-half. Do you have any theories?"

"Not a one," said Qwilleran. "I leave police work to the police."

After nailing the new letter K to the cedar post—with eight hammer strokes for each nail instead of three—he settled down to wait apprehensively for Iggy. Was the man on a binge? Had he found another job that was more congenial? And then the crucial question: Had he suffered the fate of five other carpenters?

Iggy, he reflected, was not a bad fellow. He was skilled in his craft when he chose to work, and he was neither sulky nor fractious nor dishonest—simply lazy and short on common sense, and his personal habits were annoying.

Briefly, Qwilleran considered notifying the sheriff's department about the missing carpenter. They would listen politely, but—considering the reputation of underground builders—how could they take the report seriously? And how could he identify Iggy? A skinny guy with prominent teeth and a truck that backfired a lot? What was the license number? What, for that matter, was Iggy's last name? He had no idea.

Instead, Qwilleran telephoned the Black Bear Café in Brrr and asked Gary Pratt if Iggy had been around.

"Not since I sent him to your place last week," the barkeeper said. "How's he doing?"

"When and if he works, he does a good job, but he needs constant prodding and supervision, and I never wanted to be a construction boss. By the way, do you know his last name?"

"Never heard it. And he doesn't use a credit card," said Gary with a laugh.

"I don't suppose you know where he's living."

"Sleeps in his truck, the chances are, on some back road."

"If you see him, Gary, tell him my driveway is clear now. It was blocked by a large tree as a result of the storm, but it's been trucked away."

"Sure thing," said Gary. "When are you coming in? Today's special is barbecued ribs and pecan pie—my grandma's recipe."

"I'll catch it the next time around," Qwilleran said.

On a wild hunch he jumped on his trail bike and explored the dirt roads surrounding Mooseville, where Iggy might park his truck and pass out for a couple of days. He even tried the Old Brrr Road where he had spotted Clem's abandoned pickup. The vehicle with the frantic chicken had been removed, and he saw no sign of Iggy's truck.

On another wild hunch he stopped at the lumberyard and asked if Iggy had charged any building materials to the Klingenschoen office since Thursday.

Three good-natured brothers ran the lumber business. "Hey, Joe," said brother Jim, "has old horse-face been in here the last coupla days?"

"Ain't seen him," said Joe. "Couldn't hardly miss that set of teeth."

"Ain't heard him either," said Jack. "Every time his jalopy pulls into the yard, I think we're being attacked by some nut with an Uzi."

When Qwilleran arrived at the cabin, there was a car parked in the clearing—a familiar tan four-door—and Roger was prowling around the building site.

"Trespassers will be prosecuted!" Qwilleran called out.

"Hey!" Roger greeted him. "This is the first I've seen of your building project. It's neat! And you've got a new K on the signpost."

"The old one blew away. I lost a big tree, too."

"Lucky you've got five thousand others."

"Wait till I put my horse in the stable."

Qwilleran wheeled his bike into the toolshed and hung it on padded hooks, then conducted Roger through the framework of future rooms. "And this one, with south and west windows, is the cats' apartment. There are times when we all need our privacy. Will you come in for a drink?"

"I don't think I should," Roger said. "I'm on my way to Lockmaster to pick up Mrs. Ascott, and she doesn't approve of anything stronger than hot water with lemon. She's got bad eyes but a very good nose, and Mildred doesn't want us to offend her. You're attending the meeting tonight, aren't you?"

"In a weak moment I said I would," said Qwilleran with a lack of animation.

"How would you like to come along for the ride? It's an hour's drive to Lockmaster, and we can stop for dinner on the way down. I know a good place. Coming back, she'll sit in the backseat and not say a word. Frankly, she gives me the creeps. So I'd be glad of the company."

That was all Qwilleran needed to hear: Stop for dinner at a good place.

"I'll have to shower and feed the cats," he said. "How much time do we have?"

"We ought to leave by six o'clock."

"Then would you be good enough to give them their food?"

"Me! I've never fed a cat in my life!" Roger professed to a fear of felines, and he looked about apprehensively as he entered the cabin. "Where are they?"

Qwilleran pointed to Koko on the moosehead and Yum Yum on a crossbeam spanning the dining table.

"I'd feel more comfortable, Qwill, if they were down on the floor. Isn't that where cats are supposed to hang out?"

"Not Siamese! But I'll get them down in a hurry. Watch this! . . . CEREAL!"

Koko thumped from the moosehead to the mantel to the woodbox to the floor, and Yum Yum swooped through the air from the beam to the top of the bar, causing Roger to duck and retreat toward the exit. For their prompt response they were rewarded with a few of Mildred's tasty crumbles.

"Now here's a can of salmon," Qwilleran explained, "and here's the can opener and a spoon. Just spread it on this plate, mashed up, with the dark skin removed. They don't like the dark skin."

"At our house we eat the dark skin—if we're lucky

enough to have canned salmon," said Roger. "Hey, it's *red salmon*! Mostly we buy tuna, when it's on sale."

Qwilleran said, "I notice you're wearing a coat and tie."

"Mrs. Ascott doesn't approve of casual."

"Okay, I'll be ready before six. If you want music, put a cassette on the stereo. Koko likes Brahms."

In the allotted time he emerged—coated, cravatted, and spiffily groomed except for his flamboyant moustache which always looked wayward. "I'll be glad to drive my car," he offered.

"Thanks, but Mrs. Ascott will fit better in the back-seat of my four-door. She's rather large."

"How will she get home?"

"She'll stay over, and Mildred and Sharon will drive her back in the morning."

The route to Lockmaster was sixty miles straight down the main highway, and as soon as Roger went into overdrive, Qwilleran asked, "Have the police any leads on Clem Cottle's disappearance?"

"Not that they're telling."

"Do you know his father?"

"I've met Doug Cottle, but I don't know him very well."

"What is he like? He sounded curt when I talked to him on the phone."

"Oh, he's curt, all right. Curt is something he does very well. So different from Clem. I guess Clem takes after his mother. She's nice."

"Do father and son get along together?"

"Not too good, I hear. He blamed Clem for the

fire—something he said Clem did, or didn't do, in connection with the electrical system."

"Did the state fire marshal investigate?"

"He didn't have to. No one was killed, and the fire chief didn't report any evidence of arson."

After crossing the Moose County line, the road led into hunting country with its rolling hills, opulent horse farms, and miles of fences dipping and curving across the green terrain. In the landscape and the dwellings there was an air of sophistication that Moose County lacked, and the restaurants were said to be better. Roger pulled into the parking lot of a place called the Palomino Paddock.

When Qwilleran noted the hostess in a long dress and several diners in dinner jackets and a wine steward wearing heavy chains, he began to think he should pick up the check for this meal. When they were seated (with pomp) and the menus were presented (with a flourish), he knew the Palomino Paddock was not for a young man on a tuna-fish budget. "Since you're driving tonight, Roger, dinner is my treat," he said.

They started with vichyssoise, and Qwilleran said, "What do you know about Mrs. Ascott?"

"Not much. She and my mother-in-law have been good friends for years. Mildred reads the tarot cards, you know, and I guess they have something in common. Did she ever read the cards for you?"

"Once, a couple of years ago. I hate to admit it, but she was right about everything—although I didn't think so at the time. You said Mrs. Ascott is a big woman?"

"She's huge! Not fat, just monumental, as Sharon says. There's something about a huge old woman that's more formidable than a huge young woman. Her eyes are always half closed, but they're long! Sharon thinks she uses eye makeup to make her eyes seem longer, like they do in India. She doesn't talk much in company, just monosyllables in a tiny voice. But when she goes into action and starts predicting the future, she's frightening. She sounds like a drill sergeant. I wouldn't mention this to Sharon or Mildred, but sometimes I think she's really a man."

Both men had ordered the prime rib, and Qwilleran declared it to be real beef without the hypodermic needle or irradiation or blood transfusion.

"Speaking of Mrs. Ascott," Roger said, "do you want to hear something weird? . . . When the baby was born, we asked her to be godmother. She came up here for the christening, and Mildred had a get-together for some friends, with Mrs. Ascott delivering spirit messages. It was spooky. She had a message for Sharon and me from a spirit named Harriet. This Harriet said we should move the baby's crib to another room. That's all—just move it to another room."

"How did you react?"

"I felt like a fool, but Sharon insisted, so we moved the crib from the nursery to our own bedroom, which was pretty crowded. Two nights later . . . the whole plaster ceiling of the nursery fell down!"

"Did you ever know anyone named Harriet?"

"Sharon never did," said Roger, "but that was the name of my great-great-grandmother."

Qwilleran threw a quick, incredulous glance across the dinner table. "Do you expect me to believe that?"

"It's true! Ask Sharon. Ask Mildred."

Lockmaster had been the home of wealthy lumber barons in the nineteenth century, and their mansions were fanciful examples of Victorian architecture. At one of these, which appeared to be an exclusive boarding house, Qwilleran and Roger picked up Mrs. Ascott. In her long black dress, with black crepe draped over her dyed black hair, she moved slowly and majestically to the waiting car with Roger at her elbow. They wedged her into the backseat with some embarrassment on the part of the men, and a few artfully controlled giggles from Roger. She sat in the center of the seat, staring straight ahead through eyes long and slitted.

"Are you comfortable, Mrs. Ascott?" Qwilleran asked.

"Mmmmm," she replied.

In the front seat, during the ride back to Mooseville, there were animated discussions about baseball, politics, and the prevalence of violent crime Down Below. Arriving at Mildred's cottage, the two men eased Mrs. Ascott out of the car and guided her indoors like two harbor tugs maneuvering an ocean-going liner into its berth. There she was greeted with adulation by Mildred and Sharon and ushered to a seat of honor in the middle of the living room sofa—the flowered sofa that Mildred had recently reupholstered with hours of

sweat and tears. Qwilleran thought, I hope she rein-
forced the springs.

Seated in a half circle, facing the sofa, were the
guests, speaking in hushed tones: John and Vicki Bushland, Sue Urbank without her husband, the Comptons,
and others Qwilleran had not met. It was still daylight,
but the traverse draperies had been drawn across the
window-wall, and lamps were lighted. A hint of in-
cense gave the assembly a mystical aura.

Mildred welcomed the group, saying, "We're privi-
leged to have Mrs. Ascott with us this evening. She has
so much to tell us about matters beyond our perception
that I'll waste no time in introducing this renowned
woman whose revelations speak for themselves."

The guests were asked to write their initials on slips
of paper, fold them, and drop them in a basket, which
was then placed on the coffee table in front of the seer.
There was a breathless pause. Mrs. Ascott, ignoring
the contents of the basket, gazed at a distant point
above and beyond the heads of the assemblage. Finally
she started to speak in a booming voice, addressing her
pronouncements to the initials in the basket.

"To SFU . . . I am receiving the impression . . . of a
mistake . . . You have made a drastic decision . . . not
for the best . . . Is it too late to change your plans?"

"No," said Sue Urbank in a small frightened voice.

"Then do so!"

A murmur of surprise rippled through the audience.

"To RJM . . . You have changed careers . . . with
some trepidation . . . Have no fear . . . You have acted
wisely."

Roger and Sharon exchanged happy glances.

"Remember your responsibilities . . . Avoid unnecessary risks."

"Yes. Thank you," said Roger.

Mrs. Ascott continued to stare at the opposite wall through heavy-lidded eyes. "To LMC . . . I see pain . . . Remember your age and use discretion . . . You could have trouble with . . . your knees."

Lisa Compton groaned while nodding her head.

"To SKM . . . In my mind's eye . . . I see you tormented . . . by indecision . . . Duty first, desire later."

Again the MacGillivrays exchanged glances, not happy ones.

"To JWB . . . I have a vision . . . of great loss . . . material loss . . . but you will save what really matters."

Bushy passed a nervous hand over his nearly hairless head.

"To LFC . . . I see a dwelling . . . Are you selling property?"

"I'm trying to," said Compton.

"Don't be impatient . . . Bide your time . . . A good offer is on the way."

"Thank you."

"To VRB . . . My dear . . . something you have long wanted . . . will be yours."

Vicki Bushland barely suppressed a little shriek.

At that point Mrs. Ascott asked for a glass of water, and there was a brief intermission as guests whispered to each other and Qwilleran thought, Mildred could have briefed this woman on the concerns of her friends: Sue Urbank's pending divorce, Roger's career crisis, Lisa Compton's "jogging knees." Everyone knew that Lyle wanted to sell his house in Pickax and buy a condominium, and Sharon wanted to hire a baby-sitter and return to teaching school, and Vicki desperately wanted a successful pregnancy.

Mrs. Ascott resumed with a message for MTH: "It would be wise . . . to have a complete physical examination . . . without delay!"

Qwilleran thought this a cruel pronouncement to make so abruptly and in public, and he turned to see Mildred's reaction. Her lips were pressed together.

When the session ended, there had been messages for everyone except JQ, and Qwilleran surmised that the psychic had sensed his skepticism, or Mildred had warned her.

At this point the hostess rose and said, "Mrs. Ascott has consented to answer a few direct questions if anyone cares to ask."

There was silence until, in a challenging voice, Qwilleran asked, "Can you tell us anything about the whereabouts of a young man named Clem Cottle?"

Mrs. Ascott stared at the upper wall with unseeing eyes. Finally she said, "I have a sense of distance . . . a long distance. He is very far away. Is he in the armed services?"

"No," said Qwilleran, "he's a local carpenter."

"He wishes to return . . . but he is unable."

She's bluffing, Qwilleran thought, but then the enigmatic woman added, "Are you JQ? I have a message

for you . . . from a female spirit . . . Her name is . . .
Joy . . . Take precautions . . . to protect your family.
Do you have two . . . children?"

"No, ma'am, I have two cats."

There was a suppressed tittering in the audience.

"There is another message . . . from Joy . . . not
quite clear . . . about an excavation . . . The message
is . . . fading out . . . It's gone . . . That is all."

"Thank you," said Qwilleran, somewhat shaken.

She went on with other messages from other spirits
for other guests, but he could think only of the cryptic
tidings from Joy, his boyhood sweetheart, who had
been dead for two years.

TWELVE

On Sunday morning Qwilleran recalled Mrs. Ascott's messages with mixed reactions. He suspected she had received no vibrations whatever about Clem Cottle and was only trying to save face. He resented her ominous reference to Mildred's health; there were less frightening ways of urging a friend to have a physical checkup. On the other hand, the idea of a spirit message from Joy Wheatley, with whom he had been so close for so many years, was disturbing. He remembered Roger's story about Harriet and the nursery ceiling.

He was on the porch with the Sunday papers, throwing each section on the floor as he finished reading it. Yum Yum liked to roll on them, kicking and squirming and having a good time. At one point he went indoors to call Mildred and discuss the events of the previous evening. There was no answer, of course; she and Sharon were chauffeuring Mrs. Ascott back to Lockmaster. While he was letting the phone ring the recommended number of times, however, he heard the unmistakable sound of ripping paper. Koko was standing on a newspaper with his front end down and his hind end elevated and his tail stiffened into a question mark. With teeth and claws he was shredding the *Moose County Something*. It was the second time Koko had attacked the "Qwill Pen" column.

"This has got to stop!" Qwilleran scolded. "Shape up, or we'll ship you to Washington. You can get a job at the Pentagon."

Why did that cat never shred the *Daily Fluxion* or the *Morning Rampage* or the *New York Times*? Did it have something to do with the quality of the paper or the smell of the ink? Patiently he gathered the torn scraps of newsprint. Koko had destroyed Emma Wimsey's story about Punkin.

Qwilleran had met many old-timers since moving to Moose County: the incredible Aunt Fanny; Grandma Gage, who did push-ups and headstands; Homer Tibbitt, still doing volunteer work at ninety. When he was with them, he felt he was talking with his own grandparents, whom he had never known. Now he had a sudden strong urge to drive to Pickax and visit the Senior Care Facility. He could scout the possibilities of more memoirs. He might take some flowers to Emma Wimsey. He wondered if the Chief Canary would be on duty. Smugly he groomed his moustache with his fingertips.

Sunday afternoon was a popular visiting day at the Facility. Cars filled the parking lot, and relatives were chatting with residents in the lounge, the lobby, and the dining room. The "canaries" flitted about in their yellow smocks, bringing the elderly down from their rooms, watching lest they became overtired or overexcited, then wheeling them back to the elevator.

Irma Hasselrich, in her yellow blazer, was on duty at the reception desk. "Oh, Mr. Qwilleran!" she greeted him. "We've all been reading your column about Emma and Punkin. It's delightful!"

"Thank you," he said, "but I can't take credit. It was Emma's story."

"We read it to her three times, and it brought tears to her eyes. I myself thought it was beautifully written—with such sincerity and compassion."

Qwilleran preened his moustache with pleasure. Although he affected modesty, he relished compliments about his writing. "Is she allowed to have flowers?" He was carrying a bunch of daisies in a florist's green tissue.

"Of course. She'll be thrilled! I'll have someone bring her down to the reading room, where it's quiet. We're getting awfully busy today. By the way, Emma had some discomfort this week, and the doctor is limiting her visits to ten minutes."

When Emma's wheelchair rolled into the reading room, she reached forward to clasp Qwilleran's hand with both of her shrunken ones, her thin lips trembling in a smile.

"Thank you . . . for that beautiful . . . writeup," she said, her speech faltering and her voice noticeably weaker. More than ever she appeared fragile and wispy.

"It was a pleasure to write," he said, "and here's a small thank-you for sharing your story about Punkin."

"Oh!" she cried. "I never had any . . . flowers in . . . green paper. We never had . . . money for . . . fancy things."

"May I ask, after you went to college, did you teach school?"

"Yes. The school had . . . one room. There was . . . a potbellied stove . . . and oil lamps . . ."

He tried to ask questions that would focus her attention and jog her memory, but her answers were hesitant and vague. "You told the story of Punkin very well. Do you remember any other tales?"

"I used to know . . . a lot of stories. . . . I wrote them down . . . I don't know where they are."

"Emma, honey," said the volunteer, "they're safe and sound in your room upstairs." She caught Qwilleran's eye and tapped her watch. Emma was looking weary.

"We'll have another visit someday," he said. "Until then, goodbye." He clasped her cold hands in his.

"Goodbye," she said in a wisp of a voice.

As Emma was wheeled away, clutching her daisies, he went to the reception desk to speak with Irma Hasselrich. "She seems to be failing," he said.

"But you never know!" she said brightly. "These farmwomen have tremendous stamina." Optimism was the policy of the canaries.

"The newspaper is interested in running more memoirs of old-timers. How many residents do you have?"

"Sixty-five, and others on the waiting list."

"Would it be possible to screen them? The volunteers probably know who has a reliable memory and who has a story to tell."

"I'll raise the question at a staff meeting this week," she said, "but we wouldn't want to discriminate, would we? We might hurt the feelings of some of these dear folks. They're like children."

Her gentleness was attractive, Qwilleran thought, yet she had a cultivated sophistication. He was curious about this stunning woman, probably about forty, who had never married, who dedicated her life to helping others, and who still lived with her parents in Indian Village. This much he had gleaned from her father, the jovial attorney for the Klingenschoen Fund.

He said, "You could help a great deal with this project, if you could be good enough to give me some background information on policies of the facility. Perhaps you would be free for dinner some evening."

"Unfortunately," she said, "I'll be on the desk every evening this week, but it's charming of you to ask."

"How about Saturday night?"

"I would really love it, but it's Father's birthday."

Before Qwilleran could huff into his moustache, a voice called out, "Mr. Qwilleran! Mr. Qwilleran! I'm glad I caught you." It was Emma's canary, waving a shopping bag. "Emma wants you to have these things—to keep."

"What are they?"

"Just little mementoes, and some stories about her life."

"Shouldn't she give them to her family?"

"Her family isn't really interested, but Emma says you'll think of something to do with them. There's a candybox that was a valentine from her husband, probably seventy years ago."

"Give her my thanks," he said. "Tell her I'll write her a letter."

When he turned back to finish his conversation with the Chief Canary, she had walked away from the desk, replaced by a lesser canary in a yellow smock. "Ms. Hasselrich was needed in a meeting," she said. "Is there a message?"

There was no message. He carried Emma's keepsakes to the parking lot, thinking, What am I doing here? I could have been an investigative reporter Down Below.

At the cabin Koko was immediately attracted to the shopping bag and its contents. He took a vital interest in anything new, anything different, any addition to the household, and Mrs. Wimsey's mementoes—having been on a farm for seventy years—probably retained an enticing scent. Among the notebooks and envelopes and loose papers was the candybox, covered in faded pink brocade that was almost threadbare and topped with a heart outlined in yellowed lace—a pathetic reminder of bygone happiness. Qwilleran stuffed the documents back into the shopping bag and added the candybox to the clutter on the dining table, where Koko applied his inquisitive nose to every inch of the old silk and lace, all the while tapping the table with his tail. *Tap tap tap.*

THIRTEEN

On Monday morning as Qwilleran was preparing to serve the Siamese their minced beef mixed with cottage cheese and laced with tomato sauce, there was an explosion in the woods, and a rusty pickup with camper top lurched into the clearing.

"Iggy's back!" Qwilleran proclaimed in a tone of excitement mixed with dread. "He must have run out of cigarette money."

Although eager to confront the man with questions and rebukes, he restrained his urges. He waited until the carpenter oozed out of the truck. As Iggy ambled toward the building site at the pace of a tired snail,

Qwilleran followed. "Nice day!" he remarked to the prodigal workman.

"Should be able to finish THEM SUCKERS TO-DAY," said Iggy.

"To which suckers are you referring?" Qwilleran asked politely.

"Them boards!" He pointed to the siding.

"Good! And I wish you'd dispose of that rubbish." Qwilleran indicated the scraps of shingles and torn wrappings. "I have business in Pickax today, but I'll be back in time to pay your day's wages. See you after lunch."

He strode back to the cabin to finish working on the cats' breakfast but found them on the kitchen counter, finishing the job themselves. Before leaving for Pickax he glanced automatically around the interior, checking for feline temptations, locking up toothbrushes, hiding copies of the *Moose County Something*, closing all drawers, hiding the telephone in a kitchen cabinet, and leaving no socks lying around.

"Keep an eye on the carpenter," he told them. "Don't let him burn down the house."

He locked the doors, front and back, as he left. There was no need for Iggy to have access to the cabin.

The business in Pickax was the monthly luncheon meeting of the trustees for the Klingenschoen Fund. He stopped at his apartment to pick up some more books, dropped into the newspaper office to trade comradely insults with the staff in the city room, then reported to the meeting place in the New Pickax Hotel, built in

1935. Since that time it had never been redecorated, and the menu had never changed. The natives of Pickax were creatures of habit and tradition.

At the luncheon table Qwilleran remarked, "I see they've warmed up the 1935 chicken à la king again." His humor brought no response from the bankers, accountants, investment counselors, and attorneys who administered the fund, but the high-spirited Mr. Hasselrich said he thought the chicken was rather good.

Following the luncheon the trustees reviewed the Fund's philanthropies and considered new applications for grants and loans. It was Qwilleran's money, in the long run, that they were handling, but his mind wandered from the business at hand. He kept combing his moustache with his fingers; something was calling him home to the lakeshore.

He drove back to the beach faster than usual, with the car windows wide open, and the closer he came to the lake, the fresher and more invigorating the air. When he started up the driveway, however, the atmosphere changed. His eyes started to itch and smart unaccountably. At the same time he became aware of a foul odor . . . It was smoke! But not wood smoke! He detected noxious fumes from something burning—something toxic. He took the curves and hills of the drive like a roller coaster and jammed on the brake at the top of the dune. The clearing was filled with black, acrid smoke. Iggy's truck was there, and the carpenter was behind the wheel, blissfully asleep.

"Crazy fool!" Qwilleran muttered, coughing and

choking. He jumped out of his car and banged the door of the pickup. "Wake up! Wake up! I didn't tell you to *burn* the stuff!" he yelled between fits of coughing.

Iggy climbed slowly out of the cab. The asphyxiating smoke had no effect on his leather lungs.

"Quick! Help me douse it with sand! I'll get shovels!" Qwilleran ran to the toolshed and threw open the door. What he saw was too improbable to comprehend. Staring at him from the darkness were two pairs of eyes.

"YOW!" came a voice from the depths of the shed, accompanied by a female shriek.

"How did you get out here?" Qwilleran shouted.

"YOW!" said Koko in indignation.

Qwilleran grabbed a couple of shovels and slammed the toolshed door shut in the faces of two astonished animals.

Working fast, with an occasional assist from Iggy, he smothered the smoldering pile of asphalt shingles and their waterproof wrappers.

When the job was done, he leaned on his shovel, breathing hard. "How did the cats . . . get into the shed?" he gasped.

"Cats?" asked Iggy. "WHAT CATS?"

"My cats! How did they get out here in the shed?"

"I never seen NO CATS."

"I'll show you. Get out there to the shed. Move it!"

With some persuasive shoving Iggy trotted down the narrow path to the toolshed.

Qwilleran threw open the door. "Now what do you call those animals?"

The two elegant creatures were pacing back and forth with resentment, their muscles rippling expressively under their silky fur, their whiskers bristling, their ears swiveling, their tails pointed like rapiers.

"What do you call those?" Qwilleran repeated.

"Funny-lookin' suckers, AIN'T THEY?"

Qwilleran wanted to grab the man by the seat of the pants and throw him out, but he gritted his teeth and paid him for five hours' work, after which Iggy drove away in his snorting, battered truck with a debonair wave of the hand and a toothy grin.

Seizing the two cats about the middle, Qwilleran carried them from the toolshed, opened the rattail latch of the porch door with an elbow, and tossed the two culprits on the redwood chaise. They froze in the position in which they landed and glared at him.

"Don't give me that insolent stare!" he said. "You two have some explaining to do!"

He unlocked the cabin door, stepped into the mudroom—and yelped! There was a hole in the wall, roughly three feet wide and seven feet high. Below it there was a liberal sprinkling of sawdust, with pawprints clearly defined.

"What? What?" Qwilleran spluttered, in the most inarticulate moment of his entire life.

Gradually the facts became clear. Beyond the opening was the roughed-in skeleton of the east wing. Iggy had cut a hole for the connecting door. After that, the lazy loafer had easy access to the cabin and could have napped on a white sofa or, worse yet, in Qwilleran's bed. Meanwhile, the cats had access to the east wing. Calmly they had walked through the newly sawed opening; casually they had jumped out an unframed window. But how did they end their journey in the toolshed?

In whatever way they managed the feat, it appeared that they had enjoyed the experience, because they were now peering between Qwilleran's legs, toe-deep in sawdust, ready to repeat the adventure. Grabbing them, he locked them up, announcing with a declamatory flourish, "Once more into the guestroom, dear friends!" While they howled their protests, he found a sheet of plywood left over from the subfloor and nailed it across the rectangular aperture with angry blows, smashing his thumb in the process.

Between erratic strokes of the hammer he thought he heard coughing outdoors.

Russell Simms was standing in the backyard with her hand over her nose and mouth. "Something's burning," she said in a muffled voice.

"Go around to the lake porch," he said. "I'll meet you there."

On the lake porch the air was fresh and clear, and he inhaled deeply. "Have a chair," he said to Russell, "and I'll tell you a story you won't believe. I came home from Pickax and found that idiot burning shingles! He also cut a hole in the wall of the cabin, and the cats got out."

"I saw them," she said quietly.

"You *saw them*? Where were they?"

"In the yard."

"Where was the carpenter?"

"I don't know."

"He was probably in the cabin, sleeping in my bed—that blockhead! So you're the one who put the cats in the toolshed! That was smart thinking! But how did you manage it?"

She put a hand in her sweater pocket and drew out a few morsels of the dry catfood that she fed to the seagulls.

"Fishy Fritters!" Qwilleran said in amazement. "You actually lured them into the shed with Fishy Fritters? If I try to feed them Fishy Fritters, they throw a catfit . . . Well, Russell, it's a miracle that you happened along when you did. If I had lost those cats, I would have killed that man!"

"I had a feeling I should come," she said shyly.

"I don't know how to thank you. How can I thank you?"

Hesitantly she said, "Will you tell me something?"

"Of course."

"Honestly?"

"Of course!"

"What's wrong with my cottage?" She removed her dark glasses and looked at him directly for the first time, her eyes half closed and the pupils contracted. No wonder Mildred said her eyes were weird!

Having paused too long, he said quickly, "I don't think . . . that is, I was unaware of anything wrong with the cottage. When the Dunfields lived there, it seemed to be . . . rather comfortable."

"Why are they renting it?"

"Mr. Dunfield died, and his wife doesn't care to live at the beach any more."

"When did he die?"

"About two years ago."

"What happened to him?" Her piercing eyes searched his.

"Well . . . it was most unfortunate, you see. He was a fine man, a retired police chief, a friend of mine . . . I'm sorry to say, he was murdered."

"I knew it!" Russell said with a shudder. She jumped up, rushed from the porch and ran down the steps to the beach. He watched her head for home along the shoreline, faster than she had ever traveled before.

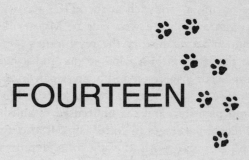

FOURTEEN

"I swear I could kill that guy!" Qwilleran said with vehemence. He was having lunch with Roger and Bushy and relating the events of the previous afternoon—how the underground builder had burned the shingles and allowed the cats to get out of the cabin. "If they had been lost in the woods, I would have clobbered him with a two-by-four—and I mean it!"

The photographer said, "When we were building our addition two years ago, our guy painted the whole thing a sick green while we were away. Our house is white, you understand! He painted the addition green because—he explained afterwards—the green paint was on sale! My wife was so upset, she almost had a miscarriage . . . What's your guy's name?"

"Iggy. That's all I know."

"Cripes! He's the one who painted us green! You have to watch him every minute."

"I know. He started to shingle my roof in a poisonous blue."

They were having a sandwich at the FOO, a down-at-the-heel restaurant on the west side of Mooseville. At some point in recent history the restaurant's large sign had lost the letter D in a wind storm, and it had never been replaced. Fishermen and boaters patronized the place because it was close to the docks, the food was cheap and plentiful, and the unlicensed establishment served illegal beverages in coffee cups. It also appeared to be popular with the sheriff's deputies, leading Qwilleran to deduce that the restaurant was under suspicion or the local law enforcers were corrupt.

The three men ate with their hats on, in accordance with FOO custom—Qwilleran in the orange hunting headgear that he liked, Roger in a Mooseville baseball cap, and Bushy with his skipper's cap at a dapper angle.

"Iggy was on the job when I left this morning," Qwilleran said, "but this time I've taken the precaution of locking up the cats in the guestroom. He's supposed to start framing the windows today. No doubt it will take him a week, allowing for catnaps and cigarette breaks."

Bushy nodded wisely. "If you ask me, it's not only tobacco he smokes."

"I wouldn't tolerate him, but he's my last resort . . . Any news about Clem, Roger?"

"Police are investigating. That's all I can find out," said the young reporter.

"That's what I guessed. Anyway, I'm stuck with Iggy. He's not only lazy and infuriating; he makes stupid mistakes, but I can't ride herd on him every minute. I'm glad to get away for a few hours."

"Have you spent much time on the lake?" the photographer asked.

"Last time was two years ago. I went out on a chartered trawler and hooked something I wasn't supposed to, and all hell broke loose. What's on the agenda, Bushy?"

"I thought we'd take off for the island right after lunch and spend a couple of hours over there investigating the situation on the shore, then do some fishing and fry up our catch on the beach. I've got a portable stove on the boat and a coffee pot, and we can slice potatoes and throw 'em in the pan."

"I brought the beer and ginger ale," said Roger.

"Have you checked the weather?" Qwilleran asked. "I hear they're having heavy winds in Canada."

"Luckily they're going to miss us," said Bushy, "but it gets cool out there on the island. You might need a sweater under your windbreaker."

"I brought one," said Roger.

"So did I," said Qwilleran.

"Then we're all set!"

The photographer's boat was a modest cabin cruiser called *Say Cheese*, and he was an experienced skipper. As they sped across the water, Qwilleran looked back at the receding shoreline, nestled at the foot of the sandhills and fringed with wharves and the masts of boats. Mooseville looked as quaint as an Italian fishing village, and he experienced a tingle of nostalgia for other times, other places, other friends.

It was one of those days when the sky was blue and the clouds were puffy, moving proudly like tall ships. They were moving fast, Qwilleran noted. The skipper had the motor wide open, and no one tried to talk against the roar. Soon the island appeared to rise out of the lake—just the tops of trees at first, then the wide beach, and then the small, flat-roofed fishing shack near the trees. He counted. There were actually three trees on Three Tree Island.

Bushy cut the motor, and they putt-putted toward a prefabricated metal pier. "They take the pier down in winter and store it in the shack," he explained. "The shack isn't much, but it's shelter. Mostly they use it to clean fish, so you won't want to spend much time inside unless you brought a clothespin." He pinched his nose.

With the boat tied up at the pier, they walked ashore. It was a low-lying island, and the beach was wide and smooth.

"Good place for a spaceship to land," Roger said. "The landing site is on the opposite side of the island, the pilot told me. Anyone want a drink before we start exploring?"

He brought a cooler from the boat, and they

stretched out on the sand. Bushy and Qwilleran stripped off their shirts, but the white-faced Roger said, "Not me! I burn!"

As Qwilleran lay on the sand he heard a whistling sound high overhead. He sat up and listened, smoothing his moustache as he vaguely remembered hearing it once before when he was vacationing at the cabin. On that occasion it was followed by a violent storm. He said nothing about it; after all, he was a city-bred land-lubber, while Roger and Bushy had known this lake all their lives. Since they showed no concern, Qwilleran lay down again.

"Okay, team," said the skipper after a half hour. "Let's hit the trail. Better put the cooler back on the boat and take your sweaters. Bring mine, will you, Rog?"

"Do we proceed clockwise or counterclockwise?" Qwilleran asked. They tossed a coin and started west-ward. It seemed like a small circle of land when viewed from the approaching boat, hardly larger than a cartoonist's idea of a desert island, but it proved to be a long way around when they trudged along the shore. The beach that appeared so hard and smooth was in actuality an expanse of deep, fine sand, and every step was a slide backward as well as a push forward. After tramping for half an hour there was still no hint of a scorched spot on the beach or even among the beach grass that covered the crown of the island.

The photographer had his camera ready. "Don't give up! We're not halfway around the island yet."

"How can you tell?" Roger asked. "It feels like we've been around twice."

They trudged on. Soon they put on their sweaters, having reached the windward side of the island. The breeze was coming from Canada across a hundred miles of water.

"Look! Did you see that?" Roger asked excitedly. "A water spout!"

"Is that a freak of nature?" Qwilleran asked. "Or does it have something to do with plumbing?" Since arriving in Mooseville he had become uncomfortably aware of plumbing.

"It's the tail of a cloud spinning around and picking up water like a fountain."

"That doesn't sound good."

Bushy had to admit that the clouds were moving faster than he would like, and Qwilleran pointed out that the sky was an unusual color in the north.

"I don't like it," said Bushy. "I think we should head back to the boat on the double and cut loose for the mainland. Storms come up fast on this lake. Let's go!"

They attempted the return trip at a trot, but the deep sand and the rising wind fought them every step of the way. The sky had changed to a yellow-gray, and the lake was whipping up a surf.

Bushy shouted against the wind, "We may have to stay on the island overnight!"

Qwilleran thought, The cats won't get their dinner. They'll be starved by morning, and they're locked up in that small bunkroom. They'll be furious.

When they arrived within sight of the boat it was

thrashing in the waves and crashing against the metal pier. Even as they watched helplessly, the lines snapped, and the *Say Cheese* shot into the air on the crest of a wave and capsized.

"Oh, my God!" the skipper groaned.

The wind caught it under the bow, and it rolled and tossed wildly like a dying shark. Bushy ran to the edge of the water and watched it go, until a giant wave caused him to dash back to safety.

"Damn shame!" Qwilleran said.

"Rotten luck!" said Roger.

The dejected skipper said, "Let's get out of this wind."

Heads down and caps jammed on, they forged up the slope to the fishing shack, a makeshift hut of wood and corrugated metal that rattled in the wind. There were two windows, but they had been boarded up for the winter and not yet uncovered. The men entered the shack and leaned against the door to close it, so strong was the force of the gale. There was no light, with the windows covered, and it was drafty. The fishy aroma was the least of their concerns. Qwilleran stumbled over a wooden crate.

"There's a wood-burning stove here somewhere," Bushy said, groping around the interior, "but I don't know if there's any wood. Do we have matches?"

The matches, unfortunately, were on the boat along with the portable cookstove and coffee pot and fishing rods and radio. And none of the three men was a smoker.

"If I can fall over two more crates, we can all sit down," said Qwilleran.

Wooden boxes scraped on the uneven floor, and the three men sat down in the dark. They were silent for a few minutes, each with his thoughts.

"Who brought the dominoes?" Qwilleran asked.

Bushy laughed. "I loved that boat, but luckily it's insured, so let's get our chins up off the floor and figure out something to do for the next few hours. When I don't show up by nightfall, my wife will call the sheriff, and they'll come looking for us with the helicopter, but it could be a long wait."

"It's four-thirty," said Roger, whose watch glowed in the dark shack.

"Time for the Happy Hour!" said Bushy. "I could use a double martini right about now."

"How long do these big blows usually last?" Qwilleran wanted to know.

"Fifteen minutes or fifteen hours."

"If I have a choice, I'll take the abbreviated version."

"I'm never going to eat fish again," Roger said. "This place is putrid!"

"Any guess about the wind velocity?"

"I'd say fifty miles an hour."

"More like sixty, if you ask me."

"Listen! Did you hear something?" Bushy said with an anxious hitch in his voice. "It sounds like a splash right outside the shack!" He opened the door a crack and peered outside. "Hell! The lake's rising!"

Qwilleran wondered if the island had ever been entirely submerged. He wondered if the others were

thinking the same thing. In the total darkness faces and
emotions were invisible.

In another half hour the spray was hitting the shack
and water was running under the door. Waves began
slamming against the building.

No one was talking. They were all waiting—waiting
for the next giant wave. The apprehension was palpa-
ble. Qwilleran had faced life-and-death situations
before—with a dogged resolve to survive or a numb
resignation. Only where Koko and Yum Yum were
concerned did he ever succumb to gut-wrenching
worry. Now, with mounting anxiety, he wondered
what would happen to them. Would Mildred adopt
them? Would they miss him? Koko would adjust, but
Yum Yum would stop eating; she was emotionally de-
pendent on Qwilleran, and she would pine away.

Another wave pounded the building, and it tilted.

"We're moving!" Bushy yelled as the shack shuddered and creaked.

"We're going to be swept into the lake!" Roger
screamed. It was the first vocal evidence of fear. "I'm
getting out!"

"Wait! Don't panic!" Qwilleran shouted. "Let's see
what's the best thing to do. Bushy, got any ideas?"

"Which way are we moving?"

"My guess is . . . toward the center of the island."

With another watery crash the cabin moved again.

"Oh, God!" Roger said with a whimper.

Qwilleran said, "If you're praying, ask for suggestions."

There was another crash, followed by another shudder, and then the shack stopped with a bump.

"What's that?"

"We hit something!"

"I think we hit a tree!"

The waves pounded and roared, and the building quaked, but its journey stopped. It was wedged between the three trees of Three Tree Island.

"We're stuck!" cried Bushy. "Now what?"

A wave pushed the door open, and water gushed into the shack.

"Get on the roof," Qwilleran said. "We can't sit here like trapped animals. The water can't rise that high . . . Can it?" he asked when the other two were silent.

"How do we get up there?"

"Pile up the crates."

"Wait until after a big wave, and then act quick before the next one."

"Okay, here goes! Somebody give me a boost."

Qwilleran was the tallest and heftiest. Standing in ice water up to his knees, he boosted Bushy and then Roger. They reached down and gave him a hand just as the next surge of cold water soaked him to the armpits. The three sprawled on the roof like drowning sailors cast upon a reef. The shack was fast between the three trees and had tilted, so the flat roof had a precarious slant.

"Make yourselves comfortable," Bushy said.

"It's cold up here," Roger whined.

"It's colder down there. Flap your arms. Flex your knees, kid, but don't rock the boat."

The wind howled and whistled; the surf crashed. As

time wore on, ominous clouds could be seen scudding toward the mainland.

"It smells better up here, if anyone cares," Roger said.

"At least we can see what's happening," said Qwilleran. "The sensory deprivation in that dark shack was giving me the willies." He had turned down the flaps of his hunting cap and was trying not to think about the cold. Compared to the frigid dunking he had suffered, the wind was not that chill, but he was soaked to the skin.

"Six o'clock. We've been marooned over an hour."

"Feels like a week," said Bushy. "I could use a shot of brandy."

"I'd settle for a cup of coffee," Qwilleran said. "Even one from the Dimsdale Diner."

"If I hadn't given up smoking, now is when I'd want a cigarette."

They clung to the roof, passing the time with meaningless chatter and attempts at brave humor.

"Seven fifteen," Roger announced.

"Am I numb from exposure, or is the wind subsiding?"

"It's dropping a little, but it's still cold."

"It's going to get colder before it gets warmer, so keep moving, fellas."

Qwilleran pictured the Siamese clamoring for their supper. Or did they raise the roof only when they had an audience? What did they do when no one was around? . . . What else was happening on shore? Soon it would be dark. Bushy's wife would notify the sheriff. Sharon would call her mother, and Mildred would call the sheriff, Mooseville police, and state troopers; she was a woman of driving action. Would it occur to her to drive to the cabin and feed the cats? She was thoughtful that way; she had even worried about Captain Phlogg's unpopular dog. But how would she get into the cabin? There was an extra key, but it was hidden under the log rack on the porch. She might look under the doormat or over the door frame, but who would think of looking in a hollow log at the bottom of the log rack? . . . Qwilleran was getting hungry. He wished he'd had the deluxe half-pound cheeseburger with fries, instead of the quarter-pounder with salad.

At eight-thirty the surf was less menacing, but the island was still flooded. An unhealthy yellow light illumined the sky, and gray funnel clouds could be seen over the mainland.

Bushy said, "I should have paid some attention to my horoscope this morning. It told me to stay home and do chores that I'd been putting off."

Roger said, "My horoscope said I'd take a trip, and this is one trip I'll never forget—that is, if I live. Something tells me I'm a candidate for pneumonia."

"Maybe I'd better start reading those things," Qwilleran said grimly.

"When I was born," Bushy said, "my parents had a neighbor who could write horoscopes, and she was supposed to be quite good. My parents had her do one for me, and she said I'd live a long life, so there's nothing for you guys to worry about tonight."

"That's your horoscope, not mine," said Roger. "I'm ready for an oxygen tent."

"This astrologer also said I'd be a portrait-painter (that's not too far off-base) and I'd marry a Capricorn (that's Vicki's sign) and my weak point would be my head. It sounded like I wouldn't have all my marbles, but I turned out to have a pretty good IQ and no hair!"

Qwilleran asked, "How did you react to Mrs. Ascott's session on Saturday night?"

"How about that?" Bushy said belligerently. "Did you get what she said about a material loss? She knew I was going to lose my boat, so why didn't she tell me to stay on dry land? I don't pretend to know how these things work, but all three of us were at that meeting and planning to embark on this damned trip. Why didn't she receive some kind of vibrations and tip us off?"

Roger said, "The girls still think she's wonderful, but I think she's slowing down. She told Mildred emphatically to get a physical checkup, and Mildred had just had her annual physical last week—the whole works—and nothing was wrong except her weight. It makes you wonder about Mrs. Ascott's other advice."

"She was off-the-track about Clem Cottle's whereabouts," Qwilleran said, "but that message from Joy rocked me back on my heels. We used to be very close."

"She said something about an excavation," Roger said. "Do you suppose she meant old Mr. Klingenschoen's buried treasure? Maybe she wants you to dig,"

"You dig, Roger, and I'll split it with you."

They had hours ahead of them, and they talked to keep their teeth from chattering. Roger talked about the crazy kids in his classes when he was teaching history. The photographer talked about his customers who wanted to look like cover girls when they really looked like prunes.

Qwilleran talked about the Siamese: how they had taken an inordinate liking to Mildred's homemade cereal . . . how Koko shredded newspaper, but only the *Something* . . . and how he had an obsession with the trap door. "He got down into the crawl space once when the plumber was working on the water heater. I don't know what he finds so engrossing down there."

Roger said, "There could be mice or chipmunks. The chipmunks could tunnel under the foundation and come up in the crawl space and spend the winter there with a few bushels of acorns."

"For all you know," said Bushy, "you've got the Chipmunk Hilton under your floor . . . Say, I read your story about the woman who heard her cat scratching under the door after it was dead. How do you explain that?"

"I don't try," Qwilleran said, "and I'll tell you something else I can't explain. You know Russell Simms, who's been renting the Dunfield cottage? She had an urge to visit my cabin yesterday, and she arrived just in time to rescue my cats. A bloody miracle! She also had bad vibrations about the Dunfield cottage."

"Did you tell her about the murder?"

"Yes, but I should have kept my mouth shut. I had a phone call from Mildred this morning; Russell moved out of the cottage suddenly last night, forfeiting a whole summer's rent."

"Strange girl," said Roger. "Did you ever notice her eyes?"

"I'll tell you one thing," said Bushy. "I'd hate to be marooned on this island with Russell Simms and Mrs. Ascott."

Roger started to giggle and laughed until he was on the verge of hysteria.

"Cut it out," Bushy ordered. "You're shaking the shack."

"Let him laugh," Qwilleran said. "It'll warm him up."

"But the shack will cut loose from the trees and float away to Canada, and I don't have my birth certificate!"

At nine-thirty dusk was beginning to fall, and the wind dropped to a stiff breeze.

"I could use a blanket," Bushy said.

"I could use a sleeping bag and hot-water bottle," Roger said.

Qwilleran said, "I could use the *Komfort-Heet.*"

On the corrugated metal roof of the shack they did push-ups to keep warm and massaged their arms and legs. At ten-thirty they were still talking.

Bushy said, "I'll tell you a true story that's kind of spooky. It happened to my aunt during the Depression. Her husband got a job in a steel mill Down Below, and they were living in a one-room furnished apartment. That's all they could afford. Her husband worked hard, came home tired, went to bed, and snored. He snored so loud and so non-stop that it drove her crazy. She couldn't sleep. It was torture! Cotton in her ears didn't help, it was so loud. She felt like killing him! One night she dreamed she beat him to death with a table lamp, and she woke up in a cold sweat. Her husband was dead in the bed beside her. He'd had a coronary thrombosis."

In the thoughtful silence that followed Bushy's story they heard the throb of the sheriff's helicopter and saw the searchlight. The pilot dropped a ladder and picked them off the roof. "Blankets there! Hot drinks in the jug!" he shouted above the noise as the craft veered toward the mainland. "Taking you to Pickax! Landing on the hospital roof!"

There was not a word from the passengers. Qwilleran felt he might never wish to talk again.

"Tornado hit the shore!" the pilot shouted. "Lots of damage! I'll buzz the beach!"

They flew low over the dune, and the searchlight exposed the destruction: large trees uprooted and the condominium site reduced to splinters.

"Down there!" the pilot shouted. His passengers looked down. The roof of the Dunfield cottage had been blown off, leaving the interior a maelstrom of rubble.

Lucky girl, Qwilleran thought. She got out just in time.

The helicopter followed the shoreline until it reached Seagull Point and the Klingenschoen property. Nestled in the trees, the cabin was not easy to spot, but he could distinguish the brown roof, the huge chimney, the two porches—all as solid as a rock, as it had been for seventy-five years. But . . .

"Where's the new addition?" Qwilleran yelled. "It's gone!"

FIFTEEN

The three men snatched from the flooded island were treated for exposure at Pickax Hospital, but Qwilleran refused even a thermometer until he had telephoned Mildred and arranged for her to pick up the key and feed the cats. When he was released on Thursday it was Mildred who drove him home through the torrential rain that was the aftermath of the windstorm.

She said, "You and Bushy must be in excellent physical shape, or they wouldn't have let you go home today. Roger has to stay in for further observation. What a horrible ordeal for you poor dears! Did you know it was in the out-of-town newspapers yesterday?"

"I didn't see a paper or use the phone after Dr. Halifax gave me his knockout drop." Qwilleran spoke in a voice more subdued than usual.

"The *Morning Rampage* had a story on page three, saying three boaters were missing, and in the afternoon the *Daily Fluxion* reported the rescue on page one: *Former Flux Staffer Rescued from Lake*."

"I hope they didn't say we were looking for the site of a UFO landing. How did they get the news? Moose County hasn't made headlines since the 1913 mine disaster."

Driving rain was beating against the windshield until the glass was virtually opaque, and Mildred pulled off the road to wait for some degree of visibility.

She said, "This is very unusual weather for July. Of course, we all know what's causing it."

"What's causing it?" he asked in all innocence.

"Why, the visitors from out there, of course!"

"You're not serious, Mildred."

"You can't expect aircraft to barge in from outer space without disturbing the atmosphere."

Earnestly he said, "Mildred, a couple of weeks ago there was a bright light pulsating outside my window at two o'clock in the morning. Do you know anything about that? Was it a trick?"

Mildred was incensed. "What do you mean?"

"I thought it might be a practical joke."

"You're really awful, Qwill, to say a thing like that . . . Are you sure you feel all right?"

"I'm okay. A little weary, that's all. The medication is sapping my energy."

The rain showed signs of abating. Mildred started the car and pulled onto the highway. "I'm sorry about what happened to your new addition, Qwill."

"Is it totally destroyed?"

"The foundation is intact, but the rest is rubble. Some of the boards have blown half a block away. And the Dunfield house is a wreck! What a blessing that the poor girl got out in time. I suppose we'll never know who she was, or where she came from, or why she was here."

They drove in silence for a few minutes, listening to the rain attack the car. Then Qwilleran said, "I nailed some plywood over the opening between the cabin and the east wing. I hope it didn't blow out."

"It's still in place. You're a better carpenter than you think you are. The tornado didn't even ruffle a shingle on the cabin. They're crazy that way. A tornado will demolish a house without touching the lilac bush at the front door."

"Imagine the cats having to live through that! They'd be terrified! They say a tornado sounds like a jet when it tears through one's property."

Mildred said, "They were still holed up in the bedroom when I went there yesterday morning, but they were like wild animals. I don't know whether they were unnerved by the storm or just plain hungry. I took them some turkey, and last night they had meatloaf, and this morning some leftover salmon mousse. They liked it."

"They'd been imprisoned in the guestroom for al-most twenty-four hours," Qwilleran said. "Luckily they had their commode and drinking water. Cats hate a closed door, you know, regardless of which side they're on. If they're out, they want to get in, and if they're in, they want to get out."

The K signpost came in view, and Mildred turned on her right-turn signal.

"My car's at the FOO. Would you mind dropping me off there?" he said. "I left it in their parking lot when we took off for Three Tree Island."

"Are you sure you should drive?" she asked. "If you feel drowsy, I'll get Sharon to drive your car back to the cabin."

"Thanks, Mildred, but I'm all right. Don't worry."

"All three times I went to your cabin there was a truck in the clearing. I suppose it belongs to your car-penter, but I didn't see him around."

"He was putting in window frames on the day of the tornado. I hope he wasn't hurt. He's so thin, a heavy wind could blow him away."

At the FOO she declined Qwilleran's invitation to have coffee and a doughnut, saying that FOO dough-nuts would make better boat anchors.

"Thanks for the ride, Mildred, and it was good of you to take care of the cats."

"No trouble at all. In fact, I enjoyed doing it."

Qwilleran bought a copy of the midweek *Something*, which had gone to press before the tornado hit. Then he drove slowly to the cabin, thinking that Mildred was a wonderful woman who would make someone a good wife if only she would unload her absentee husband. When he turned into the K driveway, he was beginning to dread the first glimpse of the destruction, but he was eager to lay eyes on the Siamese. There had been times during those long, cold, wet hours when he thought he might never see them again. He shivered at the recollection.

The scene was exactly as Mildred had described it. Iggy's truck was in the clearing, and the east wing was a shambles, but Qwilleran didn't care; he was only glad to be alive. Although the drenching rain was turning the clearing into a lake, he waded through the puddles without noticing them. After what he had been through, what was an inch of rainwater?

He unlocked the door and said dully, "I'm home."

The Siamese regarded him from a distance with an expression of silent resentment.

"You can be glad your meal ticket wasn't drowned," he said. "CEREAL!"

The two ingrates bounded across the floor, Koko walking the last few feet on his hind legs, to receive their treat.

Qwilleran made coffee for himself and was sipping it with gratitude and relief when Arch Riker phoned.

"Thank God you were all rescued, Qwill," the editor said. "I heard about it on the radio Tuesday night and called the papers Down Below. It was too late for our midweek edition. Why doesn't anything ever happen on our deadline? What were you doing out on that island anyway?"

"You may not believe this, Arch, but we were looking for scorched earth where a UFO was said to have landed."

"You're cracking up, Qwill!"

"Be that as it may," he answered wearily, "I'm thinking of moving back to Pickax and crossing off this summer as a lost cause. The east wing is ruined. The sky is gray. The lake is even grayer. The rain is beating on the roof and flooding the windows, and the rotten weather is expected to continue. And it's all on account of those lousy UFOs."

There was a brief pause before Riker asked, "What kind of medication did they give you at the hospital, Qwill?"

"Ask Dr. Halifax. It's his secret formula. Is Pickax flooded?"

"Main Street looks like the Grand Canal. All the creeks and rivers in the county are swollen, and some of the bridges may wash out. Better stay put till the rain stops. You sound tired. Get some rest. Catch up on your reading. Forget about the 'Qwill Pen.' But when you get back to normal, you can write a hair-raising column about your ordeal."

And still it rained, pounding the roof, flattening the beach grass. "Damn those visitors!" Qwilleran said, shaking his fist at the dreary sky.

He went to the back porch and looked at Iggy's pickup in the clearing. The man might be living in it! He might be asleep in the truck-bed right now! Qwilleran realized he should investigate, but the rain was descending noisily, and he felt lethargic.

After a while Yum Yum forgave him for abandoning

her, for shutting her up in a small room without food, for smelling like a hospital. When he stretched out on the sofa, she leaped lightly to his chest and uttered the seductive wail that meant she wanted to be petted. Koko, on the other hand, prowled about the cabin irritably, exploring remote corners, looking for a newspaper to shred, jumping on and off the moosehead repeatedly in a reckless waste of energy.

It was only when Koko crumpled the mudroom rug and started nosing the trap door with moist snorts that Qwilleran snapped to attention. His moustache bristled as a possibility flickered through his mind: Iggy might be under the floor, asleep! He might have seen the funnel-shaped clouds and gone under the cabin to safety. But how would he get into the cabin? The door was securely locked. . . . Well, he would knock out the temporary partition, step through the opening into the mudroom, and then nail the plywood back in place to keep out the gusting wind. He would know that all such beachhouses have crawl spaces, so he would find the trap door, go down in the hole, and close it after him. Then he would stretch out on the sand and go to sleep. Iggy could sleep anywhere! It was an interesting theory, but not plausible, Qwilleran decided. Even a somnolent carpenter wouldn't sleep thirty-six hours. Nevertheless, he shoved Koko away from the trap door, opened it a few inches, and shouted the man's name. There was no answer from Iggy but an ear-shattering yowl from Koko.

Qwilleran was aware he was not thinking clearly. He felt groggy. As he watched the rain cascading off the cabin roof, he thought, Iggy might have been injured when the roof of the east wing collapsed; he might have been killed; his body could be lying under the rubble; or it might have been blown into the woods, along with sections of the roof and siding. Qwilleran realized he should investigate, but the rain deterred him, and he lacked ambition.

His curiosity began to overwhelm his weariness, however, when Koko's behavior caused his moustache to quiver, ever so slightly. The cat was sniffing the trap door eagerly, passionately. Qwilleran remembered seeing a flashlight—somewhere—and he fumbled in drawers and cabinets before finding it in the mudroom. Koko, sensing his intention, pranced with long legs and rampant tail.

Qwilleran swung open the trap door and flashed the light into the dark hole. There was nothing in sight but sand. He tried sprawling on the mudroom floor with his head hanging over the edge in order to flash the light in several directions. He saw sand everywhere—a few rocks—a few pipes leading who-knew-where.

Koko had been racing around the mudroom, yikking and yowling at the spectacle of this large man lying on the floor. Now he peered down into the hole with his four feet tightly bunched, teetering on the edge.

"No!" Qwilleran commanded.

"Yow!" said Koko defiantly as he jumped down into the crawl space.

"Koko! Get out of there!"

The cat had disappeared into the shadows and failed to reply, much less obey.

Qwilleran tried the magic words, "Cereal! Cereal!" Yum Yum came trotting, but there was no response from Koko, the most obstinate creature he had ever encountered, and that included an ex-wife and two case-hardened editors. He flashed the light again, speculating on the feasibility of following the cat. There was about a two-foot clearance, in some spots less, between the sand and the floor joists of the cabin.

"Dammit, I'm not going after you!" he shouted to the miscreant under the floor. "You can stay there all day! I was marooned on an island; I came close to death; I narrowly avoided pneumonia; and I've lost the east wing. I'm not going to belly-crawl in the sand after a cat!"

Qwilleran scrambled to his feet, closed the heavy oak door with a crash and straightened the rug over it, leaving Koko alone in the dark. Then he drove into Mooseville for lunch, first giving Yum Yum some affectionate stroking and a tidbit of bacon salvaged from his breakfast tray at the hospital.

"I hope he can smell this bacon," he said to Yum Yum. "Let him eat his heart out!"

Qwilleran was in no mood for conversation, and he found a secluded table at the Northern Lights Hotel. Even so, the waitress wanted to know all about his experience on the island. She had heard the news on the radio and had read about it in the *Daily Fluxion*.

Qwilleran pointed to his throat and mouthed the words, "Can't talk."

"You caught cold!" she said.

He nodded.

"It must have been freezing out there, with your clothes all wet and the wind blowing fifty miles an hour!"

He nodded.

"How about some cream of mushroom soup? That should feel good going down."

He nodded and also pointed to the half-pound cheeseburger with fries and cole slaw. When he had fortified himself with solid food and three cups of coffee, he felt alive once more.

Back at the cabin the rain was still hammering the roof, soaking the remains of the east wing, drenching the woods, and blotting out the lake view. Yum Yum greeted him nervously. She disliked being alone. She cried piteously.

"Okay, sweetheart," Qwilleran said, "we'll give him another chance."

He opened the trap door, expecting a contrite Koko to bound out of the hole, shake himself, and spend the next hour cleaning his fur, but the cat did not make an appearance. Once more Qwilleran sprawled on the floor, hanging his head over the edge—a maneuver of discomfort as well as indignity. It was then that he heard a distant rumble—the kind of noise that Koko made when he was busy with some engrossing task. He was talking to himself under his breath.

"What are you doing, Koko?"

There was more mumbling, almost a growl.

Qwilleran had been born with the same kind of curiosity that has killed centuries of cats, and he threw off his waterproof jacket and lowered himself into the hole. The opening was about two feet square, and he was a big man. He made several attempts before learning the knack: squat down, slide the legs forward while chinning on the edge, then roll over. Now he could flash the light to all corners of the crawl space. It was, as he had previously surmised, mostly sand, but now he noticed some lumps of concrete or hardened mortar, a sprinkling of acorn shells left there by tunneling chipmunks, and a beer can. He hoped there would be no snakes or skunks. It was dusty, and he sneezed a few times. Cobwebs tickled his face and were vastly unpleasant when they caught on his moustache.

He had no time to wonder about the beer can. Koko's behavior was disconcerting. The cat was in the center of the crawl space, approximately under the dining table, and he was digging industriously.

With Mrs. Ascott's message ringing in his mind, Qwilleran started a torturous belly-crawl toward him. The chunks of mortar had sharp corners, and the seventy-five-year-old joists were four-by-sixes, hard and unyielding. Ahead of him, sand was flying, propelled by the cat's frantic paws.

Qwilleran's moustache prickled as he approached Koko, and he felt a peculiar sensation in his scalp. "What have you found?" he called out.

Koko ignored him and kept on digging. Qwilleran crawled closer, trying to keep the beam of the flashlight on the scene of the excavation. The cat was uncovering something that he could not identify. It was something solid, with a shape that was becoming more defined. Qwilleran inched forward. And then the light went out. He shook the flashlight, joggled the thumb-switch and cursed the thing, but the battery was obviously dead. He threw it aside.

Now he was operating in total darkness. He knew he was within reaching distance of the cat, and he extended his right arm and grabbed a handful of furry hide. Koko struggled and yowled in protest as Qwilleran hauled him back and used his other hand to feel for the treasure.

It was a shoe—a canvas shoe with shoelaces. Inside the shoe was a foot, and connected to the foot was a leg.

SIXTEEN

Upon discovering the body Qwilleran notified the sheriff, though not until he had tipped off the *Moose County Something*. Once more two protesting Siamese were locked in the guestroom as police maneuvered Koko's grisly treasure from its burial place and up through the trap door—no simple operation! There were grunts, shouts, arguments, and muttered maledictions during the process. The rain continued, and the vehicles of the sheriff department, state police, coroner and technicians churned the driveway and clearing into mud.

Unofficial visitors were stopped by a roadblock at

the entrance to the K property, Arch Riker being one of these. The editor and publisher of the *Something* chose to cover the incident himself, since Roger MacGillivray was still in the hospital. Also, Riker thought, Qwilleran might need moral support in his present medicated condition. The night on Three Tree Island and the destruction of the east wing, followed by the discovery of a dead body under the house, would be enough to shake even a veteran journalist if he happened to be taking Dr. Halifax's potent pills. The editor, showing his press card, was allowed to park on the shoulder of the highway and walk up the long muddy driveway in the rain. Upon arriving at the cabin, he was restricted to the back porch.

Indoors the mudroom was living up to its name, as feet came and went in the course of grim, official business. The atmosphere was one the cabin had never known: the awesome hush of a murder scene under investigation, punctuated by the terse comments and orders of lawmen at work, not to mention the occasional complaints of offended Siamese issuing from the guestroom. Qwilleran was asked to stand by but keep out of the way, as samples of sand were collected and the premises were photographed, measured, and dusted for prints.

Dr. Halifax's formula notwithstanding, Qwilleran's energy and alert curiosity were miraculously renewed by the excitement of the crime. When asked to identify the body, he was able to say it was the carpenter known as Iggy, an appellation that tallied with the name on the driver's license found in the pickup truck.

It surprised him that Iggy possessed anything so conventional as a driver's license, and it disturbed him—now that the man was dead—that he had never known his full name, had never asked, had never needed to ask. Despite obnoxious work habits and unattractive personal habits, Iggy was a fellow human who deserved more than a dog's name. He was Ignatius K. Small.

In Qwilleran's opinion the cause of death had been a smashing blow to the skull, although no one bothered to inform him of the coroner's decision. Today Qwilleran was not the richest man in the county; he was not the leading philanthropist; he was not the star writer for the *Something*. He was merely the occupant of a house in which the body of a murdered man had been found.

When the investigators were ready to question him, he motioned them to the pair of white sofas, but the suggestion made the occasion too social. The red-headed detective from the state police post in Pickax preferred to sit at the dining table, and the sheriff's deputy preferred to remain standing. The table was cluttered as usual with writing paraphernalia: typewriter, papers, books, files, pens and pencils, scissors, staple gun, paper clips, and rubber cement—plus the recent addition of a faded pink brocade candybox adorned with a lacy heart. It caught the detective's attention, and Qwilleran thought, Let him make of that what he will.

Everyone in Moose County knew the Klingenschoen name, the Klingenschoen property, the identity of the

Klingenschoen heir, and the size and droop of his moustache. Nevertheless, the detective asked routine questions in a polite, non-threatening way, and Qwilleran answered promptly and briefly.

"Your full name, sir?"

"James Qwilleran, spelled with a w. No initial."

"May I see your driver's license?" The detective accepted it and handed it back with barely a glance at the moustache on the card and the moustache on the face. "What is your legal address?"

"Number 315 Park Circle, Pickax."

"How long have you resided at that address?"

"Two years and one month."

"Where did you live before that?"

"Chicago, New York, Washington, San Francisco . . ."

"You moved around, Mr. Qwilleran. What kind of work did you do?"

"I was a journalist assigned to various bureaus."

"What is your occupation now?"

"Semi-retired, but I write for the *Moose County Something*."

"What are you doing in Mooseville?"

"My plan is—or was—to spend the summer months here."

"Have you changed your plans now?"

"It will depend on the weather."

"When did you arrive?"

"About three weeks ago."

"Is anyone else living here, Mr. Qwilleran?"

"Two Siamese cats."

"Do you own this property?"

"I'm heir to the property, which is currently held in trust by the Klingenschoen estate."

"What was your connection with Ignatius Small?"

"I hired him to build an addition to the cabin."

"How long have you known him, Mr. Qwilleran?"

"About ten days."

They were routine questions designed to put him off-guard, and Qwilleran was waiting for the old one-two. Finally it was delivered:

Who buried him under your house?

"I have no idea," said Qwilleran without missing a beat. "I would have preferred Mr. Small to be buried elsewhere, and I imagine your men feel the same way."

"When was the last time you saw him, Mr. Qwilleran?"

"Tuesday morning."

"Under what circumstances?"

"He reported for work shortly before I left to have lunch in town. He said he was going to start framing the windows, and I paid him in advance for the day's work."

"Did you pay him in cash?"

"Yes."

"What was the amount?"

Qwilleran reached for a notebook on the table. "Fifty-five dollars."

"Were you expecting any other workmen on Tuesday?"

"No."

"And where were you between the time you left for the lunch and the time you found the body?"

"I had lunch with friends—John Bushland and Roger MacGillivray at the FOO. Then we boarded Bushland's boat and went out to Three Tree Island. For some fishing," he added. "But a storm came up, and we lost our boat. After being marooned for several hours, we were rescued by the sheriff's helicopter. All of this is on record in the *Morning Rampage* and *Daily Fluxion.*"

"When did you return to this house?"

"About four hours ago."

"Where were you between the hour of your rescue and your return this morning?"

"In the Pickax Hospital under the care of Dr. Halifax."

"Have you any knowledge of what happened in your absence?"

"I certainly have! A tornado wrecked the new addition I was building."

"How did you happen to find the body?"

"My male cat was acting suspiciously, scratching the floor and trying to get down into the crawl space. I opened the trap door to see what was bothering him, and he jumped into the hole and refused to come out, so I left him under the floor and went to lunch."

There was a sharp cry from the guestroom. Koko knew he was the subject of the discussion.

"How long were you gone?"

"About an hour."

"And what happened when you returned?"

"The female was making a fuss about the male being underground, so I opened the trap door and found him digging in the sand and growling. I went after him and discovered he had disinterred a foot."

The trooper turned to the sheriff, who exhibited a chrome flashlight in a clear plastic bag. "Have you seen this flashlight before, Mr. Qwilleran?"

"It's a common style, but it looks like the one I was using in the crawl space until it suddenly blacked out. Dead battery."

The sheriff removed the flashlight from its bag gingerly and pressed the thumb-switch; the light flashed on.

Qwilleran shrugged. "Well, that's the way they manufacture everything these days."

"When you came home from the hospital, Mr. Qwilleran, did you find the plywood panel nailed up as it is now?"

"Exactly."

"Is that how you left it on Tuesday?"

"Exactly."

"When you left on Tuesday, did you lock the door?"

"Yes. I always take great care to lock up."

"Does anyone else have a key?"

"I subscribe to the Glinko service, so they have a key. Also, there's a spare hidden on the screened porch in case I lose my keycase or lock myself out."

"Where is it?"

"Follow me."

They trooped out to the porch where Riker was waiting patiently and straining his ears to hear.

Qwilleran—with a wink at the editor—reached toward the top of the doorframe.

"Don't touch it," said the sheriff, and he climbed up to look. "It's not here," he announced.

"Look under the doormat," Qwilleran suggested.

"Not there either," said the deputy.

"That's unusual."

The detective made a note. "Are you going to be around for a while, Mr. Qwilleran?"

"Around where?"

"Here at this address."

"I may move back to Pickax if the weather doesn't improve."

"Please keep us informed of your whereabouts. You might be able to help us further. And we'd appreciate it if you'd come in for prints, to check against those we've found . . . One more thing," he added, glancing over his shoulder at Riker. "Please don't discuss this case with anyone."

Taking the flashlight, beer can, mudrug, and other evidence in plastic bags, the officers left, only to be intercepted by the editor, who fired questions.

Meanwhile Qwilleran released the long-suffering animals from their prison. "You've lost your rug," he said to Koko.

He poured a double Scotch for his friend, a glass of white grape juice for himself, and a saucer of the same for Koko. "Care to wet your whiskers?" he asked as he placed the saucer on the floor.

The police cars soon pulled away, and the editor

shambled into the cabin, dropping disconsolately on a sofa. "They wouldn't talk."

"Just tell your readers that the police are investigating."

"You dirty rat! For this I walked half a mile up your drive in rain and mud?"

"If a dead body turned up in your basement," Qwilleran told his old friend, "you too would keep your mouth shut."

"They don't suspect *you*, do they?"

"They suspect everyone, including the little green men in the UFOs."

"I'm your oldest friend," Riker continued persuasively. "You've always discussed cases with me."

"Heretofore, I was never personally involved. This is the first time I've had a dead body of my own. But I'll tell you one thing: Someone around here hates carpenters!"

The editor drained his glass and stood up. "How do *you* feel about carpenters, Qwill?"

"The same way I feel about editors. There are times when I've wanted to *kill them*!"

It was still raining, and Qwilleran drove Riker to his car parked on the highway. "How about having dinner somewhere tonight, scout?"

"Well, it's like this," said Riker. "My horoscope in today's *Rampage* said I'd resume relations with an estranged friend, so I'm taking Amanda to dinner tonight."

When Qwilleran returned to the cabin, he took care of one small detail. He reached into the lograck on the porch and withdrew a doorkey. After eradicating Mildred's fingerprints and replacing them with plenty of his own, he returned the key to its niche in a hollow log. Then he telephoned Mildred. "How's Roger?"

"He's one sick boy. Sharon is at the hospital now, and I'm keeping the baby. How do you feel?"

"I'm fine, thanks." The murder had not yet been announced on the radio, and Qwilleran had no intention of breaking the news. "Do you have today's papers from Down Below?" he asked her.

"I have the *Fluxion*."

"What's my horoscope for today?"

"Hold the line. I'll get it." There was a rustling of newspaper pages. "Here it is. For Gemini it says, 'Don't complain about the lack of excitement today. Take a trip! Visit a friend! Do something you've been wanting to do.' How about that?"

After thanking Mildred and hanging up, Qwilleran pondered the advice for a while and telephoned Bushy, but the answering machine said that he and Vicki had gone back to Lockmaster and could be reached there. He found the photographer's business card and dialed the number. Bushy answered, sounding none the worse for a night on Three Tree.

"How are you doing?" Qwilleran asked.

"I'm so glad to be warm and dry and alive, I'm walking two feet off the ground. How about you?"

"No more than nineteen inches."

"That's true, you lost part of your house, didn't you? How were the cats when you got home?"

"They were in good shape. Mildred had fed them an epicurean menu."

"Don't forget, you're going to bring them down here for a studio portrait. How about tonight? It's only an hour's drive. We can talk about Three Tree. It'll do us both good to get it off our chests."

Qwilleran agreed. After all, his horoscope had suggested it.

"How would you like to go for a ride?" he asked the Siamese as he thawed two cartons of beef stew for his dinner and theirs. "You can have your picture taken by a professional photographer and entered in a calendar contest. You'll win hands-down."

They approached their share of the feast fastidiously, gobbling the meat and licking up the gravy but leaving the carrot and potato and onion high and dry on the rim of the plate. Then they washed up in perfect unison like a well-rehearsed chorus line: lick-the-paw three four . . . over-the-nose three four . . . over-the-ear three four. When the wicker picnic hamper appeared, they hopped into it and settled on the down-filled cushion as if they knew they were about to pose for calendar art. By the time they reached Lockmaster they were both comfortably asleep.

The lumber barons' mansions in Lockmaster had been lavished with turrets, gables, oriel windows, and verandas. Now they housed a funeral home, a museum, two insurance companies, three real estate agencies, a clinic, and the Bushland Photo Studio.

Bushy and his wife met Qwilleran at the door and

clutched him in a triangular embrace as if the ordeal had made them old friends.

Vicki said, with tears in her eyes, "I was almost out of my mind Tuesday night."

"At least you were warm and dry," Qwilleran reminded her.

"It's amazing that you and Bushy pulled through better than Roger, although he's much younger."

Bushy said, "Roger is anemic. He needs a good slug of red wine every day. My mother was Italian, and that was her cure for everything. Why didn't I rub some on my head?"

"Bring the cats into the studio, Qwill," said Vicki.

The front parlor was furnished in updated Victorian, to provide quaint settings for contemporary photos. Qwilleran set down the hamper in front of the marble fireplace and opened the lid. Everyone was quiet, waiting for the Siamese to emerge, but not so much as an ear appeared above the rim of the hamper. Qwilleran peered into its depths and found both cats curled up like a single fur pillow with heads, legs, and tails tucked out of sight.

"Wake up!" he shouted at them. "You're on camera!"

Two heads materialized from the fur pillow—Koko bright-eyed and instantly alert, Yum Yum groggy and cross-eyed.

Bushy said, "Let's go in the other room and have a drink and leave them to get familiar with the place."

For the next half hour he and Qwilleran re-lived the horrors of the island experience.

"Now that I recall," Qwilleran said, "I pulled through with more fortitude than I showed when there was a dead spider in the *Komfort-Heet*."

Bushy said, "I felt a kind of inner force fighting the cold."

The more they talked, the less horrifying it became. The ironic humor of the situation emerged. They could laugh about it and probably would, for years to come. When they returned to the front parlor to start the photo session, the Siamese were still asleep in the bottom of the hamper.

"Okay, you guys, cooperate!" Qwilleran said. He reached in with both hands and grasped Koko about the middle, thinking to lift him out, but Koko's claws hooked into the wicker and could not be dislodged.

"Come on, sweetheart," he said, putting his hands gently under Yum Yum's body, but she also had eighteen functional hooks that engaged the open weave of the hamper. "I'm going to need help," he said.

Vicki reached into the hamper, murmuring soothing words, and carefully unhooked Yum Yum's left paw from the wicker while Qwilleran did the same for the right paw. Then they lifted, but her rear claws were firmly anchored. By the time they disengaged the rear end, the front end was again attached to the hamper.

Qwilleran's back was beginning to ache. He stood up, stretched his spine, and took a few deep breaths. "There must be a way," he said. "Three intelligent adults can't be outwitted by two cats who don't have university degrees and don't even have drivers' licenses."

"Let's turn the thing upside-down and shake them out," Bushy suggested.

They tried it, and the down cushion fell out but not the cats.

"I say we should go back and have another drink," said Bushy. They did, and Koko and Yum Yum remained riveted to their travel coop for the remainder of the evening.

On the way home Qwilleran tuned in WPKX for the eleven o'clock news and heard this: "Police report that the body of a man identified as Ignatius K. Small, itinerant carpenter, was found buried under a lakeside residence east of Mooseville. According to the medical examiner, death was caused by a blow to the head, and the time of death was established as four o'clock Tuesday. The property is owned by the Klingenschoen estate. James Qwilleran of Pickax is currently living there."

"Dunderheads!" Qwilleran said. "They make me sound like the number-one suspect!"

SEVENTEEN

After WPKX had broadcast the news of the carpenter's murder every half hour, Qwilleran's telephone began to ring and he found himself fielding calls from concerned friends and friendly kidders. "No, I didn't do it, and if I did, do you think I'd tell you?" . . . "Thanks, but I'm not ready for an attorney yet; go chase an ambulance." There were crank calls also, but he had learned how to handle those when he worked for big-city newspapers.

While watching the Siamese eat their breakfast, he reconstructed the murder scene from their viewpoint. They were locked in the guestroom with their water dish and commode. For a while they sat on the windowsill and watched the carpenter, Koko probably tapping his tail in unison with the hammer. They had a couple of drinks of water, scratched the gravel in their commode, and catnapped on the guestbed . . . Perhaps a vehicle of some kind arrived and alerted them—alerted Koko, at any rate. Had he heard that particular motor before? What did he hear next? Voices? An argument? A fight? Did he see anything through the window? Did he hear the door being unlocked? The trap door being opened? After that there were indistinct noises under the floor. Eventually the trap door banged again and the vehicle drove away . . . Or did the murderer arrive on foot via the beach? That was a possibility . . . Everything was quiet, and Koko had another drink of water, after which he slept until wakened by the roar of the tornado and the terrifying crash of the east wing. Both cats scuttled under the bed. Later they heard the rain slamming the roof. It was dark, and they were hungry.

That had happened three days ago. Now they were satiated with white meat of tuna and were perched somewhere overhead, communing with their contented innards. Koko was on the moosehead, while Yum Yum crouched on a crossbeam overlooking the dining table where Qwilleran often did interesting things with typewriter, scissors, and rubber cement. The cats stayed at their posts even when the two state police officers were admitted to the cabin.

This time the red-haired detective from the Pickax post introduced an inspector from Down Below, evidently a homicide specialist. He explained that they needed a little more information. Qwilleran found it unusual that the state would fly a man four hundred miles north to investigate the murder of an itinerant carpenter, while hundreds of murders in the state capital itself went unsolved. With a cynical huff into his moustache he suspected that the homicide man wanted to get away from city heat for a while and possibly do a little fishing.

"Have a seat," said Qwilleran, pushing back some of the clutter on the table. The inspector pulled up a chair, while the local officer remained standing.

After some repetitious preliminaries the inspector asked, "Was Ignatius Small a good carpenter in your estimation, sir?"

"He seemed to know his craft."

"Was he recommended to you?"

"No. He was an itinerant carpenter and the only one available. There's a shortage of carpenters in this neck of the woods during the summer months."

"How did you find him, sir?"

"These underground builders, as they're called, hang around the bars. A barkeeper sent him over here."

"Could you describe his personality?"

"He smiled a lot . . . and accepted orders and suggestions well enough."

"Did he always carry out orders?"

"To the best of his ability, I would say. He wasn't a sharp thinker, and he had very little energy."

"Would you say he was . . . *lazy*, sir?"

"If that denotes falling asleep while shingling the roof, yes, you could say he was lazy, or narcoleptic."

"How did you feel about that, sir?"

Qwilleran thought, He's fishing; watch your step . . . To the inspector he said, "I was grateful to find anyone at all to do my work. Beggars can't be choosy."

"Did he ever make mistakes?"

"Occasionally, but it was always something that could be corrected."

"Did he ever cause you to lose your temper?"

"What do you mean?"

"Did you ever threaten him physically?"

Qwilleran looked at the detective with expressionless eyes, mournfully lidded. "Would you elucidate?"

"Did you ever . . . threaten to . . . *clobber him with a two-by-four?*"

Instantly Qwilleran recalled lunch at the FOO with Bushy and Roger. They had been overheard!

At the same moment the telephone rang, and a fur body dropped from the overhead beam, landed on the table, panicked, kicked wildly, scattered papers and pens, flew past the inspector's head to a nearby bookshelf, leaped to the bar and collided with another fur body that had swooped down from the moosehead, bounced off the sofaback, whizzed past the dining table, skimmed across the chairbacks, and crashed into a lamp. The phone continued to ring. Fur bodies were flying in every direction. Zip! Whoosh! The three men were ducking. Then the ringing stopped, and the two cats came to rest on the sofa, where they engaged in mutual licking of imaginary wounds.

"Sorry," Qwilleran said. "They were having a cat-fit."

"The phone scared them," said the local officer.

The inspector stood up. "Thank you for your cooperation, sir. We may want to talk to you again."

When the detectives had left, Qwilleran said to the cats, "You two have never been scared by the telephone in your lives!" He gave them a few crunchy crumbles for a treat.

After starting a blaze in the fireplace to dispel the gloom of an overcast sky and the dampness of two non-stop rainy days, he sprawled on the sofa with a cup of coffee. The Siamese arranged themselves in cozy bundles on the hearth rug nearby—their backs to the warmth and their blue eyes fixed on his face, waiting for conversation.

"The thought occurs to me," said Qwilleran, stroking his moustache, "that Mooseville might be in the grip of a serial killer—an out and-out sociopath."

There was a decisive "YOW!" from Koko.

"Thank you, sir, for your vote of confidence. Unlike you, the chamber of commerce will resist the idea; it's a bad image for a tourist town. But I suspect the police are on to something. Otherwise, why would they bring in their big guns? There's plenty for them to do Down Below. It's my belief that they suspect, as I do, that several isolated incidents up here are actually serial killings."

"YOW!" said Koko again, showing an unusual interest in the topic.

"Sorry, old boy," Qwilleran said to him, "one body is enough. You'll do no more excavating!" He massaged his moustache intently. "Where will they look for suspects? It could be an ordinary individual with a hidden personality disorder who kills and doesn't even know he's killing. That's happened elsewhere. It could be the superintendent of schools; it could be the president of the chamber of commerce! That's why it's hard to catch this kind of criminal. I say the police have a tricky job ahead of them. The killer could be someone who's had a twisted relationship with a specific carpenter and proceeds to transfer his animosity to all carpenters. Or he could be another carpenter—a monomaniac who wants the field all to himself. If this is the case, where was he when I needed a builder?"

Qwilleran got up to refill his coffee mug. The cats remained where they were.

Returning he said, "It's the logistics of this latest crime that boggle my mind: how to lower the body through the trap door, convey it to the middle of the crawl space without leaving a distinct trail, and bury it under loose sand—all with only two feet of headroom, or less. Of course, Iggy was as thin as a potato chip; he can't have weighed more than ninety pounds."

Qwilleran began to massage his moustache vigorously. "Could it be that Iggy was already in the center of the crawl space when he was attacked? Could it be that the killer lured him down there with the story of the Klingenschoen treasure? ... Koko, did you hear two voices under the floor? If the answer is yes, tap your tail three times."

There was not even a whisker stirring on the hearth rug; both cats were having their afternoon nap.

Qwilleran screened the fireplace without disturbing

them and drove to Mooseville to pick up his mail and replace certain items confiscated by the police.

In the post office he found the patrons talking about the murder as they licked their stamps and unlocked their boxes, but they quickly changed the subject when he approached. His mail was plentiful—too plentiful, considering that his secretary had gone on vacation. It always happened that way. And now his narrow escape on Three Tree Island would bring another flood of letters from well-wishers, and the publicity on the murder would result in yet another wave of correspondence.

When Qwilleran entered the hardware store he was aware he was being ogled by other customers. To the proprietor he said, "Thanks for turning off the rain, Cecil." Huggins was president of the chamber of commerce, and he regarded the weather as one of his responsibilities of office.

"Too late!" he said dolefully. "The tourists are leaving in droves, and the fishermen are giving me hell. We haven't seen the sun for three days . . . Say," he added in a lower voice, "is it true what they said on the radio?"

"Sad but true."

"Murder is bad for business, you know. Even worse than rain. Tourists don't like the idea of a killer running around loose. How'd the body get underneath your house, Mr. Q?"

"I wish I knew."

"Are the police bothering you?"

"I daresay they're bothering everyone."

"Do they have any suspects?"

Another customer barged into the conversation—a big man in a flashy cowboy outfit and expensive boots. "Hey, are you the fella with a dead body under the floor?" he asked with a pudding-face smile.

"I'm glad to say," Qwilleran said politely, "that it's no longer under the floor."

"How'd it get there?"

"Lou," said the storekeeper gently, taking the man's arm, "look over there in the tool department. There's a new kind of saber saw that we just got in stock. You'll like it. I'll give you a five-percent discount as a good customer."

The big man drifted away to the other side of the store.

The hardwareman shook his head and said to Qwilleran, "He's a nuisance sometimes, but he spends a lot of money on tools, so I try not to offend him. Sometimes I feel guilty, because I know he never uses them, but a fella with his money is going to spend it on something, so let him spend it on electric saws. That's what I say. Am I right?"

"It makes sense," said Qwilleran. "What do you hear about the flooding?"

"Worst ever! The creeks in three counties are dumping into the Ittibittiwassee. It's flooding farms and washing out bridges. Very bad! They're announcing on the radio which roads are closed."

Qwilleran bought a new flashlight and had another key made. "Do you keep a record, Cecil, of people who buy duplicate keys?"

"Not a chance, Mr. Q. With all the records I have to keep for the government, I can't keep tabs on folks who lose their keys." The storekeeper accompanied Qwilleran to the door, and when they were beyond earshot of the clerks and customers he said, "There's something I should tell you, Mr. Q. Certain local folks are talking about you this morning in a way I don't like. You're a great guy when you're giving the K money away, but get a little mud splashed on your trouser cuffs, and they're ready to trample you in the gutter."

"Interesting observation," said Qwilleran, "but I don't get the point."

Cecil glanced hastily around the store and whispered, "A certain element around here—troublemakers and not very bright—would like to think you're the one who killed the carpenter and buried the body. If they don't know the truth, they invent it, and they like to do mischief."

Qwilleran took it lightly. "Perhaps I should call Glinko and requisition a bodyguard."

"If I were you, Mr. Q," said Cecil, "I'd go back to Pickax until it blows over. There's something else, too, that's being whispered: When Clem Cottle was last seen, he was working for you."

Qwilleran thanked him for his concern and left the store. This, he thought, is a new slant on Mooseville society—an idea for the "Qwill Pen."

When he arrived at the cabin, however, he momentarily lost his detachment. The interior was a wreck! Cecil's words flashed into his mind . . . until he recognized the nature of the damage and identified the culprits. The dining table had been swept clean, except for his typewriter; all the Indian rugs had been pushed into corners, their fringes chewed; Emma Wimsey's shopping bag was overturned and the contents scattered.

"Bad cats!" Qwilleran bellowed. Yum Yum went slinking under the sofa; Koko leaped from floor to woodbox to mantel to moosehead in a swift, guilty blur of light-and-dark brown. Scolding would accomplish nothing. This was a Siamese protest against the incarceration and neglect of the last few days. Perhaps the cats were even blaming him for the lack of sunshine.

Patiently Qwilleran collected the desktop clutter from the floor. Patiently he straightened the rugs. Patiently he collected Emma's papers. "I hope you cats know," he said, "that I'm bucking for sainthood when I do this with such forbearance."

Half the pens and pencils were missing, but he knew where they were. With a broom from the mudroom he made several swipes under Yum Yum's favorite sofa and retrieved the following:

A few balls of cat hair.

A toothbrush with a red handle.

Two felt-tip pens and one gold ballpoint.

Three pencils.

A postcard from Polly Duncan, perforated with fangmarks.

A cheap lipstick case, evidently Joanna's.

A white sock with green sports stripe.

Qwilleran assuaged his own damaged feelings with a cup of coffee and a session with the letter opener. First he read the latest postcard from Polly Duncan. She was having difficulty adjusting to the English climate; she was having respiratory problems. "She thinks *she's* got problems!" he said to anyone who cared to hear. Next he opened a letter from the Senior Care Facility:

Dear Mr. Qwilleran,
I think you will want to know this. Yesterday our dear Emma Wimsey celebrated her birthday. She had a birthday cake with candles and wore a paper hat. As the aide was putting her to bed, Emma said, "I hear scratching under the door." Shortly after, she passed away quietly in her sleep. She had just turned ninety.

Sincerely,
Irma Hasselrich, MCSCF
Chief Canary

Emma Wimsey had lived a long life, Qwilleran reflected. She had secured an education, raised a family, performed her farm chores, worshipped her Lord, collected her little stories, and passed her final days among those caring canaries in yellow smocks. Only when he visualized the diminutive woman in a paper hat on her ninetieth birthday did he feel a degree of sorrow. Opening her valentine box, he regretted that none of her family wanted this paltry legacy. If she had left a grandfather clock and a rosewood piano, they would have fought for their inheritance—a bitter idea for the "Qwill Pen."

The box contained trinkets and scraps of paper, including one yellowed clipping from the old *Pickax Picayune*, probably seventy years old:

NUPTIALS CELEBRATED

Emma Huggins and Horace Wimsey of Black Creek were united in marriage at the Mooseville Church Saturday at four o'clock. There were six in the wedding party. Refreshments were served in the church basement.

Among the mementos were a buffalo nickel and a Lincoln-head penny; a tiny locket; a blue ribbon won at a county fair for home canning; a thin ring set with a few garnets, one missing; a bit of ivory that could be nothing but a baby tooth, probably that of her firstborn.

The Siamese had come out of seclusion to watch the excitement, and when Qwilleran tackled the contents of Emma's shopping bag, they wriggled in anticipation. They knew reading material when they saw it, and they liked him to read aloud. In the bag were school notebooks filled with daily thoughts and bundles of hand-written manuscripts on lined paper.

"This appears to be," Qwilleran told his listeners, "the lifework of a north-country farmwife who attended teacher's college, taught school for a while, and retired to raise a family. She never forgot how to spell and punctuate and compose a good sentence, and she obviously had an urge to write."

Leafing through the collection, he found one tale titled "The Face at the Bridge." It was footnoted, "A true story which I told to my children many times. It always scared them."

"Here's a story that will curl your whiskers," he said to the cats, and he read it aloud.

THE FACE AT THE BRIDGE

When I started teaching in a one-room school-house near Black Creek, I lived with a farm family and had to walk three miles to school in all kinds of weather. I always went early because I had to make a fire in the wood stove and trim the lamps and wash the glass chimneys and sweep the floor.

One day in late November before snow had started to turn the brown landscape white, I set out for school in pitch-darkness. There was a covered bridge over the creek, and oh! how I dreaded crossing that bridge in the dark! On this particular day, as I entered the dark tunnel, I saw something that made my knees shake. There was a white object at the far end—small and round and white and floating in the air. I stood stockstill with my mouth open as it came closer, bobbing gently. I wanted to turn around and run, but my feet were rooted to the ground. And then I realized it was a FACE—no body, just a white face! It started to make noises: "U-u-ugh! U-u-ugh!"

I tried to scream, but no sound came from my mouth. Then two white hands reached for me. "U-u-ugh! U-u-ugh!"

As the white face came close to mine, I was about to faint, but then I recognized it. I recognized a pale young girl from our church. She was wearing black garments and a black shawl over her head, and she was trying to tell me not to be afraid. She was a deaf-mute.

Qwilleran smoothed his moustache with satisfaction. This was the kind of stuff his readers would enjoy, and it actually happened in Black Creek; the bridge might still be there. With his interest piqued, he delved into the bagful of manuscripts, reading how Emma's son had been attacked by a swarm of wild bees who chased him all the way home, and how Emma's cousin had caught her hands in the wringer of an early electric washing machine. There were local legends, mining and lumbering adventures, and the account of Punkin, the cat who scratched under the door.

The possibilities raced through Qwilleran's mind. The *Moose County Something* could feature these country tales with Emma's by-line on page two alongside the "Qwill Pen"; he would write an introduction for each one. Arch Riker might be able to syndicate them; there was a growing interest in country lore. If the Klingenschoen Fund would publish them in book form, the royalties could establish an Emma Wimsey Scholarship—unless greedy heirs tried to get into the act; Hasselrich would have to deal with that aspect.

"If we publish a book, that little lady will be dancing in her grave," Qwilleran told the cats, "and I hope her insensitive relatives choke on it!"

As he read on, he was able to identify the early and late periods of Emma's writing. In the older manuscripts the paper was yellowed and the ink was fading. Those of a later date were written by a hand that was beginning to shake with age or infirmity.

There was one work in poignant contrast to the others in the collection. Scribbled on the stationery of the Senior Care Facility, it was apparently written after Emma entered the nursing home. The handwriting was almost illegible, and Emma's story-telling talent had faded. Titled "A Family Tragedy," it was a mere statement of facts without style or grace or emotion. Qwilleran had no desire to read it aloud.

My husband was a farmer. We had four sons and one daughter. She was beautiful. Her name was Violet. She could have had a fine young man, but she fell in love with a rough fellow. Her brothers pleaded with her, but she wouldn't listen, so her father disowned her. Violet's husband never built her a proper house. They lived in a shack. Their little girl went to school in rags. My menfolk wouldn't let me visit them. I used to peek in the school window to look at my granddaughter. I gave the teacher clothes for her to wear. One day the girl went to school crying. Her mother was sick and all black and blue. The teacher called the sheriff. He arrested Violet's husband for beating her. He wasn't in jail long. Violet was pregnant. She died when the baby came. The older girl had to keep house and tend the baby. The teacher said she changed overnight from a child to a woman. There was a lot of gossip. The baby grew to be a beautiful child. I knew something terrible was happening. When the child was twelve she shot herself with her father's gun. I prayed that the Lord would punish him. My prayers were answered. The back of a dump truck fell on him and killed him.

Qwilleran lost no time in phoning the hardware merchant, who was related to the Wimseys by marriage. He put a blunt question to Cecil.

"Yes," was the answer. "Little Joe is Emma's granddaughter. Her real name is Joanna. Joanna Trupp. She doesn't have anything to do with the Wimsey or Huggins family—just keeps pretty much to herself. I don't know why. We've never given her any cause. All the relatives feel sorry for her. It's a sad case. But she's a pretty good plumber, I hear."

"Why do you call it a sad case?" Qwilleran asked.

"Well, you know, Big Joe abused both his daughters sexually after his wife died. That's probably why the younger girl killed herself. She was only twelve. Did it with her daddy's gun. Big Joe was just no good! Everybody knew that. God knows every family tree has one branch that's unhealthy and withers away. I hope Little Joe makes it."

EIGHTEEN

As soon as Qwilleran confirmed that Joanna was Emma Wimsey's granddaughter, he knew what to do with the valentine box. She might not care about it, but it included two small items of jewelry, and he ought to offer it to her. Adding the lipstick that Yum Yum had hidden under the sofa, he put the box in his bicycle knapsack.

Joanna lived on Hogback, one of the roads officially closed by the swollen river, but with his trail bike he could skirt the inundated areas. He had never experienced a flood. During his career as a newsman he had covered fires, riots, plane crashes, earthquakes, and the fringes of war, but never a flood. It was difficult to imagine the friendly Ittibittiwassee overflowing its banks, going crazy, drowning farms and destroying bridges. Now he could make a firsthand observation, and it might be a subject for the "Qwill Pen."

He biked up the paved Sandpit Road and east on the gravel Dumpy and was still a quarter-mile from the riverbed when he noticed a change in the atmosphere. The chirping, rustling, cawing, chattering sounds of dry land were deadened and replaced by the silence of flooded fields under a heavy sky. When the Ittibittiwassee came into view, it was no longer a river; it was a lake with trees and barns and sheds tilting far out on its glassy surface. Hawks were circling over the wetlands, looking for drowned carrion. The scene was unhealthily quiet.

Hogback Road was impassable, but he cut through the woods on the high ground that paralleled it. As he zoomed up over the last sandhill he had a view of the plumbing graveyard. Most of the old plumbing fixtures in the yard were submerged. The animal cages had washed away entirely, and Joanna's flat-roofed shack was dangerously tilted and about to collapse. The van was not there; neither was she. Still he felt compelled to call her name two or three times, and his voice sounded eerily loud across the counterfeit lake.

A spongy margin at the edge of the flood indicated that the water was beginning to recede or drain into the sandy soil, leaving debris in its wake: sodden papers and rags, bits of wood, food wrappers, beer cans, and a muddied plaid that looked like Joanna's everyday shirt. He picked up a crude wooden cross that had marked an animal's grave and lifted a large red rag from the mud. Then he jumped back on his bike and plunged back into the woods, heading for town.

Dumpy Road with its dreary trailer homes surrounded by junk cars was even more depressing on a gray day. It was rutted and treacherous after the rain, and he had to concentrate on the roadbed. Just then something whizzed past his ear, alarmingly close, and he saw a rock as big as a grapefruit hitting the ground. He turned to find its source, and a second rock grazed his shoulder. At the same time he saw two figures ducking behind a shed.

Qwilleran did no more sightseeing that day. He pedaled back to the cabin and telephoned Mrs. Glinko. "Have you seen Little Joe lately?" he asked.

"You got another leak?" she said with her perpetual good humor.

"No, but her house was destroyed by the flood, and I'm worried about her. We wouldn't want to lose a first-rate plumber, would we?"

"She's okay. She's around somewheres. Want me to dispatch her for anything? Ha ha ha!"

"No, thanks."

Qwilleran turned to the Siamese, who were attending him closely as if concerned—or hungry. "This is not the vacation paradise I envisioned," he told them. "I'd like to read my horoscope for today."

He picked up the phone again and called Mildred Hanstable. "Qwill here. How's Roger? . . . That's good. I was worried about him . . . No, not a thing.

No mention of suspects. When Roger gets back on the beat, we may hear something. By the way, do you have any papers from Down Below? . . . Good! What's my horoscope for today?" There followed a long wait and a sound of rustling newsprint. He listened and then said, "Well, thanks, Mildred. And let's have dinner one night next week."

He tamped his moustache. In the *Morning Rampage* the forecast read, "Interesting developments are in the offing. Hang in there a little longer." The *Daily Fluxion*, on the other hand, advised, "Know when to wash your hands of a bad situation. Cut your losses."

Qwilleran gave the contradictory counsel some serious thought as he heated two cartons of chili for himself and opened a can of crabmeat for the Siamese, and he was inclined to go along with the *Rampage*. His ruminations were interrupted by the sound of a vehicle moving up the drive. He went to the back porch to investigate. It was a recreation vehicle of modest size, and the driver in camping attire who jumped out of it was Nick Bamba.

"Hi!" he said. "I'm on my way Down Below to pick up Lori and the baby, and I decided to drop by and see how you're doing. Hey! What happened to your new addition?"

"It was redesigned by the tornado," Qwilleran informed him. "Come in and have a bourbon. Have you had dinner?"

"No, I'll grab something on the road."

"I'm thawing some packaged chili. How about a bowl? It's not bad. Even Koko will eat it in a pinch."

Qwilleran poured the drinks and set out some cheese and crackers. "Who'll take care of your cats while you're gone?"

"One of our neighbors at the condo. Mighty Lou."

Qwilleran looked dubious. "You mean the one-and-only original Mighty Lou? Is he reliable?"

"Oh, sure. He's very good with cats."

"He doesn't resemble your average cat-sitter."

"No, but he's a good guy—brushes them, talks to them, and everything. The cats like him." Nick took a sip of his drink, expressed satisfaction, and then said, "You came up with a couple of shockers this week, Qwill. First you're marooned on a desert island, and then you find a dead body under your house! Are there any suspects?"

"All I know is what I hear on the radio. The police don't confide in me."

"But you must have some noodles of your own." Nick knew that Qwilleran's suspicions had paid off in the past.

"I don't know. I'm up a tree. Someone must have had a key to get in and bury the body. I subscribe to the Glinko service, and all their service personnel have access to my key—and God knows who else can borrow it. What do you know about the Glinko operation, Nick? Is it all legal and aboveboard?"

"As far as I know."

"They're raking in the dough—dues from summer people and commissions from their workers. What do they do with all their money? They live like paupers."

"They've got a lot of expenses," Nick said, "what with three kids in college, one of them in Harvard."

Qwilleran tried not to appear stunned. "Harvard, did you say? Harvard University?"

"Those eastern schools don't come cheap."

Qwilleran put the bourbon bottle and ice bucket on the coffee table. "Help yourself, Nick."

"Are you going to stay in Mooseville?" the young man asked.

"If the weather doesn't get any worse."

"I wasn't thinking about the weather."

"What's on your mind? Out with it!"

Nick hesitated before saying, "I think you'd be wise to pack up the cats and beat it back to Pickax. We have some riffraff around here, and I've heard some nasty rumblings. Don't forget, I work at the state prison, and there's no better place to hear rumblings."

Qwilleran stroked his moustache. Cecil had warned him; a small boulder had been aimed at him on Dumpy Road; and there had been several crank calls on the phone. "What is this riffraff you mention?"

"They hate the summer people, because they think they have money. The chamber of commerce keeps the lid on them in tourist season, but the town has emptied out since the storm, and the troublemakers are more visible. They gang together, get a few drinks, and cut loose. I'm warning you, Qwill. Go back to Pickax tonight!"

"I have yet to run away from a situation, my boy, and I've lived through some hairy ones."

"You're isolated here. There's only one driveway and

no escape route. They can vandalize the cabin—start a fire—do something to the cats."

At the mention of the Siamese—Koko perched on the moosehead, Yum Yum looking fragile and precious on the sofa—Qwilleran grew pensive. He was so deep in thought that he jumped when the telephone rang. "Hello?" he said warily.

"Hey, Qwill, this is Gary at the Black Bear," said the barkeeper.

Qwilleran responded with some surprise. Gary had never phoned him before.

"How's everything in Mooseville?"

"Apart from the rain, the mosquitoes, and the tornado, everything's fine."

"Sorry to hear about Iggy. He wasn't a bad guy. Dumb, but not bad."

"Yes, it's unfortunate," said Qwilleran with less than his usual verve.

"Are you moving back to Pickax?"

"I haven't made any plans."

"I would if I were you," said Gary, his voice muffled as if he were cupping his hand around the mouthpiece. "A bunch of rowdies are gathering around here, and they've got something cooking. Take my advice and get out! . . . Gotta hang up now."

Qwilleran replaced the receiver slowly, and Nick observed his mood. "Trouble?" he asked.

"Another warning—from Gary Pratt."

"See? What did I tell you? If you don't leave," Nick said vehemently, "I'm staying here tonight. I've got a police radio, and I'm going to block the drive with my

RV and sit up with my shotgun." Without waiting for
an objection he dashed out to the clearing and moved
his camper. When he returned, he had a portable spotlight, a shotgun, and a rifle. "I've alerted the sheriff,"
he said.

They ate chili and drank coffee, and Qwilleran recounted his adventure on Three Tree Island, his tribu-
lations with the underground builder, and Koko's
discovery of the body. The sky darkened early at the
end of that gloomy day, and he turned on some lamps.

"No lights!" Nick ordered. "And we'll close the inside shutters."

The Siamese sensed the mood of watchful waiting;
they too watched and waited. As they all sat there
in the dark Qwilleran asked, "What do you know
about the buried treasure on this property?"

"I've heard that rumor all my life. Some think the
old man buried jewelry or gold. Some say it was stock
certificates that would be worthless now."

"Has anyone tried to dig it up?"

"Where would they dig? You've got about forty
acres of woodland here and half a mile of beach."

"Wouldn't the crawl space be a logical place to bury
the stuff?"

"Hey, man! You've got something there," said Nick.
"Gotta shovel?"

Qwilleran smoothed his moustache. "Suppose some
local person, who guessed the loot might be under the
house, lured the carpenter down there with the promise of a split, got him digging for the treasure, hit him

on the head after he found it, and pushed him into the hole he had dug!"

"And then left with the whole caboodle! Neat trick!" Nick said.

"If it's true, it might explain how Iggy's body got down there. But if it's true, I suspect it's only part of the story," Qwilleran said. "It's my guess that the murderer is a serial killer operating in Mooseville."

"What!"

"YOW!" came a voice from the moosehead.

"Koko agrees with me. I contend that the victims were not only my builder but Clem Cottle and Buddy Yarrow and—"

He was interrupted by a triple-thump as the cat came down from his lofty perch, growling a gutteral threat.

"What's that?" Nick snapped. "He hears someone coming up the drive!"

"No, look at him! He's sniffing the trap door. It's the same performance he staged before he found Iggy's body."

Nick jumped to his feet. "There's something else down there. Want me to go and see?"

"I'll go," Qwilleran said.

"No, I'll go. I'm smaller." Nick grabbed his spotlight, threw open the trap door, and slipped through the hole nimbly. Koko streaked after him.

Yum Yum approached the scene cautiously, but Qwilleran intercepted her and shut her up in the guestroom. "Sorry, sweetheart. This is no business for a sensitive cat."

Down in the crawl space Nick was talking to Koko and getting an occasional "ik ik ik" in reply.

"Find anything?" Qwilleran shouted. "What's he doing?"

"He's at the far end," Nick yelled. "Come on, Koko ol' boy. Whatcha got over there?"

"YOW!"

"Is he digging?"

"No. Not digging. But excited." Nick's voice became more and more remote as he worked his way toward the far end of the crawl space.

The wait seemed interminable. "Any luck?"

There was no answer.

"Nick! What's going on down there?"

"Hey, Qwill!" shouted a muffled voice. "Come on down here!"

Qwilleran lowered himself through the trap door, thrusting his legs out as he had learned to do, chinning on the edge, then rolling over. The far end of the crawl space was brightly illuminated by the high-powered light. Nick and Koko had progressed as far as they could go. They were up against the fieldstone foundation, the man staring at the floor joists above him and the cat on his hind legs, pawing the air.

Qwilleran scudded across the sand like a lizard, amazed at his own agility, ignoring the cobwebs that clung to his face, and inching through tight spots with only a twelve-inch overhead.

"Get a load of this!" Nick said as Qwilleran approached. "You have to squeeze in between the foundation and the first joist, or you can't see it. Only a cat could have found it!"

Qwilleran twisted his body into the tight space and looked up as Nick swept his spotlight across the overhead timber. There were marks on the joist, but the wood was dark with age, and they were hard to decipher.

"It's written in *blood*!" Nick said. "Koko must have smelled the *blood*!"

"I was right!" Qwilleran exulted as he spelled out the obscure message. "They were serial killings!"

"YOW!" said Koko, racing across the sand to the trap door and hopping out of the crawl space.

"Let's get out of this damned hole," Nick said. "The cobwebs make me itch all over. You bring the spotlight."

He started to belly-crawl across the sand, and Qwilleran followed with the light, but not until he had reached up and touched the lettering on the joist. It wasn't blood; it was lipstick.

The two men brushed the sand off their clothing, then sprawled on the white sofas, talking and drinking coffee and listening for prowlers, their firearms close at hand. The Siamese, sensing the tension, sat on the sofas with their haunches elevated as if ready to spring. Twice the sheriff's helicopter buzzed the shoreline and searchlighted the Klingenschoen property.

At dawn Nick announced he would continue his journey Down Below if Qwilleran would promise to return to the safety of Pickax. "And when are you going to report to the police what we found?"

"As soon as I've put some food in my stomach and splashed some cold water on my face," said Qwilleran, who was adept at inventing false replies when the occasion demanded.

As soon as the camper pulled away from the cabin he telephoned the Glinko night number. "Qwilleran again," he said with the clipped speech of urgency. "We've got a plumbing emergency!"

"Allrighty. I'll dispatch Ralph," said Mrs. Glinko as if 5 a.m. emergencies were routine.

"Couldn't you dispatch Little Joe? She knows the plumbing setup here."

"Oh, so you want Little Joe, do you?" the woman said with a leering laugh. "You want her in a hurry, eh?"

"The toilet's backed up," Qwilleran said sternly.

"Okay, I'll try to find her. No tellin' where that babe is shackin' up now."

By the time Qwilleran had pacified the Siamese with an early breakfast and had started a blaze in the fireplace to dispel the dawn chill, Joanna's van pulled into the clearing. Although her attire was never neat, at this hour it looked slept-in, and her eyes were bleary. "Toilet backed up?" she asked with a yawn.

"I have to apologize," he said. "It was a false alarm. It corrected itself, but I appreciate your quick response, and I'll pay your bill for an after-hours housecall."

"I was sleepin' in my van on the Old Brrr Road when she buzzed me. My house washed out."

"I'm sorry to hear that. Will you rebuild?"

"Yeah, I'm gonna build a nice place like this." She swept admiring eyes over the cabin interior.

"May I offer you some breakfast? Coffee and a cinnamon roll?"

"Sure," she said, suddenly more awake.

"Or would you prefer an apple turnover?"

"Can I have both?"

"Why not? I can make them in a jiffy. How do you like your coffee?"

Joanna was fascinated by the microwave oven and computerized coffeemaker, and Qwilleran knew how to play the gracious host. They ate at the bar, and she talked about the tornado, and her animals, and how the flood had swept away their cages. When he suggested a second cup of coffee in front of the fire, she hesitated, looking at the white linen sofas and then down at her work clothes. "I'm too dirty."

"Not at all. Sit down and make yourself comfortable. And prepare for a surprise." He handed her Emma Wimsey's valentine box. "This belonged to your grandmother. Perhaps she never visited you, but she loved you very much. It contains some keepsakes she would want you to have."

She examined the trinkets and souvenirs in the box and glowed with pleasure. If she found Qwilleran's sudden hospitality a suspicious right-about-face, she gave no indication. After all, she was having breakfast with the richest man in the county—in a setting that was the epitome of glamor to a resident of Hogback Road.

Qwilleran, on the other hand, dreaded the confrontation that was coming and deplored the means he had taken to accomplish it. Finally he said, "I'm not going to rebuild my new addition. My carpenter was murdered. Did you know he was murdered?"

"Iggy?" she said without surprise.

"Ignatius K. Small was his name. And a few days before that, Clem Cottle disappeared. Yesterday I biked out Hogback Road to look at the flood damage, and I found Clem's jacket in the mud near your house." When she looked bewildered, he added casually, "Clem's red softball jacket with the rooster on it. How do you suppose it got there?"

"Mmmm . . . Clem was going to . . . build a new house for me," she said uncertainly. "He came out to tell me . . . how much it would cost."

In the same conversational tone Qwilleran went on. "Well, I'm afraid you've lost a good carpenter. I'm sure Clem is dead. Buddy Yarrow was another fine young man who was killed; he fell in the river near your house. And then there was a carpenter named Mert who disappeared, although they found his truck in a junkyard. And didn't you tell me your father was a carpenter?" He waited for a reaction but none came. Altering his tone to one of accusation and looking steadily into her eyes, he said, "Doesn't it seem strange, Joanna, that so many carpenters have died or disappeared? How do you explain it?"

Her eyes shifted as she tried to find an answer. "I don't know," she said in a small voice.

"I think you know how Clem's truck ended up in a

ditch on the Old Brrr Road. Did you bury his body on your property?"

Joanna gazed at him, paralyzed with shock.

"And how about Mert? Did you invite him home for a beer and hit him on the head with a lead pipe?"

"NO!" She was looking frightened.

"Did you have the hardware store make a duplicate key to my cabin so you could go down into the crawl space? I think you got Iggy to go down there during the tornado—for safety—and he never came out."

Her expression changed from fright to menace—she was a big strong girl—and Qwilleran thought it wise to move toward the fireplace in reach of the poker. As he paced back and forth on the hearth he said, "You know all about this, Joanna! Down in the crawl space there's a list of all five carpenters and the dates they were murdered."

Her eyes were moving wildly. "I didn't do it!"

"But you know something about it. Did you have a partner?"

"I didn't have nothin' to do with it!"

"The police are going to suspect you because the names in the crawl space are written with your lipstick."

"Someone else did it!" she cried. "She stole my lipstick!"

"Who?"

"Louise!" She was moistening her lips anxiously.

"Who's Louise?"

"A girl. She does . . . bad things."

"Why would she kill five carpenters?"

Her voice became hysterical. "They're bad! Her daddy was a carpenter! He was a bad man!" Suddenly she jumped up and rushed to the door.

"Don't forget your grandmother's box," Qwilleran said.

Joanna ran from the cabin and drove away in her van, spraying gravel.

Slowly and with regret Qwilleran dialed the number of the state police.

NINETEEN

The sun was shining, Pickax was drying out, and bells in the Old Stone Church on Park Circle were ringing joyously as Qwilleran arrived at his apartment over the Klingenschoen garage. In his car were his typewriter, summer clothes, coffeemaker, the Siamese in their travel coop, and of course their turkey roaster.

He consulted his horoscope in the weekend edition of the *Moose County Something*, which now carried a syndicated astrology column in response to reader demand. "You have some explaining to do, Gemini," said the anonymous astrologer. "Socialize with an old friend and get it off your mind."

Qwilleran telephoned Arch Riker. "Okay, boss, I'm back in Pickax and ready to talk. Why don't you come over for a drink tonight? The refrigerator man came back from vacation, and we have ice cubes."

"Do you mind if I bring Amanda with me?"

"If you can stand her, I can stand her," said Qwilleran with the breezy candor of a lifelong friend. "I assume your off-again romance is on again."

"We're having dinner with the Hasselriches at six, so we'll have to see you later, about ten. And do me a favor, Qwill. I'd appreciate it if you'd water her drinks. She's bad enough when she's sober."

"Tell me one thing, Arch. How come you broke down and bought a horoscope column for the *Something*?"

"I read a survey. The horoscopes get a larger percentage of readership than anything else in the paper, including the weather."

At ten o'clock the couple climbed the stairs leading to the former servants' quarters over the garage, Amanda scowling and grumbling about the narrowness of the treads and the steepness of the flight.

Riker said confidently, "I knew you wouldn't last long in Mooseville, Qwill. You've lived too long with concrete sidewalks, traffic lights, and fire hydrants."

"How could you stand the damned mosquitoes?" Amanda said. "And all that sand! And all those noisy birds! They'd drive me crazy! And all that water! Who wants to look at a flat body of water all the time?"

"I'm glad my return has your blessing," said

Qwilleran cheerfully as he served the refreshments with a flourish of cocktail napkins, coasters, and nut bowls.

"You're in a good mood tonight," the editor said.

"I talked to Polly in England. The doctors have advised her to cut her visit short. She's got a bad case of bronchitis and asthma. Wrong climate, I guess."

"Too bad she had to lose such a good opportunity," said Riker, "but for your sake I'm glad she's coming home. A woman with bronchitis and asthma is better than no woman at all." He chuckled, and Amanda glared at him.

Qwilleran asked, "How did you enjoy your dinner with the Hasselriches?"

"They're charming hosts," Riker said. "No doubt about it."

"They're so charming, I could throw up!" his companion growled.

"Was their unmarried daughter there?"

"Irma? Yes, she's just as cordial as her parents," the editor said. "Attractive woman, too."

Amanda made an unpleasant noise.

Qwilleran said, "Irma is a mystery to me. I wish I knew what she's all about."

"I'll tell you what she's all about," said Amanda with her usual belligerence. "When she was eighteen she killed her boyfriend, and old Judge Goodwinter—before he went off his rocker completely—sentenced her to twenty years in prison, but the Hasselriches made it worth his while to reduce the sentence. She got probation in the custody of her parents, plus orders to do ten years of community service. She's been serving the community *ad nauseam* every since!"

Riker glanced at Qwilleran and rolled his eyes expressively. "So, let's have the latest news on the Mooseville murder beat, Qwill. As usual it happened after our weekend issue had gone to press. I'll be glad when the new building's finished and we can start printing five days a week."

"First I'll let the cats out of their apartment. Otherwise Koko will raise the roof when he hears us talking about him." He opened a door at the end of a hall, and two proud Siamese paraded into the living room with tails and whiskers perpendicular. Yum Yum commenced an investigation of shoelaces. Koko rose effortlessly to a bookshelf six feet off the floor and settled down between Simenon and Conan Doyle.

"Well, Nick Bamba came over Friday night," Qwilleran began, "and we were having a quiet evening with the lights out and loaded firearms across our knees, in case anything happened, when Koko suddenly started making an ungodly fuss. He wanted to go underground! We let him go, and he led us to the names of the five carpenters who are alleged murder victims: Joe, Mert, Buddy, Clem, and Iggy— together with the dates of their demise. Captain Phlogg wasn't included; apparently the old soak really drank himself to death, as everyone thought."

"Where were the names?" Riker asked.

"Daubed on a floor joist in a tight spot where only a cat would find them. Nick thought the names were written in blood, but it was lipstick. That's when I knew the killer was Joanna Trupp."

Amanda snorted in disdain. "What's to stop a man from buying a lipstick if he wants to write on joists?"

"True," said Qwilleran, "but the first three names matched the purplish-red lipstick that Joanna lost in my cabin. Yum Yum had hidden it under the sofa. The last two names, apparently written after she bought a new lipstick, were in a different color—more orange."

"Why do you suppose she wrote with lipstick?" Riker asked. "Or is that question too naive?"

"For the same reason that people use lipstick to write farewell messages on bathroom mirrors: It's handy. If Little Joe were a house-painter instead of a plumber, she might have used red enamel. Don't overlook the significance of the color . . . The question next arises: Why did she keep a tally of her victims?"

"Because women like to make lists," Riker said archly, and Amanda scowled at him.

"Because each murder boosted her ego. It was a scorecard of her victories in a private war she was waging."

Riker said, "I'll bet she conked those guys with a lead pipe or a monkey wrench."

"We can assume she conked her father with the tailgate of a dump truck. Mert and Clem are unaccounted for; there'll be a search for their buried bodies on her property when the water recedes. Their trucks were found within walking distance of her private graveyard. Likewise, the mudslide where Buddy Yarrow went into the river was nearby."

"Question!" said Riker. "Since the first four were reported as accidents or missing persons, when did you first suspect murder?"

"Subliminally, I suppose, when Koko started tapping his tail. He'd been watching the carpenter drive nails *bang bang bang*, and when the man failed to report for work, Koko's tail started going *tap tap tap*."

"Sounds like hogwash to me," Amanda muttered. "How about a refill, Sherlock? The Squunk water was delicious, but don't forget the bourbon this time."

Qwilleran refreshed her drink but not without a wink at Riker. "Perhaps it was none of my business," he said, "but I went around asking questions yesterday. Cecil Huggins remembers making a duplicate key for Joanna; it could have been a key to my cabin. The guys at the lumberyard remember Clem saying he was going to build a house on Hogback Road. The night bartender at the Shipwreck Tavern remembers the last time Mert came into the bar; Joanna was buying his drinks."

"Convenient recall!" Amanda protested. "Hearsay! Circumstantial evidence!"

"I admit it, but you can be sure that the mortality rate for carpenters will decline now that Joanna—and Louise—are in custody."

"Louise! Who's Louise?" Riker asked.

"Ah! Now we come to the curious part. Little Joe didn't know she was killing. She had invented another self— another girl—to do the dirty work. No doubt it was the only way she could cope with her intolerable homelife. For years both she and her sister were sexually abused by their father. When the younger girl killed herself—out of desperation, guilt, self-loathing, or whatever—it must have triggered a murderous hate in Joanna. Shortly after, 'Louise' engineered the tailgate accident that killed Big Joe. Little Joe's twisted reasoning would go something like this: Big Joe was a carpenter; he was a bad man; therefore all carpenters are bad men. It became the holy mission of 'Louise' to wipe them out, one by one."

"Shocking!" said Riker.

"That's what serial killers are all about," Qwilleran said. "Their motivation doesn't make sense. That's why they're so hard to catch."

"YOW!" came a loud voice from the bookshelf, and three heads turned to look.

Qwilleran said, "Koko no longer taps with his tail, now that the carpenter-killer has been apprehended. And I'm glad it's over. My only regret is that the murderer turned out to be Little Joe."

"What will happen to her?"

"Her fate now, I suppose, is in the hands of the courts and the doctors. It will take a lot of psychiatric treatment to straighten her out and get some answers to questions."

In the moment of silence that followed, a faint but distinct sound came from the Conan Doyle shelf: *tap tap tap*.

Amanda crowed with delight. "I always knew you were a windbag, Qwill, but I like your moustache."

After his guests had gone, Qwilleran made coffee for himself, poured a saucer of white grape juice for Koko, and gave Yum Yum a crumb of cheese. Then he sprawled in the big chair in his writing studio, while the Siamese arranged themselves on his desk in photogenic poses, waiting for the conversation to begin.

"Now that we're back in Pickax," he said, "I can't believe we spent those three lunatic weeks in Mooseville. There's something intoxicating about the atmosphere up there that distorts reality. It should be investigated by the narcs . . . Or even the EPA; it could be radioactivity from those UFOs."

Koko squeezed his eyes in agreement.

"And the behavior of you two was enough to unhinge a rational mind. When you staged your catfit, were you really alarmed by the ringing phone? Or were you trying to distract the inspector in a tense moment?"

Koko blinked innocently, and Yum Yum yawned.

"I'd also like to know, young man, why you reacted to Russell Simms in such an ungentlemanly manner. You embarrassed me! It's true there was something weird about her; she moved like a cat and had eyes like a cat, and she seemed to have a sixth sense . . . Hey, where are you going? Come back here!"

Koko had jumped down from the desk and was walking from the room with that particular stiff-legged gait that denoted supercilious disapproval. He paused in the doorway only long enough to switch his tail contemptuously—twice—before completing his haughty exit.

"I guess I offended him," Qwilleran said to Yum Yum. "He's temperamental, but we have to make allowances for genius, don't we? Koko was obsessed by the trap door long before Iggy was murdered and even before Clem disappeared, and it wasn't because of mice in the crawl space; he knew something *abnormal* was going to happen down there. Koko could teach Mrs. Ascott a thing or two."

Yum Yum purred delicately.

"That rascal made a fool of me when Arch and Amanda were here. He's developing a mischievous sense of humor. But I still maintain that his tail-tapping had something to do with the serial killings."

"YOW!" Koko reappeared in the doorway, standing on his hind legs and pawing the air.

"I said s-e-r-i-a-l," Qwilleran told him. "Not c-e-r-e-a-l."

Both cats stared at him with expectation in every whisker.

Qwilleran looked at his watch. "Okay, you guys, it's time for your bedtime treat!" He gave them a handful of Mildred's crunchy breakfast food.